DEN OF DEATH

DEN OF DEATH

ALI ARCHER

Den of Death (Minnie Kim: Vampire Girl #5) © 2020 Ali Archer
ISBN: 979-8-9860954-9-3

Cover Design by Kuro Ishi Cover Design
Editing by Lorie Humpherys

www.aliarcher.com

THE ULTIMATE GUIDE
TO BECOMING A VAMPIRE

I'm on my way to Italy to find Philo &
hopefully bring him home. & David's
already there, but I have to go. I can't
just stay home & wait.

The flight's really long, so I thought I'd
finally go through the Guide. Somebody's
gotta be able to do a better job than
this. (David thinks that somebody
will be me. Ugh.)

Anyway. Maybe it'll help me stay busy/
distracted until I find him.

I can't wait until I do.   I'm gonna hug
The International   & hug that
Council of Vampires   boy &
                      never let him go!

If I ever do a reVamp (ha!) of this Guide, I want to focus on the struggles we face in trying to be good citizens. I just don't want to:
① ruin the good name of progressive vampires who are trying to become non-predators
② romanticize what vamps really are.

INTRODUCTION

Think vampires are pale, pointy-teethed monsters? Think again. When the London vampires first revealed their identity, what surprised humans most was not that vampires exist, but that they have been living among them all along. Vampire legends have been told since the beginning of time, and hold both truth and fiction.

The purpose of this guide to give you — both the inquiring human and the new vampire — an overview of the vampire world so you may either choose what is best for yourself, or learn how best to adapt.

We are eager to share our truths with the world and hope that we may all live and work peaceably together.

CHAPTER ONE

TRAVELING TO ITALY HAD SEEMED LIKE A GOOD IDEA back in my room at the Aristos house, but now? Not so much.

Back there, I thought coming to Italy to find the Master and rescue Philo was my only choice, but who'd I been kidding? I didn't even know where the Master lived, or where he'd be holding Philo, let alone have any chance of sneaking him out of there.

Where the heck had my brains gone? It seemed like I'd only gotten stupider since becoming a vampire.

Take on an old, obsessed vampire at a school dance? *Sure.*

Help an imugi level up just to impress my dad? *Why not?*

Take in a werewolf boy? *Of course!*

Sneak off to Italy to face the Master of vampires? *Might as well!*

Now here I was, walking through the enormous Leonardo da Vinci International Airport to get to the immigration station and I had no plan for how I was gonna get through. Or even what to do once I did.

The TSA workers at the American security gates made me recite the dreadful "I promise not to kill anyone" pledge and had accepted the travel papers I'd used when I left for Seoul, since they were good for six months, but I was nervous about what the immigration people here might say. My papers were for Seoul specifically, and while it allowed for some travel, I was pretty sure that was for inside South Korea—not for travel anywhere else. All I could do was cross my fingers and pretend to have misunderstood the documents, which, given my lack of brain cells lately, I could probably pull off.

The truth was, I was desperate. I'd do anything to get into this country.

Instead of thinking about the logistics of what was going to happen once I deplaned, I'd spent the last thirty-six hours since I decided to follow David to Rome, thinking about Philo. Thinking about how I'd get the Master to release him, and how I'd help him get his strength back. I'd need blood. A lot of blood. And I hadn't registered with the Italian Council to let them know I was coming. I honestly didn't know if the Master *was* the Council here, or if there was a separate group, but I hadn't wanted to alert him that I was coming.

From what I'd gleaned about David and our family being on the Master's hit list, he wasn't exactly gonna roll out the red carpet for me. For all I knew, he'd kill me on the spot.

Yeah, this was definitely not my best plan ever.

But Philo was here and I had to help him. What other choice did I have?

Sure, David had come to try to patch things up with the Master, but how long was that gonna take? I knew Philo wouldn't die from starvation, but…

I shook my head and straightened my shoulders. I'd never been a worry-wart, and I wasn't gonna start now. Up ahead, I saw a sign with the American flag on it and heaved a sigh of relief. My shoulders were already killing me under the weight of my backpack and from sitting on a plane for the last eleven hours. I got into line with everyone else and offered a smile to a woman I'd seen on my plane. She and her husband were on their third trip here, she'd told me, and I'd gratefully followed them through the airport since they knew where they were going.

The memory of Philo in his cell, and the feeling of pain and unbearable hunger, had me donning an air of confidence I didn't feel. I had to get through customs and I had to get to Philo. There just wasn't any other option.

"Don't worry, hon," the woman from the plane said. She'd glanced back at me and must have noticed the tension in my face. "This'll be a piece of cake, just you see." Her warm Southern drawl was comforting, and I tried to offer her a grateful smile, but the look of concern in her eyes when she turned away told me I hadn't been too convincing. She had no way of knowing that I had just made a difficult decision and only had a few seconds to figure out how to do it.

My turn came. I stepped up to the counter and handed over my documents to the middle-aged woman behind it. She looked up in surprise and I smiled, this time putting all my acting skills to the test. It had to be the best, most convincing smile of my life.

To her credit, the agent was all business once more and proceeded to inspect my passport and travel papers. "These papers are for Seoul—" She looked back up at me, and I was ready.

I'd promised myself I'd never use my gifts against humans, but I was quickly learning that in the supernatural world, promises were foolish things. When I'd been human, I couldn't imagine a time when I would lie to my parents, skip school, or talk back to grown-ups. Back then, there'd been a lot of things I swore I'd never do.

Things were different now.

As soon as the agent's dark blue eyes met mine, I threw my mind into hers. Immediately I knew I'd gone too far, done too much, because she staggered back and her mind sort of panicked and began to shut down. I released a long, slow breath and gently pulled my influence back as I glanced around. I don't think anyone had noticed, or thought anything about the agent's reaction, thank goodness.

Her mind began to relax, and now that I was being more careful, I could hear her thinking. I inserted myself into her thoughts and tried to change them.

The agent frowned and glanced back down at the papers again. When she read Seoul, Korea, I changed her thoughts. Despite what she read, she said, "How long do you plan to be in Rome?"

Her gaze was wary as she met mine, but it was only because apparently Rome had a vampire problem, and she didn't like that yet another bloodsucker was coming into her city.

"Just ten days," I said.

"Business or…pleasure?" She stumbled a little on that one, her mind filling in all sorts of unpleasant things a vampire might do for pleasure. I wanted to replace her terrible thoughts with more innocent ones, but I'd never influenced anyone like this before and I was afraid to do too much.

Instead, I gave her my best I'm just an innocent girl smile. "Sort of business, I guess. I'm here to interview with Rome University for a scholarship," I lied. I hoped she didn't ask me any questions about it because I only knew what I read in the brochure on the plane.

"Oh." The agent was actually stunned by my response. She hadn't really thought of vampires as regular people who wanted to pursue higher education. She thought, *But you're so young! And you're already thinking about university?* Until she remembered I was a vampire and so I probably wasn't really as young as I looked. She narrowed her eyes, suspicious of me and vampire-kind once again, but she stamped my passport.

I sagged with relief, and gratefully took my stuff back from her. "Thank you," I said. "Have a great day!" I slipped out of her mind and began to walk away, but I felt her staring after me for a good fifteen seconds. My relief fled as I feared her coming to her senses and calling down the *polizia* on me. Note to self: *Don't stop the influence until you know you're totally in the clear.*

Thankfully no *polizia* came after me, and I was able to buy my bus ticket and start yet another long walk toward the station. When I got on the bus without any trouble, I shoved my suitcase onto the shelf and sank down into an empty seat with a long sigh of relief. It was the nicest bus I'd ever seen, with reasonably comfortable seats, lots of leg room, and adjustable headrests—*if* you were tall enough to rest your head on them, which I was not.

I startled when a girl a few years older than me, with curly brown hair, warm skin and blue-jean eyes flopped onto the seat next to me. She leaned into my personal space. "Hey! *Sei americano?*"

Two guys dropped onto the seats across from me and now I had three intense Italian people grinning at me. It was a little intimidating.

"Uh." I looked at all their smiling faces and attempted to match their friendly demeanors. Responding to the girl, I said, "Yeah. I'm American."

The girl turned from me and a flurry of words flew between her and the guys. From their rolling eyes and sheepish grins, I wondered if they'd bet I wasn't American, but the girl had guessed right. I felt a little sorry for them. I mean, my appearance didn't exactly scream *American.*

"Boys," the girl huffed, turning a conspiratorial smile on me. She stuck out her hand. "I'm Bianca Marino. And these are my brothers, Freddy and Luca." Her English was laden with a thick Italian accent, but otherwise very good.

"Hi." I gave them a little wave. Why was I so lame?

The boys each nodded at me, wide grins spread across their faces. They might not have been supermodel gorgeous, but they were still plenty attractive enough to make me uncomfortable. I always forgot that I was attractive now, too—thanks to my vampire blood. Now that I knew they were siblings, I could definitely see the resemblance in the thick, chocolate brown hair, straight noses, wide, full lips and those denim-blue eyes. Freddy wore his hair long, so it fell in waves to his shoulders. It wasn't a look I was generally fond of, but it suited him. Made him look very Italian. Luca wore his hair shorter, with one side very tall—more like how the boys at home wore theirs.

"I'm Minnie," I said, after a stretch of silence. I figured it must have been my turn to speak. I did my little wave again, which made me feel stupid and embarrassed, but whatever. "Hey."

"Minnie, eh?" Freddy said as he leaned forward. "Is that a…uh…*un soprannome*? Because you are so small?" He pinched his finger and thumb together indicating something very, very small, then raked his gaze up and down my body. "Or are you a fan of Minnie Mouse?" The way he said it was so insulting. I mean, I wasn't a huge Disney fan, but so what if I was? Minnie was the boss.

Bianca hit him with her sizable handbag while presumably reaming him off in Italian. Meanwhile, I tried do a clothing check to make sure there wasn't anything suggestive about what I was wearing. My determination: If Freddy found torn black Chucks, torn skinny jeans and my Garfield the cat T-shirt that said "Feed me" a turn-on, then he had bigger problems than just Bianca. I didn't even have any makeup on, I'd thrown my hair up into a messy bun while on the plane, and I'd been traveling for twenty-four hours. Despite my vampire glam, I'm sure I didn't look that hot.

"Never mind him," Bianca said in a stage-whisper as she once again leaned in too close to me. I'd read about Italians and their lack of personal space, but experiencing it was something else altogether. My parents would have died. They didn't even like to touch each other, let alone complete strangers. "So! Are you here for your backpacking?"

Luca said something to Bianca, then Bianca said to me, "Oh, not backpacking, then. That's what most young Americans come to Italy for, but you do seem a little young for that. What are you doing here? Are you all alone?"

I knew better than to admit I was actually all alone to complete strangers, but I didn't have an answer ready. I hadn't expected anyone to give me the fifth degree like this, or else I would have been better prepared. "How'd you know I wasn't backpacking?" I asked.

"You have a suitcase," Luca answered with a shrug. His body language was ultra casual, but I got the sense he was keen to know the answer to Bianca's questions.

I took a deep breath and mentally crossed my fingers that these people would buy the lie I was about to spin. "I'm here for an interview with the dean at Rome University."

The three shared a look, then Bianca turned back to me, an expression of disbelief on her face. "Really? Signor Abrama? *We* go to RUFA!" she moved her hand back and forth between her and the boys while my heart sank down to my toes. This was my punishment for telling so many lies—how the heck was I gonna get around this one? "We are just getting back from our summer travels. I cannot believe school starts next week! What will you be studying? We are all in the sculpture and installations school. I—" she pointed at her chest, "am a sculptor, but these two idiots make monstrosities out of metal." She gave a pretend shiver.

"Hey." Luca kicked her foot with his. "We are sculptors, too. Just because we do not get our hands dirty with clay does not mean we are not artists."

Bianca flicked her hand in the air, as if dismissing Luca's words. "Whatever. In case you have not guessed it, the three of us are triplets. We spend *way* too much time together. I thought I could break free of them when I went to university, but no. All three of us got scholarships to the same school!" She threw her hands up in the air. "Can you believe it?"

I laughed with her, feeling myself relax. I liked this girl. She was fun and fierce and reminded me a lot of Stacey. And Luca seemed cool, too. But Freddy…He didn't seem to be enjoying himself the way the rest of us were.

He eyed me suspiciously. "You look too young to be going to university." He sat back against the seat and rested his arm on the tiny window ledge. He stared at me. In fact, they all stared at me. At least Luca and Bianca were just curious. Freddy stared as if he could see into my brain and read all the lies piling up in there.

I glanced out the window, at the Italian landscape zooming by, and felt a pang of regret that I hadn't been able to enjoy the view because of these nosey people. I sighed, knowing that wasn't entirely true. I'd have totally enjoyed their company if it weren't for all the stress I was under and all the lies I'd told.

And especially if it hadn't been for Freddy.

"Are you sure you are even old enough to travel alone?" Freddy chuckled, then made a point of sitting up tall and looking around the train. "Or maybe your daddy is here somewhere?"

I turned my attention back to Freddy. You know, I pride myself on being a nice person. I liked being nice. But right then, I found I didn't care a whole lot about hurting Luca and Bianca's feelings—okay, I did have a prickle of regret, but this Freddy guy deserved a kick in the pants. But I wasn't quite ready to go that far.

Instead, I gave Freddy my best smile. "Oh," I said airily. "I'm older than I look." This time I was the one to lean forward, my gaze glued to his. "I'm a vampire."

*★ look into this
• The Council should write a Complete History or something
• There's gotta be some amazing vamps who've
  done amazing things!

A BRIEF HISTORY OF VAMPIRES

At least!
(I hope so!

CHAPTER ONE

Most people attribute vampirism to ★Vlad the Impaler, c. 1450, however vampires have roamed the Earth since long before humankind. The fact that we only gained public attention after Vlad's incorrigible deeds, is proof that vampires in and of themselves are not evil. Just like human beings, vampires can be both good and evil. If a human was evil upon their reMaking, they will

1

likely remain so. But the stories of good vampires are not nearly as titillating as the atrocities committed by the bad, so our myths and legends tend to be built around them, which is a source of great frustration for vampires. No matter how long we live, we can never really escape the childhood adage of "one bad apple spoils the bunch."

It is true that Vlad III, was a particularly vicious man, but he was not made vampire until after the atrocious acts for which he is most known for. Following that event, he

CHAPTER TWO

It seemed as if the whole bus went dead quiet. I didn't think I'd spoken loudly at all, but human beings had been prey to vampires forever, so I suppose it made some evolutionary sense that their ears would pick up the word *vampire*, even in a crowded bus.

I leaned back in my seat, keeping my eyes glued to Freddy's, even though I really wanted to check on Bianca and Luca to see how freaked out they were. I'd probably never see them again, but I liked them and I didn't want to frighten them. Freddy hadn't even flinched. I had the feeling if I dropped my gaze first, he'd take it as some kind of victory and the predator in me couldn't allow that.

Luca shoved Freddy hard enough that Freddy conked his head against the window and I bent my head to hide my grin. "What did you do that for, you *coglione*! She's a nice girl. Why do you have to ruin everything?"

Bianca pushed on Freddy's knee with her foot while he glowered at Luca. "Yeah, Freddy. I am trying to make a friend. You always ruin it for me." She turned to me with a slightly over-bright smile, that I guessed meant she was nervous to have me so near, but she was trying to keep an open mind. "Usually, he just hits on girls, and since these two are always around, it makes it hard for me to find friends."

I relaxed a little and sighed, trying to ease out the rest of the tension. "It's okay. He knew something was different about me, and he wanted to protect you, that's all."

"*Si*," Freddy said, leaning into the space between his siblings. He pointed his finger between the two of them. "*E non vali la pena.*"

"Me? *Non ho bisogno della tua protezione?*" Bianca laughed and shook her head. Luca just knocked Freddy's finger away.

I didn't understand the words flying out of their mouths, but I figured it had to do a lot more with them than me. I glanced past them to the other passengers on the bus and only caught a couple people still watching me. So much for flying under the radar. But once I thought about it, I realized it wouldn't be a bad thing if everyone knew I was a vampire. I mean, that's what I'd come here for—to find other vampires. Since I didn't know where the Master lived, my grand plan was basically to find where the vampires were and ask them. It hadn't seemed like a bad idea on the plane, but now I realized that short of standing in the middle of *Piazza del Popolo* and calling, "Here, vampire, vampire!" there was no good way to go about this.

I glanced around the packed bus again, this time hoping to get a *hey, you're the same as me* kind of vibe but…nothin'. It seemed I was the only vamp on the bus. I sighed.

I turned back to Bianca. "So…" I waited until she broke off her conversation with her brothers and glanced back to me, bright spots of color high on her cheeks. I got the impression she enjoyed bantering with her brothers. "Do you know of any decent hotels near the school?" Thank goodness I didn't have to stay in a hostel since I had the limitless credit card David had given me, but I wasn't about to be all posh like Audrey Hepburn in *Roman Holiday*. I'd grown up believing that extravagance was foolish, and I really tried hard not to be foolish.

Bianca gasped, a horrified expression on her face. "You do not have a reservation?" At the blank look on my face, she went on. "What were you thinking coming all this way without a reservation? This is Rome, *sorellina*! There are never any free rooms in the hotels. You have to book them in advance."

"Oh." *What was it I'd just been thinking about not being foolish?* I looked down at my hands, absently rubbing them and trying madly to think up a plan. I could maybe rent an apartment. I wouldn't be here for a whole month, but it was better than the streets. Or, maybe I would have to check out the hostels after all and see if they had any room. I was about to ask Bianca if she knew any good ones, but she spoke first.

"Do not even worry about it." She slung a long, slender arm around my shoulders. "You can stay with us. Right, *Fratelli*?" She glared at each of her brothers. Luca glanced at me and shrugged, but Freddy was definitely ticked off. I thought he'd reject the idea, but instead he mumbled something under his breath and fixed his gaze somewhere beyond the window.

"See?" Bianca turned a beaming smile on me. "You can stay with us. We do not live on campus, but we have an apartment that is very close. You never did say which art school you will be in."

My mind felt like it had whiplash and I blinked at her for a second before I found my voice. "Oh, um." *What was it she said they did?* I remembered that the Rome University of Fine Arts had different schools for different specialties. *Oh!* Sculpting, and whatever it was the boys did, but something like sculpting.

22

"Painting!" I practically shouted. Then, quieter, "Painting. And drawing. Painting and drawing. That's what I do!" *Ah. Just shoot me now!* I needed to stop talking. Every time I did, I just made it worse for myself. I hoped I'd be able to move on with my quest before my lies caught up to me.

Bianca's face fell, but her smile soon returned. "Ah. I was hoping you would be in the sculpting and installation school, but it is fine. You will have a little bit longer walk to get to the painting and visual arts building, but it won't be too bad." She smiled and it reached her eyes, making them sparkle. Luca caught my eye again, his expression nearly mirroring his sister's. I didn't think he was bugged at all to have me stay with them. Freddy, however, was busy scowling out the window. Frustration and anger radiated off of him like a fever. "Will you stay with us? Please say you will."

"Thank you," I said with complete sincerity. "You don't have to do this, but I can't say how much I appreciate it."

Bianca waved her hand, dismissing my concern. "We are happy to do it! And all of our friends will think we are so cool to have a vampire friend." She winked at me.

"Oh." I chuckled, not sure what to say to that. "I won't stay long. I promise. I'll get my own place right away."

"Do not even worry about it. You can stay with us for as long as you like." She grinned then flopped back into her seat, her arms folding over her chest, and gave her brothers a look of smug satisfaction. I smiled a little shyly at Luca, which he returned, then closed my eyes and pretended I was really tired.

I wasn't physically tired but emotionally? Mentally? My lack of a plan definitely made me feel tired.

I'd have to find a hotel room just as soon as I could. If Bianca hadn't been sitting right beside me, I would have been on Expedia looking for a room right then. There was no way I could stay with these guys while I hunted for the Master. I had to be flexible, able to follow any leads I found to the places the vamps called home. If I disappeared, Bianca would probably call the police—or worse, the university. As weird as it might seem, I didn't want to give her or Luca, even Freddy, if I were being honest, a reason to think badly about me.

It seemed like I was the first vampire they'd ever met and I felt like I had an obligation to make a good impression. Vampires had a bad rap, and I was determined to change that. So now, on top of everything else, I needed to make sure Bianca and her brothers had no reason to complain about me, no reason to worry about me, and most of all, no reason to fear me.

At least that last one was easy enough. There wasn't a single scary thing about me.

A voice came over the intercom, speaking Italian. "This is us," Bianca said.

The intercom voice spoke in English next, saying, "Rome City Center," and a thrill of excitement went through me. I hadn't been able to see much more than farmland on the way here, but now here I was—in *Rome!*

My excitement waned though when everyone seemed to press themselves toward the door, as if they couldn't get away from the scary little vampire fast enough. I swear, when we reached the terminal in Rome, that bus emptied out faster than any public transportation I'd ever been on. And that included all the Korean ones, which is saying something, trust me.

"Wow," Bianca said, looping her arm through mine as we leisurely walked inside our own little bubble of space through the terminal. "Having a vampire in my circle of friends has its advantages, I see."

Freddy and Luca walked ahead of us. Luca even volunteered to carry my backpack, so all I had to do was drag my rolling suitcase along behind me. The boys talked together in fast-flowing Italian, but I didn't get the impression they were talking about me or anything. Even Freddy seemed to be resigned to bringing me home with them.

I chuckled, then frowned. "Isn't Rome kinda full of vampires? I mean…" *Doesn't the Master of vampires live here?*

Bianca laughed. "Rome? I don't think so. Hey, Luca. Freddy. Is Rome full of vampires?"

They glanced over their shoulders, then looked at each other and shrugged.

"I do not know of any," Luca said.

"Neither do I," Freddy said. "Until now, that is." He grinned wickedly at me and I had the feeling I shouldn't let my guard down around him. No sir-ee.

"Does that answer your question?" Bianca squeezed my arm and leaned closer. "Were you hoping to snag a hot Italian vampire, hmm? Rome is called the eternal city—perhaps that is why!"

I laughed, but worry formed a hard nugget in my stomach, making me feel a little nauseous. How was I gonna find the Master now? How would I find other vampires if I was staying with these guys? And how was I gonna get away from them long enough to even try to find the city's vampires? Bianca and her brothers might think there weren't any vampires in Rome, but they had to be wrong. Maybe Roman vampires just weren't that modernized and hadn't come out of the closet.

I thought the Master had been instrumental in establishing Councils around the world, and those had been created to ensure vampires complied with the treaties. Right? A nugget of worry became a nugget of doubt—if the vampires were so far on the down-low, would it be hard to find the Italian Council? Because I was gonna need a blood supply soon and there was no way I was gonna go *foraging*, so to speak. I wanted my blood packaged up in plastic, just like it should be.

I took in the scenery as we walked and felt kind of disappointed in Rome. That part at least, looked like any other major city. Behind the bus terminal was a giant mall, with Starbucks and McDonalds across the street. I even saw a sign for Victoria's Secret. I snapped a picture, and Luca caught me doing it. He gave me a funny look.

I held up my phone for some dumb reason. "My best friend's mom owns a Victoria's Secret. I thought she'd get a kick out of knowing that one of the first stores I saw was a Victoria's Secret." Luca just stared at me like I was an alien or something. Did he not understand me?

Bianca came up beside me again. "She does? Do you get all the best things for free?"

I laughed and shook my head. "Nope. Her mom makes her buy it. But she does get a good discount." The memory of Stacey giving me that Miracle Bra last Halloween flashed through my mind. It made me miss Stacey all the more—but I did not miss those tiny micro-boobs I had when I was human! Nowadays, every day was a Miracle Bra day *without* the bra.

The walk seemed to take forever, but had probably only been ten minutes or so, and then we arrived at the famed *Termini*—the main bus terminal in Rome. We got on a city bus, and this time when we pulled out of the terminal, I finally got to see a bit of Rome. The triplets let me sit by the window again, and Bianca pointed out things to see as the bus drove through the city. I didn't see anything too amazing—except for all the things we had back home. Like a Harley Davidson store. I had to shake my head at that one.

"This is us!" Bianca said.

I followed her off the bus, the boys close behind me. Bianca bounced on the balls of her feet, a wide smile on her face. She was tall and willowy and I thought she probably could have been a dancer if she hadn't decided to be a sculptor. "Come on! We do not live far from here."

"Do you live in the dorms?" I suddenly hoped that was true because they probably weren't allowed to have guests.

Freddy came up beside me and gave me a gentle shoulder-bump. The shocked expression I turned on him was probably cartoon-worthy, but he didn't see it, thank goodness. "No. Our parents bought us a small condo when they found out we were all going here. Said it would be a good investment." I nodded at him. That was probably the most normal thing he'd said to me since I met him. Progress? Maybe. But I'd still be keeping my guard up with that guy.

I'd have to keep my guard up with all of them, which made me sad. I felt comfortable with them and I hated that all I'd done was lie.

All the buildings we walked past seemed to be newish apartment buildings built to fit in with the older architecture. Or were they all old, but some had been updated? It seemed rude to ask, so I contented myself with soaking in all the new sights, sounds and smells. Funny how every country had its own smell. Or maybe that's just me.

Then Luca was pulling open a beautiful wooden double door in the middle of the long wall. There was no signage, no number, not even a welcome mat to tell you what it was, as far as I could see. We went inside and proceeded to climb the stairs. If it weren't for my vampire stamina, I'd have been huffing and puffing by now, but neither Bianca nor her brothers seemed at all tired. On the fourth floor we finally left the stairs behind and walked down a long hallway that was as unadorned as the building's exterior. I thought everything would be beautiful and romantic here, but it wasn't that different from Seoul, really. Tiny cramped housing on tiny cramped streets.

And the hallway wasn't the only thing that was tiny and cramped.

"Here we are!" Bianca stood by an open door and spread her arm in a grand gesture. "Welcome to our humble abode." That's what she said, but her expression—even those of her brothers—showed just how proud they all were of the apartment.

"Wow," I said as I stepped inside. It was nicely decorated, and had all the Italian touches I'd expected, but man it was small.

The apartment seemed to be one long galley. We walked straight into the kitchen, with coat hooks on the wall to my right, and a short counter with cabinets above and below and a small fridge on the left. Then you walked into the dining room, which had a small round smokey-glass table with pretty place settings for four and an arrangement of fake flowers in the middle.

Scratch that. As I walked past the table, I caught the unmistakable whiff of some kind of heady flower I didn't actually know. *Wow*. Did someone come in and get the place ready for these guys? Did that mean they were rich or something?

Past the table was the living room, I guessed, since there was a couch on the right wall facing a giant flat screen TV. Two small-ish bean bag chairs flanked the couch. Beyond that, there was a wall. I made it that far before stopping and turning back to look at the siblings.

"Wow," I said again. "This is great!" I really did try to sound sincere, but inside I was kinda freaking out. How were we all to live in this tiny apartment? Even if the couch pulled out to a bed, that only accounted for one person, but there were four of us.

"Come on," Bianca said. "You can either sleep out here on the couch, or, if you don't mind, you can sleep with me." She pushed through a door in the wall that had been invisible to me at first since it had the same molding around it as the wall itself.

It led into a small bedroom—and I mean *small*. Two twin beds took up the entire space with barely enough room for a nightstand between them. It was decorated in browns and golds—definitely a boy's room. A few photos of complex metal sculptures hung on the wall next to photos of skydivers. I wished I could get a better look at the sculptures because they were probably pics of the boys' work. I wondered if the skydivers were them, or just images they liked.

"We are through here." Bianca pushed open another door that had been smartly hidden among the pattern of molding. The door led into an extremely small bathroom. It had all the necessary equipment—including a bidet— but it was definitely a one-person-at-a-time deal.

The bathroom had another door that led into a very feminine room done in colors of plum and ivory, with a bed dominating it. It looked to be only a double, but the room was just that small. Bianca had managed to tuck a v-shaped vanity into one corner, and there was just room for a small but comfy looking chair in the corner by the window. Bird sculptures were everywhere—on the vanity, on the nightstand, even hanging from ribbons in front of the window.

"Did you make these?" I asked, turning to Bianca and pointing at the pretty little birds in front of the window.

She blushed and rolled onto her toes and back. "I did. Do you like them?"

I glanced around appreciatively. "I really do."

I turned toward the window and looked out. The view was of another building and another window just like this one. The buildings were so close, I could probably jump from one to the other without my vampire abilities. And straight down was, well, straight down. I sighed. I hadn't done much jumping in my training this summer, and the ground looked awfully far away. Assuming the window even opened. I eyed it suspiciously.

"You can have whichever side of the bed you want," Bianca said. She sounded nervous and when I glanced back at her, I saw she had one corner of her bottom lip caught between her teeth and she was massaging her hand. "Unless you would rather sleep on the couch?"

I wanted to sleep on the couch—that way I could sneak out of the apartment after they all went to bed and try to find the local vampires—but I also didn't want to be in the way. Then again, maybe she was hoping I'd choose the couch, too.

"I'm happy for anything," I said. "I'm totally good with the couch."

One of her eyebrows twitched down. "Is that what you would prefer? Because I really do not mind you sharing with me. The bed is a lot more comfortable than the couch. Plus, the boys sometimes stay up very late playing video games, so…"

Dangit. I glanced at the window again. *It better open, man.* "Oh, sure. I can stay here. I really, really appreciate it. Thanks."

Bianca's whole body seemed to relax. "It really is no problem! Pick whichever side you like."

"I'll take this side," I said without pause. I sat on the edge of the bed closest to the window. "It does feel super comfy." It wasn't a lie, but I was barely thinking about the bed. I was thinking about the window and how likely it would be that I could get it open in the middle of the night without waking Bianca.

"*Eccezionale*," Bianca said. "You probably want to have a nap. Or, um…do vampires take naps?"

I sighed and scooted further onto the bed, letting my head find the pillow. "We sure do. At least, after more than twenty-four hours of travel, this one does." I sure was tired, but my brain just couldn't stop whirling, whirling, whirling around the vampire problem. How was I gonna find them? How was I gonna get out of this apartment to even try?

She laughed lightly and I closed my eyes. "No *problema*. I'll just…"

I didn't hear the rest of her words as I sank into sleep.

went in search of immortality — and
eventually found it.

Becoming a vampire is not what
makes you evil. It's the man or woman
you are in life that determines the
vampire you will become.

Our true beginning is unknown, as it
predates modern history. However,
vampire — and   some   human —
scholars have verified that vampires
existed before man — in his present
state, at least.

Without the aid of modern donation centers, many vampires resorted to hunting for their food, which is where the fear of vampires comes from. Many more, however, developed meaningful relationships with humans who became willing donors.

We encourage you to read Appendix C of this book for the list of famous vampires throughout history. While the few indulged in the careless use of human life, others valued it and strived to live worthy lives in service of humanity.

CHAPTER
THREE

I WOKE TO BIANCA'S LIGHT SNORES AND A WARM BREEZE skimming over the light blanket someone had draped over me. I was still dressed—shoes and all—but Bianca was under the covers, her legs and arms sprawled. I felt bad that I'd been such an ungrateful guest. My mom would have been mortified. And I could only imagine how I'd creeped out my hosts—vampires quite literally "sleep like the dead."

But my shame was short-lived as I got my bearings. The apartment was quiet, and I could identify the soft snores and deep breaths of three distinct people, which meant everyone was fast asleep.

And the window was cracked open.

I didn't waste any more time thinking about it.

After a quick glance at Bianca's sleeping form, I slipped off the bed and crept to the window.

And nearly tripped over my backpack.

Man, I was smooth.

A rush of hunger welled up inside me, sudden and intense, and I had to clutch at my stomach and breathe carefully through my mouth for several long seconds. It had been too long since I'd had anything to eat and I was running dangerously low on the supplies I'd brought. I crouched down and carefully, slowly, unzipped the zipper on my pack. Of course the sound seemed to creak so loudly through the room that I was positive Bianca would wake. Finally I just yanked it quickly open, then stared at Bianca for any indication she was awake.

Still sleeping, thank goodness.

Inside my thermal pack were five large thermal water bottles and four containers of blood pudding. I'd raided our stash at home, nearly cleaning us out of donor blood. I hoped Manuella wouldn't be too mad at me.

Scratch that. She'd be livid.

And then she'd be worried out of her head.

It took me a long minute while I carefully lifted each bottle to check for which one still had some blood left. I'd packed more than enough to get me through the journey plus a little to tide me over until I connected with the local Council—which I'd planned on doing just as soon as I reached Rome.

But that hadn't exactly gone as planned.

Why had I let myself get swept along with the Marinos?

I didn't have to think about it very hard. I'd been overwhelmed and basically homeless and Bianca had made it easy to let her take care of me. Finding the one remaining full bottle, I shook it a little and smelled it, just in case it had spoiled. Grateful it was still cool, I drank down just enough to ease the hunger, in case I wasn't able to find a blood bank open this late. Assuming they had such things here.

I needed to quit acting like a kid. Stop needing people to take care of me. I silently replaced the bottle and re-zipped the pack, then crept past it to the window. It was time for me to trust myself.

The window creaked some as I pushed it open wider but the sound didn't seem to disturb anyone. And wonder of wonders—there wasn't a screen on the window. I briefly wondered why, before dismissing it. No screen certainly made it easier for me. Silently stepping into the window frame, I glanced back at the bed. Still no movement. It occurred to me that this was probably the most vampire-like thing I'd ever done. Sleep during the day, sneak out by jumping out of a four-story window at night. Scary. And also kinda cool.

Well, I thought as I contemplated the ground four stories below. *I am a vampire. And maybe it's time I started acting like one. Like Minnie Aristos instead of Minnie Kim.*

I stood, the window almost tall enough for me to stand up straight, and stepped out into the air.

Landing silently in a crouch, I grinned. Grinned like a crazy idiot. Man, I wished Philo had been there to see that. Or David. Or Siobhan or Fearghus—anyone who knew and loved me and could appreciate that this was the furthest I'd ever jumped and that I'd done it with ease.

I stood and swiped my hands together, then began strolling down the street just as cool as could be. The night was warm and there was a heady smell of flowers in the air. Not everyone was asleep, as many windows shone with light from the apartments surrounding me, and I didn't need my special skills to hear the murmur of voices and televisions drifting through the night.

I'd only taken a few steps before I realized I had no idea where I was or where I was going. I dug my phone out of my back pocket, but even though I'd charged it while in the airport, the battery was nearly dead. Plus, I realized with a stab of chagrin, I apparently didn't have service in Italy. **Nice**. I couldn't even search the internet! The only information my phone was able to give me was that it was not quite midnight. *Woo.*

So I closed my eyes and focused my senses as Sang had been trying to teach me this summer.

I'd learned that the vampire was the perfect predator, able to move freely in society, able to hunt without alerting her prey. We could hear heartbeats through walls, smell fresh blood a mile or so away—depending on the environment—and smell humans even further away than that.

I'd never really tested my abilities, beyond what Sang required of me when we practiced. I always preferred to be more human than vampire. Sang accused me of trying to cling to my old life and…maybe he was right. It's just that I'd loved my old life.

Maybe, since I was here and far away from anything I knew, I could practice being Minnie Aristos before I did anything drastic like give up on my old life. Maybe, despite what Sang thought, I'd be able to find a way to be both Minnie Kim the *girl* and the *vampire*.

At least Philo had led me to believe it was possible.

Thinking of him was just what I needed, and I shut out my mind chatter to focus on the world around me. I needed to find a hospital, or at least another vampire. Despite what the Marinos had said, there had to be vampires here.

Squeezing my eyes tightly closed, I slowed my heart and stopped breathing, focusing all my attention on sound and smell.

There was a party somewhere, a big one. I began walking toward it before I'd even opened my eyes. At least I could maybe make inquiries about a local hospital.

I moved off the sidewalk and into the shadows of the buildings crowding the narrow streets so I could speed toward the party sounds without being obvious about it. Soon, I discovered it wasn't a party at all, but a night club. It was a pretty big club, and judging by the general age of the people hanging around outside, it primarily served the college crowd. That suited me just fine, as it'd be hard enough to fit in among them, since I looked so young.

I drew some attention as I approached the door. Maybe they didn't have a super large Korean population among the students? Whatever the reason, I ignored the curious looks and pushed through the heavy steel door.

Inside, the music was so loud, I felt it through my feet and in my teeth. It moved through me and made my fingers tingle. I stood still for a moment, trying to dim the sound within me so I could focus instead on the conversations, and the heartbeats, around me.

"*Yo, signorina. Ho bisogno di vedere la tua identificazione.*" The loud words cut through my concentration and I turned my head to see a burly man, his polo shirt stretched tight over his enormous biceps and pecs, a dismissive expression on his face.

"I'm sorry," I said, turning toward him and stepping closer.

He huffed and shook his head a little, as if he couldn't believe how dense I was. "*La tua carta d'identità*," he said in a condescending tone while flicking his fingers at me.

I narrowed my eyes and frowned. I knew what he meant, now that I was paying attention. But he didn't have to be so rude about it. I pulled out my phone and then my ID from its slot on the back of my phone case. As I handed it over, though, I realized I didn't know what the legal age was in Italy, and either way, at sixteen I probably wasn't it.

The guy took the card and shone his flashlight on it while I prepared myself to influence his mind so he'd let me in.

He glanced up, and I was ready. "*Americano*, eh?"

I smiled a little and nodded, sending a small stream of *trust* into his mind.

He handed my card back and waved his flashlight toward the party. A moment later, he said, "*Buon compleanno*."

I stopped and turned back. "I'm sorry, what? Um, *mi scusi?*" I mean, I'd played a little Duo Lingo on the trip over here.

The big man smiled, completely transforming his face into one of pleasant kindness. He gestured to my card, that I'd been in the process of tucking back into my phone case. "Happy birthday," he said in careful, choppy English.

I had to think for a second. What day was it? "Oh!" I'd completely forgotten about my birthday. "Thanks!"

As I turned away, I checked my phone. Holy smokes, it was already September 3rd? Just barely, since it was just 12:15 a.m., but still. It really was my birthday. How…then I remembered it was tomorrow in Rome.

But that still only made me seventeen.

Again I turned back to the bouncer. "Excuse me?" I waited for him to stop glaring at a couple who were making out rather, um, intensely, and to face me. "What's the, um, drinking age here?" I pantomimed holding a cup to my mouth and throwing it back. Had he only let me in because it was my birthday? If so, it was probably stupid of me to be pointing it out.

He seemed to understand me just fine because he grinned merrily at my improvised sign language. "*Sedici.*" He held up ten fingers, then six fingers.

My mouth fell open. "Really?"

His grin grew and I found my own smile matching his. He might be a bit dangerous looking and at least as wide as two of me, but I liked him. "*Sì davvero.*"

I grinned madly back at him and bounced a little on my toes. "Awesome, thanks!" I spun around to face the dance floor, then whirled back again. "*Grazie!*" I told the bouncer brightly. He gave a slight bow and I returned to the crowd, feeling a lot lighter and relaxed than I had since arriving in Rome.

I began walking around the large dance floor with its crush of bodies moving, bouncing and grinding. The main floor was mainly a dance floor, with a slightly raised section with round tables and a railing flanking it on two sides. At the far end of the dance floor was a DJ booth where a real-live DJ cranked out some electric dance music I couldn't recognize. It was no BTS, that's for sure. Still, I found myself bobbing my head along with the infectious beat as I took stock of the layout.

Above the dance floor, the second floor looked out over the dancers. I made my way toward the stairs and had my foot on the first step, when a cold shiver crept up my neck and the fine hairs there stood at attention. I slowly removed my foot and turned, my back to the wall as I scanned the room for the source of that eerie feeling.

I knew what it meant, and the knowledge filled me with excitement and dread.

Another vampire was near.

It took me a minute to pinpoint who the vampire was, but then I saw him talking to the bouncer. A good-looking guy wearing a rugby shirt and deck shorts, he seemed to take up more space than a regular person. I heard the slow thump…thump…of a vampire and not the normal thrum of a human's heart.

A couple on their way up the stairs bumped into me, then sort of used me as a wall for a second as they tried to swallow each other's faces, before I managed to get away with an audible, "Ew!" They didn't acknowledge me. And…now I couldn't see the vamp. Great!

But I did see Bianca.

"Bianca!" I called over the noise, and started to push through the crowd between us. I wanted to get to her before she got to the dance floor or I'd lose her for sure. But the club was getting busier and louder by the second and hey, let's face it. I'm short. I couldn't see a thing past all the bodies.

I finally made it to the spot where I'd last seen her and…nothing.

"Dangit," I muttered, scanning the bodies as best I could.

"*Ti terrò compagnia, piccola.*" Some guy began grinding against me and I whirled, pushing him away with both hands.

"Ew!" I said again. I gave him a hate-filled glare and he backed up, his hands in the air, all while smiling and saying naughty things by the way he raked his gaze over my body.

Ugh, I thought. I turned back to my search, hugging my arms around me. I was in way over my head here and feeling more and more like Minnie *Kim* than *Aristos*. I couldn't see the vampire, I couldn't see Bianca, and I was obviously not cut out for an Italian night club.

After another few minutes, and a random butt-squeeze—someone totally grabbed my butt, but when I whirled around, no one seemed to be paying me any attention—I decided to cut my losses and go outside. Maybe I'd wait out there, or maybe I'd try just walking around and hope I bumped into a vamp. Couldn't be any worse of a plan than this was. I'd read about how touchy-feely Italian men could be, but the reality—yikes.

I squeezed my way toward the front door. The bouncer noticed me and called out—of course I didn't understand what he said, but by the look on his face and his tone of voice, I think he was asking if I was okay or something. I tried to smile brightly and waved, but he only frowned. I don't think he bought it, but there wasn't anything he could do, so I pressed on out the door.

There was a line of people waiting to get in. What the heck? I might not be positive what day of the week or even day of the month it was, but I was pretty sure it was a weekday. I hadn't lost track of that much time.

Once I got past the throng of people in line, I found an empty section of wall to lean against. There were still way too many people out here, and apparently I must have chosen the smoking section or something, because it seemed like every person I glanced at had a cigarette, or even a cigar, sticking out of their mouth. I'd looked forward to some fresh air, but there wouldn't be any here.

A group of guys and girls walked past me, and one of the guys slowed to look at me. He winked, then moved on.

It wasn't until he'd passed that I realized he was a vampire.

I jerked off the wall and tried to scan the crowd and line for the winking guy. Of course I couldn't see him.

With a huff I leaned back against the wall. Maybe I would stay here. I'd just wait outside until one vampire or another went past, then I'd follow them. I could do that. So I slid down the wall and settled on the ground for a long session of people watching and vampire hunting.

Queen Elizabeth I is a prime example—while she was persecuted for her unusual habits and her intimacy with men she did not marry, she gave her life—and her immortality—in the service of her kingdom.

Queen Elizabeth is but one example. As you'll note, many of the great men and women throughout the ages that humans admire, were in fact vampires.

Balanced against the whole, vampires have done more good than harm.

Humans are naturally wary of vampires and you shouldn't let that trouble you. They have endured centuries of violence at the hands of supernatural creatures, and since vampires are the only ones who have had the courage to reveal themselves to the world, it's only natural they blame us. <u>But there are worse things</u> than vampires in this world. *What's worse? I get why they said this but it's scary to think about what else is out there. Plus, it comes off as kinda snooty.* V

CHAPTER
FOUR

I'D NEVER TURNED DOWN SO MANY GUYS IN MY LIFE. I'D never been *approached* by so many guys in my life. It might have been flattering if they weren't all stinkin' drunk.

"*Ciao bella. Sembri così triste. Lascia che ti rallegri.*" A boy collapsed to the ground next to me and attempted to wrap his arm around me. He'd have been cute if his whole face hadn't been melting due to him being excessively drunk. I struggled to push him off of me without using too much vampire strength—his friends had congregated near us and at least one of them seemed to be sober enough to take note of such a thing.

"Ugh," I grunted. "Get. Off. Me."

The boy laughed and leaned back, a hand over his heart. He said something in a wounded tone of voice, but

I didn't hear him. Over his shoulder, I saw Bianca staggering out of the club. She was clinging to some guy, barely able to keep herself upright.

"I've gotta go," I said to the groper, and jumped to my feet. I was about to call out to Bianca, when I noticed she was with the rugby guy. The sporty vampire.

I froze, which gave the groper another chance to try to convince me of his undying love. I shrugged him off, doing my best to ignore him and his friends while I watched Bianca and the vamp slowly make their way down the street. I didn't know what to do. I mean, maybe this guy was her boyfriend. Maybe he was just gonna take her home.

And even if he took her to his place, there were…other things a boy and girl could do together that had nothing to do with drinking her blood.

Then again, I'd seen enough of Philo's memories to know that was usually what a vampire wanted from a human.

As soon as they turned the corner at the end of the street, I sprinted after them.

The guys at the club called after me, but I ignored them, focusing solely on the sound of Bianca's laughter. I kept my own self as soundless as I could—the last thing I wanted was to give myself away. If this was innocent, then I did not want to offend my new friend—and my only friend in this whole country at the moment—by causing a scene. I just needed to know for sure that it was…well, innocent. Or, at least as innocent as any relationship can be between two consenting adults.

Bianca told me she and her brothers were nineteen, and in their second year at RUFA. She hadn't mentioned a boyfriend, but she'd spent most of our time together asking me all sorts of questions. I'd barely had any chance at all to ask her many.

The problem was, I had asked if they knew any vampires, and she had specifically said no. Which either meant she had lied to me about her boyfriend, which was entirely possible of course, but didn't really make sense, or she didn't know. I mean, why would she lie about that? She was talking to me, a vampire. At that point, she'd already invited me to stay with them, so I figured they didn't have any prejudices against my kind. Unless of course they didn't have a problem generally, but maybe her brothers had a problem with their sister specifically, dating one.

I didn't want to think about the other possibility.

I didn't want to think what it might mean if Bianca didn't know this guy was a vamp.

If she was his girlfriend, wouldn't she know? Wouldn't he tell her?

And if he hadn't told her, well, that was a problem. Wasn't it?

Didn't a person have a right to know if their partner relied on human blood to survive?

For someone like me, someone reMade since the Treaty of London, it seemed perfectly acceptable to drink from legally sourced blood. But for someone older…for someone who maybe had a different kind of sire, a different kind of family than the Aristos clan, bagged blood might not be acceptable.

David had told me once that the Councils had largely been formed to identify the vampires in their jurisdictions and to ensure they changed their eating habits to meet the newly legislated standards.

Bianca's guy didn't look like an old vampire about to suck her dry. He looked like a European poster boy for healthy, active living.

But he *was* a vampire and knew better than most that looks could be deceiving.

I got to the corner, grateful to see them still slowly making their way down the block. She seemed to be walking a little straighter, which gave me a sense of relief. Maybe she'd just stumbled trying to get through the crowd that still clung to the club, even though it was two in the morning.

And what if he'd just picked her up and she had no idea what she was getting into?

I followed at a long distance from them, anxious not to get too close and give my presence away. Problem was, it meant if I stayed far enough back that the vamp couldn't sense me, then I couldn't hear what they were talking about. Not that that was any of my business, but it might have helped me know what to do.

After some walking, I realized we were heading in the direction of Bianca's apartment, which went a long way to easing my worries. I could meet up with her before she opened the apartment door maybe, which would save me the trouble of trying to figure out how to scale the side of the building and get back in through the window—something I hadn't been looking forward to at all.

I still didn't know how I was gonna explain my disappearance through her bedroom window in the middle of the night, but maybe I could explain it away by saying I felt like checking out the night life and didn't want to wake her. Though, since she'd done the exact same thing, she'd probably just be disappointed I didn't wake her so we could go together.

Ugh. I sucked at lying. I'd just never had much use for it. Well, beyond the little ones I told my parents like when I said I'd been studying, when really I'd spent the whole night watching BlackPink videos and stalking the BTS boys on Instagram. I never felt like those little lies were a big deal because I'd done the studying—I just hadn't needed to do it for hours and hours every single night. And since I got A's, my parents never knew the difference.

Somehow, I felt like any lies I told Bianca were a much bigger deal. Just by virtue of being a vampire, I felt like any lies I told were a bigger deal.

Wait.

Where did they go?

I'd been a little lost in my own thoughts, but I could only have looked away for a second, how could they have gotten so far ahead?

Oh, right.

Vampire.

He only needed a second to do...well, just about anything. A second to speed away, out of my line of sight. A second to disappear. A second to bite into Bianca's neck and...

I ran toward where I'd last seen them and stumbled to a stop when I reached the spot. They were nowhere in sight.

My nerves were on fire, every part of me anxious to find and protect Bianca. The thought reminded me of Veyo and my heart constricted a little. If only he were here with me; we'd have no trouble following their trail, then.

Still, I worked on calming my nerves while I asked myself what Veyo would do. Veyo had said he knew he needed to find and protect me, and because he'd been in wolf shape at that time, he'd just let his instincts take over. *Instincts.*

It was really hard for me to do that, to just relinquish thought for the sake of instinct. My whole upbringing had been about self-control and using one's mind rather than one's heart. But I'd also spent two glorious weeks every summer at drama camp since I was eight, so I'd learned a little about loosening up.

I repeated my little *drama llama* mantra and gently tried to push down my conscious mind while I opened myself up to my senses.

It gave me a little jolt when I realized just how much of my vampire self I suppressed, because now that I let go of some of my control, I felt this well of power and strength fill me. It reminded me of the first time one of the camp counselors tried to teach me how to project. Unsurprisingly, I'd been somewhat reserved as a child. Not a pushover by any means, but I didn't use my voice very much.

In this one exercise he gave us, we were supposed to say our lines out loud. Like, really loud. We weren't supposed to worry about how we sounded, or about speaking the line perfectly or anything, we just needed to "release our voice."

That exercise had been the single most difficult thing I'd ever done in drama, but it had been the best thing for me, too.

It took me nearly the full two weeks to get it. I'd get louder, but the counselor would keep telling me to "let go!" and to quit holding myself back. It was so infuriating! I *was* letting go! I wasn't holding back!

At least, that's what I told her and everyone else who would listen. But even Stacey, who was supposed to be my best friend, agreed with the counselor. When Stacey told me I should do something differently, I tended to believe her. She knew, better than anyone, what my parents were like and what *I* was like. She knew how hard it was for me to relinquish control to something that felt so wild. With Stace to cheer me on, I kept trying.

And on the second-to-last day of the camp, I did it.

Of course I was so mad with myself for not getting it sooner, because speaking with my full voice felt so freeing and powerful. It almost made me feel like a different person. Like a real actor.

And now, as I let the suppressed vampire within me rise to the surface, filling my whole body and mind with power and strength and freedom, I felt that same sensation. I was still me. I didn't feel like going on a blood hunger rampage or anything. But I felt *more*. I felt everything. Like I was a *real* vampire.

And I could smell Bianca's unique scent of bergamot and lemon. I'd know that scent anywhere as her whole room had been drenched in it (not in a bad way, but the room was small). The scent came alive to my eyes as if I had synesthesia, revealing a path to my right in the pale yellow my mind associated with Bianca's scent. I had no idea I could do that—it was remarkable!

With the yellow glow leading me, I didn't have to be careful with my speed, and at this point, I didn't care who might still be awake and spot me zooming by. Bianca's life might be in danger at that very moment. Besides, with my inhibitions stripped away I was able to run much faster than usual. Maybe even fast enough that a human wouldn't see me, only feel the wind gust as I rushed past.

The trail led down a narrow alley between two apartment buildings, down a street, then diagonally across an intersection. Then the vamp had actually doubled back on the opposite side of the street for a while, which really made me nervous. He knew I'd been following him, then, otherwise, why go to such lengths to evade me? What burned me most was that Bianca must be in his thrall because he'd have to pick her up in order to move so fast.

Also, didn't they say only the guilty run?

He obviously wasn't taking Bianca back to our apartment, either.

The path of Bianca's scent led me through a warren of buildings until I was completely lost. Did the vamp not know I could track them this way? Or maybe he'd thought I'd give up. If he didn't know Bianca meant something to me, I suppose he might think that.

I lurched to a stop when the trail disappeared inside an old house. I wasn't breathing hard, but I still placed my hand over my heart as I took in my surroundings and considered what to do next. I didn't know how long the scent trail would last, but either way, I needed to hurry before…

I shook my head, refusing to consider the worst.

I needed to hurry. *Period.*

There were a lot more trees here than in Bianca's neighborhood and I sensed a large green space—a park, maybe?—to my left. The apartment building seemed to be an old home that had been redeveloped into an apartment complex. It might not have been crappy once, but it was definitely in bad shape now. All the windows were dark, which struck me as odd. From what I'd seen so far, Italians were night owls and every building I'd passed had at least one light on. If vampires lived here, there was no doubt they were awake. So why the dark windows?

I picked my way over the crumbling cement walkway up to the front door where Bianca had gone in. I couldn't hear a thing. Even when I pressed my ear to the splintering front door, I heard nothing. How was that possible? I knew Bianca and her vampire were inside—I should at least be able to hear them, or her heartbeat and breathing.

Unless…

No. No unless. Bianca was still alive and I was going in there. I had to go in there.

Vamped out or not, though, I was terrified. What would I find inside that building?

What would I do if I really was too late?

What would I do if I wasn't?

With a deep breath for courage, I turned the old brass doorknob, found it unlocked, and stepped inside.

VAMPIRE SOCIETY

CHAPTER TWO

Traditionally, vampires have avoided others of their kind, with the only exception being those in their own family. Even then, many vampires have sought out a solitary life.

The Treaty of London, however, has already begun to change the way vampires interact with one another. Since they are able settle down into one place, vampires are finding themselves turning to some of their more human behaviors, including associating with one another far more regularly than at any time in our history.

Association generally happens at council meetings, which have begun to be arranged to allow for socializing, though as more vampires come into populated areas, they may run into others more often than before.

CHAPTER FIVE

IT WASN'T AT ALL LIKE I EXPECTED.

I'd expected, oh I don't know—a lush entryway filled with red velvet loungers and scads of scantily clad vampires and their thralls draped all over the place.

I blinked. Yeah, this wasn't at all like that.

Somewhere in the past, these apartments had once been a home, so an empty, unassuming entryway faced me, with nothing but closed doors on every side. But which one would lead me to Bianca? I focused on my hearing, but the sound felt muffled, as if my head was underwater. It had to be someone's gift here, something they used to keep the outside world from hearing what went on inside these walls. I had no idea such a gift existed, and it really creeped me out that it would be needed here. I paused before each door on the main floor, listening for Bianca's voice, but I still heard nothing.

There wasn't anything interfering with my sense of smell though, and this place reeked of blood.

I was about to go up to the second floor and try my luck there, when a door opened on the floor above, and music and voices spilled out. I ran behind the stairs in a flash, still unsure of what kind of welcome I'd receive if any of the vampires living here found me lurking around.

It wasn't long before I felt immensely grateful to have slipped out of view, because Bianca and her fangy boyfriend were coming down the stairs.

They chatted away in Italian, so of course I couldn't understand a thing, but their conversation was animated which led me to guess he hadn't drunk from her—at least not much. Bianca was the one doing most of the talking and she sounded just like she had on the bus, not like someone who'd just been in a vampire's thrall.

I watched as the vampire held the door open for her, then followed her out onto the quiet street. After a beat, I silently trailed after. Once outside, I saw them retracing their steps and I decided Bianca was safe—for now. I sped home, grateful for my vampire sense of direction. Turns out, scaling the outside of Bianca's building was way easier than I thought it would be, thank goodness. I'd just slipped under the bed covers when I heard the front door quietly snick open.

I listened while Bianca snuck into the apartment, her feet silent as if she'd taken off her shoes before coming inside. I listened while she undressed and used the washroom. I was busy debating whether I should say anything to her, whether I should pretend to be asleep, when she let out a long, satisfied sigh as she relaxed onto the bed.

"Hey," I said into the darkness, my voice barely above a whisper. I still hadn't decided what I should do, but as usual, my mouth made up my mind for me. Once, I read that extroverts think out loud—that they often don't know what they think or even feel about something until they've said it. I'd scoffed at the idea at the time. I mean, the human brain was the most amazing supercomputer on the planet—the idea that words could tumble out without you first choosing to say them seemed ludicrous to me. Except here I was, talking before I'd made up my mind to do so.

"Oh, hey!" Bianca turned on her side to face me, so I did the same. She didn't look at all sleepy. She'd scrubbed the makeup off her face and in the dim moonlight she appeared younger than before and full of shiny excitement. "You're back."

"Sorry about that." *What next?* I furiously asked my mouth. Of course when I needed it to decide for me, nothing came out. Typical. "I…uh…heard from a friend. And they, um, wanted to meet up." Ah! That was the worst lie—now I'd probably have to come up with who the friend was, what we did, and why wasn't I staying with her/him instead of total strangers?

"Oh, don't even worry about it. But, how did you get out?"

I glanced over my shoulder to the window and gave a one-shoulder shrug.

Bianca covered her mouth with a hand, her smile growing wide behind it. "Really? I'm so sorry. Next time, just tell me and you can leave through the front door and I'll lock up after you. Though usually we are still awake until the early morning hours, so you won't have any trouble getting out. It's only because we were all so tired from our travels tonight."

I grinned at her. "But you went out." I bit my lower lip, worried she'd see me as accusatory (which I kinda was), rather than conspiratorial.

Bianca squeaked out a sound of happiness and flopped onto her back, her hands flailing until one came to rest against me. She really was so much like Stacey. Stacey had no problem touching people, and I'd gotten used to it—from her. I was not so comfortable with strangers touching me.

"I did." Bianca snort-giggled. A moment later she swiveled her head to face me. "His name is Matteo. We've been seeing each other off and on for the past year, but we really missed each other while I was away.

I think it is time for us to take it to the next level." Her eyes sparkled with excitement.

I debated whether or not to ask if she knew Matteo was a vampire, but Bianca took care of that for me. She rolled onto her side again, placing both her hands beneath her cheek as she stared at me.

"Actually, that is why I was so very pleased to meet you today, and then to have you stay with us. I have so many questions for you. Do you mind?"

I quirked one eyebrow downward, as if I was unsure what she might want to talk to me about.

"Matteo is a vampire," she said. "Like you."

I felt my eyebrows rise, even though I suspected this was what she was about to say. "Really?" I drawled. "Wow."

Bianca placed a hand on my wrist. "The two of you are very much alike." I opened my mouth to ask how she knew that, since she'd only just met me, but she kept talking. "At least, I think you are alike. I think you would like him. He's not scary like you imagine vampires to be—he's a modern vampire. He only drinks donated blood, too. That's what you do, isn't it?"

I nodded slowly, but my mind was racing. That house had been full of vampires, and while I didn't see any blood orgies going on, I'd smelled blood. Donated blood, blood bags, blood warmers; there was really no mess with that kind of blood use. My house certainly didn't smell like layers and layers of blood, both old and new.

Sure, maybe Bianca's Matteo was different. Maybe he really was telling her the truth. I just knew that it would be very, very hard to live in a place that smelled like that, with people who lived like the others did in his building and still abstain from joining the others. I didn't know if her Matteo could do that.

But, I needed an in with the local vamps if I was gonna figure out where the Master was, so I smiled and said, "I'd love to meet him."

Bianca's grip on my wrist tightened. "Really? I was hoping you would! I told him all about you, and he'd love to meet you, too. He has something going on tonight, but we could meet up with him tomorrow." She peered hopefully into my eyes.

I felt as if the blood had stopped flowing into my veins. Why would this vamp want to meet me? Why would he care? I tried to soothe the fear that threatened to dominate by telling myself he was probably just worried I'd eat his girlfriend. I mean, he didn't know me, either. For all he knew, Bianca wasn't safe with *me*.

"That would be great."

Bianca didn't seem to notice the flat tone in my voice because she squeezed my wrist again, then leaned forward and kissed my cheek. I was still staring at her, stunned for more than one reason, as she rolled over to her side and pulled the sheet up to her chin.

"I'm glad you're here, Minnie. I just know we are going to be great friends."

I was still staring at her back long after her breathing told me she'd fallen deep asleep.

사랑해

It wasn't easy, but the next day I managed to convince the family to go about their normal life while I met with the dean and did some other boring stuff. I had to promise them I wouldn't do any sight-seeing though, which was a promise I couldn't exactly keep. At least, not in the strictest sense. I wasn't going sight-seeing per se, but I did plan to do some looking around.

I got ready, and left the apartment before ten in the morning, while the three of them were still lounging around, barely awake. I told them I was off to see the dean, when really, I was off to find one of the Council-run donor places. This summer I'd learned a lot about self-control and how to manage my hunger, but it had been over thirty-six hours since I finished off the last of the blood in the thermoses I'd brought with me, and this morning I'd eaten my last piece of pudding. I wasn't quite hangry, but I definitely needed blood. Soon.

I'd spent most of the night pondering what to do and finally come to the conclusion that in all likelihood, the Master knew I was here. That is, if he cared. Maybe I had it all wrong and he couldn't give a flying fig about me, but if he did, then he'd know I'd come to Italy. So there wasn't any point to starving myself just for the sake of stealth.

This morning I looked up the location of the Council Headquarters and found that it was actually several hours south of here, but there were offices scattered around the city where you could register your presence and arrange for donor blood. The closest place was a hotel just fifteen minutes away from the apartment.

I hadn't thought to bring any fancy clothes—just stuffed things into my bag—so I had to try to make what I had look artsy. Still, Bianca gave me a quizzical look when I pulled on a black pleated mini skirt, my Drama Llama T-shirt (for luck) and wove a random pink scarf I'd stuffed into my bag around my throat. My knee-high socks and pink high-top sneakers looked fun with the outfit, but I had the feeling Bianca thought I should be a lot more dressed up for a meeting with the dean. I pretended not to notice her disapproval, opting for an air of confidence as I said my goodbyes.

It was getting easier and easier to act, and feel, confident the more I used my vampire abilities. It was like putting on a costume and acting a part in a play—

when I allowed myself to be vampire, I glided as I walked, and felt capable of just about everything. I caught snippets of thoughts as I passed by, all of them taking note of me and not seeing the geeky high school girl, but someone confident and beautiful instead.

It had been coming on for a while now, the blurring of the line between vampire and human. I wondered if there would come a time when I didn't feel human anymore, at all. That's what all my family said. In fact, they'd all been mystified that I'd held onto my humanity for so long. Everyone except for Philo, anyway. He seemed to understand. And David, too.

But now, I wondered if I should just stop pretending to be what I'd always been and embrace what I was becoming. Even if I allowed myself to be more vampire, that didn't mean I had to abandon my humanity. Ugh. My brain was getting all twisted around.

I gave myself a mental shake and decided that for now, for as long as I was in Italy, it was probably a good idea to embrace the vampire. I knew how, now. My training this summer hadn't been long, but it had been thorough, I was sure. And I was gonna need every bit of advantage I could get if I was going to find where the Master was holding Philo and set him free.

First things first, though—blood.

Using Bianca's laptop, I located the nearest Council office—the hotel was within walking distance, so I set out. The Mercure Roma Corsa Trieste was a surprise. Nestled amongst old, classical buildings, it had a smoky glass and steel façade with a rotating door. I pushed through and found myself in a small, ultra-modern lobby in bold colors. I might have gaped for a moment, taking in the mural that dominated the far wall. I guessed it was a photograph of the hotel's exterior before its modern makeover, with pop culture references splashed over it. It was kinda cool, but also weird. I wondered what the Marinos would say about it. Finally, my gaze swung to the desk and the vampire waiting there with a smile.

A vamp I recognized.

I walked toward him, watching as he abandoned his human façade just as I'd decided to do moments earlier. This guy had a cocky attitude and I'd been so surprised to see him here that had I been *Minnie the human*, I would have tripped all over myself, I'm sure. But I was *Minnie the vampire* now, and she was all boss. Plus, I had the advantage over him. I knew he was Matteo, Bianca's boyfriend and I knew where he lived.

Not that I could imagine using that information in any nefarious way. It just made me feel cooler, thinking it.

"Ah," Matteo said in a beautiful Italian accent. "You must be Minnie. Bianca told me you were staying with her."

I smiled graciously and hoped my face didn't show my surprise. Of course she would have told him. Having a vampire friend probably made Bianca feel cooler and as if it made her more worthy of a vampire boyfriend. "Yeah!" I said brightly. "I'm Minnie Kim Aristos." I added that last on a whim, suddenly feeling that I needed the weight of that ancient name to give me clout.

I held out my hand, but instead of shaking it like I thought he'd do, he turned it and kissed my knuckles. He lingered there, looking up at me through hooded eyes and said, "I am Matteo Valerius. It is a pleasure to meet you."

Remaining still and accepting this oddly formal and old-fashioned greeting was a great test of my acting skills because inside I was squirming and squealing *Ew!* I wondered if I'd ever get used to the idiosyncrasies of old vamps.

Instead, I took a deep breath, reminded myself that I was the boss of my hand, *thankyouverymuch*, and I withdrew it without any fuss. "Well that certainly makes this easy. I haven't done much traveling, so I wasn't sure how to go about finding what I'm looking for." If Matteo noticed my snub, he let it slide right off him, because he was all suave charm as he opened the swinging gate at the end of the desk and invited me to join him in the back room.

It was just a small office or break room—a few chairs, some boxes that, judging by the open ones I saw, held supplies for the front counter, including key card folders and pamphlets boasting the local sights.

Matteo took one of the gray folding chairs and indicated for me to join him, then he began fussing with his phone. I sat, and just as I was about to ask him what he was doing, he finally spoke.

"Okay. What is your full name, again?" He had his thumbs poised over his phone and when I gave him my name, he typed it in. "You said a different last name a moment ago. Was that your clan name?"

Dangit. My boss self was off her game. "Yes," I confirmed smoothly. "Aristos."

One of his eyebrows quirked up, but otherwise, he didn't comment. "And where do you live?"

"Meyers Town, Utah. In the States."

"How long will you be here?" His accent was strong, but his English smooth—probably from working at the hotel.

"That…I'm not sure."

He looked up from his phone. "You're not sure?"

"No. I'm not here for a vacation. I'm here on business, I guess you could say." I looked down and realized I'd been twisting the edge of my T-shirt around and around. I smoothed it as best I could and folded my hands loosely together in my lap. I had to keep my cool. Be a boss.

"Bianca said you were going to RUFA." His eyebrows drew down low over his eyes as he watched me.

I decided to take a chance, and let a tiny tendril of my awareness trickle into his mind. I wanted to know if he was close to the Master, or if it would be safe to tell him a portion of the truth. I was only in his mind for a moment, but it was long enough to learn what I needed to know.

Turns out, Matteo wasn't the older, experienced vampire he'd wanted me to believe. I mean, yes, he was a hundred years old or so, but he lived like a college student—one who drank blood instead of beer. And he was exactly the kind of vampire I thought he was—the kind who picked up girls on campus or at parties and took them home to drink from them. The desire to kick his butt roiled fiercely within me.

I smoothed my hands down my mini-skirt and gave Matteo what I hoped would be a coy smile. By the way his gaze dropped to my lips and his tongue darted out to moisten his own, I think I succeeded.

"Actually," I said. "I came to Italy to meet the Master."

His gaze flicked up to mine, his eyes widening. "Why would you want to do that?"

I gave a little shrug. "I hardly know anything about him. But I want to know. My gifts are…special." I inwardly cringed and worried I was coming on too strong, but I was all in now. "I think he might be able to use me."

Matteo scoffed. "He'll have you for breakfast and toss you into the sea. What makes you think he will want you around?" He folded his arms, his phone forgotten, but my awareness of him told me it was all bravado. He didn't like the idea that I actually wanted to meet the Master, as it seemed he'd actively tried to stay under the Master's radar.

"Have you met him?" I turned my charm on full blast and leaned forward intently. "Can you introduce me to him?"

My ploy worked. My guess that he was a bit of a player and wanted people to see him as The Guy, proved accurate. He gave me a wolfish grin. "I have never met him, but my sire is his child, and knows him personally. Why don't you come over tonight and I can introduce you to him? Demitri will be able to tell you all you need to know."

My insides turned to ice as I returned Matteo's grin.

So grateful for my fam. Everyone is so cool – even ones who were harder to get to know, like Mrs. Hamburg. I still can't believe she's gone. She was angry a lot but she also CARED a lot.

It is often difficult for young and old vampires to comingle. There are many reasons for this, including, but not limited to social, cultural and gender norms practiced in the time they came of age. Asking an ancient vampire to share his feelings can be akin to asking a young vampire to devour a village. Each era has its own accepted practices and must be respected. ♡

But maybe my fam isn't normal?

Young vampires, in particular, have a tendency to assume that vampires should be like them — which is to say, like humans. Yet most vampires did not grow up in this generation, or even in this century.

It cannot be stressed enough: You must be on your best behavior when socializing with other vampires. You cannot be too formal or too exacting in your politeness. If you must err, always err on the side of caution.

Always keep in mind that most vampires you meet will be accustomed to a life of solitude. Some may not be

CHAPTER
SIX

I MANAGED TO KEEP MY ACT TOGETHER UNTIL I STEPPED outside the hotel and rounded the corner, out of sight of the hotel's wall of windows. Then I sagged against the old stone wall and breathed out a long sigh of relief. I'd done it. I'd actually come face to face with an Italian vampire, and I think I totally managed to come off as *adult* and *in control*. At least I really hoped so.

It hadn't been as hard as I thought it would be. All I did was channel my inner debate team captain and I was in the zone. As long as I remembered to keep that persona, I thought I could actually pull this whole thing off. Whatever that was.

With everything in motion, and my blood supply lined up—Matteo had said he'd have my first delivery sent to Bianca's apartment within the hour—I decided to take the scenic route on the way home. Tonight, Matteo would take me to meet his sire who might be able to help me find the Master.

As I slowly walked the old streets, enjoying the architecture and the lovely weather, I felt a sort of buoyant joy. I came across a tree with a sign saying it was over six hundred years old. With my hand pressed to its rough, deeply grooved bark, I looked up and up and up and still couldn't see the top of its branches.

"You are a beautiful thing," I whispered to it, awed by its strength and longevity as much as by its incredible height and the breadth of its canopy. The realization that the Master was far older than this tree, with a reach that far surpassed it, left me feeling a little disheartened.

"I'm coming for you, Philo." I sent my promise winging along with the wind, needing to hear myself say it in order to combat the sudden force of my fear and doubt.

When the startling sound of BlackPink's *Ddu-du Ddu-du* punched into the quiet air I literally jumped and wrapped my arms around myself. I wasn't alone on the street, but I was in a residential area so at least there weren't a ton of tourists crowding the sidewalk to witness my embarrassing moment. Once I'd calmed my heart enough to think clearly, I dug into my front pocket and pulled out my phone. I already knew whose name would be on the caller ID; the question was, was I ready to talk to her—or anyone from home.

In the end, it was a dirty look from an older couple strolling by with a pair of little dogs at their feet that had me pushing the answer button. I just wanted to stop the noise.

Except, I didn't put the phone to my ear right away.

"Minnie? Minnie! Yer aff yer heid ta be runnin' awah an' yer bum's oot the windae if ya think yer after gettin' awah with it."

By the time I had the phone to my ear, I was laughing my head off. It wasn't unusual to hear Fearghus go off with his Irish nonsense, but something else entirely to hear Siobhan talk like this.

"Yah better be dyin' there and not laughin' like I think ye are, cuz if yer not, I'm a comin' ta wring yer neck, ya better believe it."

I was bent at the waist now, one hand braced against the ancient tree for support, I was laughing so hard.

Siobhan went silent.

I continued laughing for several long minutes and all the while, Siobhan remained silent. As the laughter subsided, dread filled the empty spaces inside me. Oh crap, I was gonna get it now, I thought, as I listened to the silence on the other end of the line.

"Are ye quite done?" Siobhan asked in her usual dry tone.

Another giggle burst out, but I clamped a hand over my mouth, took a deep breath in through my nose and answered, "Yes."

"Then are ya ready to tell me what in the blazes ya think yer doin' sneakin' off to Italy of all places in the middle of the night? Did ya not think we'd be worried sick about ya? Did ya not stop to think for one second that ya ought to tell someone where you were headed and why?

"What do ya hope to accomplish there all by yer lonesome?"

Her words had struck me rapid-fire until, when she finally fell silent, I couldn't help but snark, "Are *you* quite done?"

There was a long pause, then she said in a dark tone, "Well aren't you mighty full of yerself? I've never known you to be so careless and so…stupid."

Her words hit me like a physical punch in the gut, and it took me a minute to process them. At first, I bristled—I was never, ever careless and certainly never stupid.

But as I processed, I moved around the trunk of the great tree so my back was to the sidewalk and stared up at a beautiful old house behind a wrought iron fence. Siobhan was right. I was being careless and even stupid. I'd come here without a plan. Without any knowledge of the Master whatsoever, and without a single clue how I'd achieve what I came here to do.

Siobhan must have sensed the direction my thoughts had taken me, because when she spoke again, her tone was soft. "Minnie?"

"I'm here." Just minutes ago, I'd felt like a boss and totally like I had everything under control. Now I felt like a child who'd just burned her hand on the stove despite being told it was hot.

"Look, squirt. I get why you did it. When I was young like you, I probably would've done the same thing. But you're way smarter than I ever was—it's not like you to do somethin' so impulsive as this."

"I know, but—" I hated the childish tone in my voice, but Siobhan didn't give me a chance to say anything else.

"I can guess what you thought, but that isn't the point. This thing you want to do—because you want to go rescue Philo, don't you?—Never mind, I know that's what you're planning. Thing is, it's the most idiotic thing you've probably ever done. The Master is…well, he's not like anything you've ever seen before, Min. He's not like Ying Yue or Hashiki. If you thought they were cruel and sadistic, the Master's far, far worse.

"He'll smell you from a mile away. He probably already knows you're in Rome. He probably already has people watching you, people who will oh-so-helpfully lead you directly to his door."

I started to tremble as I listened, as I considered Matteo and what he'd said about coming over and

83

talking to his sire, Demitri. Matteo said he didn't know the Master, but this was the Master's personal domain. What was the chance he'd been telling the truth?

"And once you get there—if he lets you live that long—it'll be nothing at all like you've seen before. Imagine the worst thing that happened to you—the kids teasing you with blood and chasing you out of school, or Ying Yue coming after you in Seoul, or the way Hashiki manipulated your nerves—that was really painful, wasn't it?"

"Yeah," I murmured in a tiny, high voice.

"Well," Siobhan continued brutally, like she was determined to drive home her point no matter how well it was received. "That'll be like tender hugs and kisses compared to what the Master will do to you. If you're lucky, he'll throw you into the cell next to Philo's so you can both starve for eternity. If you're not so lucky, he might eat your face off—for starters."

"Ew," I said with a soft chuckle.

"I'm not jokin' here, Min. I'm deadly serious and I suggest you take it seriously, too. The Master is the devil, Min. Truly. He's been on this Earth longer than anyone else, longer than any other supernatural creature. He's the thing that inspired all our darkest legends—from devil to vampire to monster. Except where the Greek and Roman gods were imaginary, he was not.

"David makes being a vampire look good, look decent and respectable—but that is how he and his family has chosen to evolve. Other vampires…well, you've seen a little of what they can be, but you cannot imagine the hell—the literal hell—you will find in the Master's lair."

I held my stomach with one hand splayed over my belly, while the rest of me trembled. I wanted to throw up, but I couldn't allow myself the luxury. I didn't deserve to be sick to my stomach. I'd walked right into this with my eyes wide open—I only had myself to blame.

But what other choice did I have except to keep going? I knew my plan was dangerous. I knew it would be scary—I'd just been working really hard not to think too hard on all that because it didn't matter. "I have to do it," I said. "I can't leave him there. Not like he is. I just can't, Siobhan. I have to get him out. No matter what."

Siobhan sighed and I could just imagine her tapping the wall with her fist or running her hand through her short, spiky black hair. "I know you need him free. We all need him free. I know you care for Philo in a romantic sort of way, but never for one second believe that we don't all love him as much—maybe even more—than you, little sister. I have known Philo for centuries. I have fought beside him, protected him, and been protected by him. And the thought that he is, even now, starving and dying but never findin' release from his constant hunger is eatin' me up inside. But David knows what he's doing. You have to trust him—we all do."

"But David said I could go with him, and then he just left! He lied to me! He probably just wants to clear his own name with the Master and he'll just figure Philo was the cost of doing business or something."

Silence fell between us and I wished I could take back my words, even though there was a part of me that believed them.

"Don't you dare speak of our sire like that. You have no right. No right at all to speak so ill of him. If it weren't for David, you'd be dead by now. You'd have either killed yourself a helpless little child or somethin' and gotten yourself arrested, or more likely, killed by one of us as a liability, or you'd have refused to eat in those first twenty-four hours and truly died.

"You owe everything to David. Everything. Don't you dare forget it."

Now it was my turn to go all silent as Siobhan's remarks hit their mark. My chest felt as if a giant held my ribcage in its fists and the bones were shattering, cutting deep into my flesh. I didn't know what to say, I could only listen to the silence. She was right again, of course. And even though David really had lied, I knew he'd done it to protect me. I was beyond grateful for him, my clan, and everything they'd done to help me this past year.

The fact remained though, that Philo was still a prisoner, and from the way the *kynigoi* talked, David would be lucky to get out of his encounter with the Master alive, let alone with Philo by his side.

"You're still goin' to do it, aren't ya?" Siobhan said, her accent slipping again.

I nodded, then said, "Yes. I have to."

Siobhan breathed out a string of gaelic that probably an elaborate curse. "Just…Use your gift, then. Use every dirty trick Thorstein taught you and don't ever let down yer guard. And…" Siobhan's voice cut off just then, as if interrupted by a sob—but this was Siobhan I was talking to, and she wasn't a crier. "And you better bloody well stay safe."

I opened my mouth to assure her, but the line went dead.

I dropped to my bum, my back pressed against the ancient tree, and pulled my knees to my chest. At first, my brain was numb and I didn't think of anything at all. When it kicked back into gear, it wasn't to moan about the state I was in, it was to figure out how to take Siobhan's advice and still make a plan for rescuing Philo.

Thor was forever accusing me of holding back my gift, and I'd long since figured out from him and David both that I had more natural ability than most vampires had. This summer I'd studied with Thor and learned a lot, but Siobhan was right—I had held back. Mostly because Thor's training usually involved taking over someone's mind and making them do my bidding and I'd never been willing to do that to my family, or to some unsuspecting human. I'd had my morals to think about. My sensibilities.

I realized now, though, that I'd have to ignore my morals for now. If I wanted even half a chance of rescuing Philo, I'd have to be as ruthless and cunning as anyone else.

No, I'd have to be *more* ruthless.

If the Master would eat my face, as Siobhan said, then I'd have to stay out of his way. And if he'd never release Philo, then I'd have to go behind his back. And if the Master caught me? Then I'd have to be the one to devour him.

"*Mi scusi signora. Va tutto bene?*" The words, spoken kindly but far too near, penetrated my dark thoughts and I opened my eyes to see an old Italian lady stooping down, her face a mask of concern, a conciliatory hand on my shoulder.

"Thank you," I said. "But I'm fine."

The woman didn't seem to hear me, though. She stood so quickly that she stumbled back and the man with her had to hold her steady in his arms.

"*Mio Dio. Proteggimi.*" She repeated the words over and over, while genuflecting. The man with her glared at me as he hurried the woman away.

It wasn't until they were gone, and I leaned my head back against the tree, that I realized what had scared her. Black veins marred the fair skin on my arms and hands and a bit of blood welled up in my mouth from where my fangs had cut me.

Omo, I thought. That poor old lady. She'd seen me in full vamp mode, and I hadn't even realized I'd changed.

ready to be recognized as a vampire, especially around humans, and others may not wish for company.

The older a vampire gets, the more set in their ways they become, so try not to be offended if they're not interested in joining you in this bright new age of where vampires live in the light of acknowledgement. Some individuals might actually prefer the anonymity they've enjoyed in their lifetime.

Should you have the chance to meet a vampire, take advantage of the opportunity to learn from them.

Many vampires are dedicated collectors. The hobby is a wonderful and healthy way to mark the passage of time. But be warned: never take another vampire's things. It will not end well. *This is weird!*

Assuming you are an honest individual, you may find a vampire's collection to exceed the riches of any of the major museums around the world,

CHAPTER SEVEN

WHEN I GOT BACK TO THE MARINOS' APARTMENT, I passed an older man carrying a cooler on the stairs. Three steps past him I realized he must be the courier sent with my order. I whirled and called down, "Excuse me? Do you have a delivery for Minnie Kim?" My nostrils flared as I picked up the scent of blood—I was hungry enough that even through all the packaging and the thick cooler walls, I caught just the hint of delicious, fresh blood.

The man—the human, I noted with some surprise—stopped and half-turned to look up at me. "*Si Signora. Sei Minnie Kim?*"

I nearly tripped down the stairs in my effort to reach him. "I'm Minnie Kim." I smiled widely at him, but he didn't reciprocate. There was something off about him, like he was a robot or something. He just stared at me with a placid expression that hadn't changed at all during our brief exchange.

"*Ho bisogno di vedere l'identificazione*," he said in a flat tone.

My brows drew down as I tried to puzzle out his Italian. "Pardon?" I peered at his face and noticed his pupils were fully dilated. Like he was high or something—but what drug made you act like a robot?

"*Iden-ti-fi-caz-ione*," he said like I was a child. At least that showed a bit of personality. And, I finally understood what the heck he was saying.

"Oh!" I shrugged out of my backpack purse and dug inside for my wallet. Once I'd retrieved my ID, I held it in front of his face with a positively gleeful smile on my face.

The man grunted something, then shoved the cooler at me. As soon as my hand was wrapped around the handle, he turned and left the building without another word.

"*Grazie!*" I called out, even though the door had already closed behind him. Then I ran up the next three flights, hurriedly unlocked the apartment door and flung myself onto the couch, so intent on devouring at least half of whatever was in the cooler, that I didn't take even a second to consider whether or not anyone was home.

I'd just figured that, since the delivery guy had been leaving without delivering, no one was here.

Until a man cleared his throat, very near my ear.

I nearly jumped out of my skin and was standing, my cooler held behind my back, before my brain fully processed the scene.

Freddy sat in a low sling-back chair right beside the couch, the remote control in his hand and a scowl on his face. He wore light gray sweatpants with a white tank undershirt, while his feet were bare and his hair lay about his head in tousled waves. Like he'd just rolled out of bed.

I glanced at the television which was, I now realized, playing local news, then back at Freddy.

He made a point of looking at where the cooler would be if I were holding it in front of me. "Don't worry. I don't think anyone here is in danger of stealing your..." he grimaced and looked away, "whatever that is."

"Oh, haha," I responded stupidly. "Good to know." I crossed the room as quickly as I could without using my vamp speed. "Sorry to bother you." I slipped through the doorway that led into his and Luke's bedroom. Thankfully, Luke was gone, his bed neatly made, while Freddy's lay in a rumpled heap. Seeing it made me uncomfortable and even once I'd made it into Bianca's room, I was keenly aware that I wasn't alone in the apartment. And not only that, but that the one I shared the space with, was the one sibling who seemed to hate my guts.

I sat on the edge of Bianca's pristine white bed and looked down at the cooler which I'd set on the floor at my feet. I desperately wanted—needed—to drink, but it seemed somehow wrong to do it while a human was around—particularly that human. As I gazed around the room, my heart sank. With the exception of the one chair by the vanity, everything was white, white, white. How was I supposed to drink without getting blood on something? Not that I was an animal or anything, but the blood bags weren't exactly the easiest to manage and it wasn't like I was gonna go back out there and warm up some blood in the microwave. Not while Freddy was there. Watching me. Judging me.

But I was so desperately hungry.

I didn't know how sound-proof the apartment was— not very, I suspected, since I could hear the news playing on the TV—so I'd have to do this as quietly as possible.

I moved the chair to the corner it had been in last night, then set the cooler down in front of it. Glancing toward the doorway, I sat down and opened the cooler. Inside sat another cooler—one of those Styrofoam ones, since I had told Matteo I didn't want to have to store my blood in the apartment's fridge. I pried open the lid, and there was just no way to do it quietly. It screeched and squeaked, every sound making me cringe anew. Finally I was in, and the glorious sight of six blood bags, frosted with ice and nestled together like good friends, greeted me. I sighed and most of the tension in my body slipped away.

Eagerly, and with slightly trembling fingers, I reached inside and pulled out one of the bags. I made quick work of slicing off the short nub of tubing with a vampiric fingernail, and inserted it into the side of the bag like a makeshift juice box. I had just sucked down my first long gulps of the delicious stuff, when I became aware that I was not alone.

With the bag still pressed close to my mouth, I looked up—to see stupid Freddy leaning against the open doorway with a look of disgust on his face.

I let the little straw go and dropped the bag to my lap, feeling suddenly exposed and vulnerable, as if I'd been caught doing something naughty.

Which. I. *Hadn't*. Thankyouverymuch.

"That's disgusting." He crossed his arms over his chest as if in challenge. I narrowed my eyes at him, then licked off a bead of blood on my lower lip.

"It's better than the alternative." I gave a little shrug like I didn't care one way or the other. "Besides, you don't have to watch. In fact, I don't recall inviting you in."

He smirked. "It's my place. I already belong here. In fact, you're the one who shouldn't be here."

Ugh. I hated confrontations. I looked down at the bag in my hands. I desperately wanted more. *Needed* more.

"If Bianca hadn't invited you in, would you be able to come in?" he pushed off from the door, and pushed his hands into his pockets.

"What, are you gonna kick me out and uninvite me?" I was talking a good talk, but I felt incredibly uncomfortable. Freddy was right—I didn't belong here and challenging him went against everything I'd been taught growing up.

"Would that work?" he asked.

My left eyebrow quirked as I considered his question. I wanted to scare him, to push him, though I had no idea why. In the end, though, I could only give him the truth. "No. There's no truth at all to the myth that a vampire can't enter your house without an invitation. Sorry to disappoint you."

He slumped against the door frame again. "Well, you're not staying long, right? When will you be gone?"

Rude, I thought. But then Freddy hadn't made any pretenses about what he thought of me and my kind. Then a naughty part of me was speaking before my good sense had a chance to reel it in. "I'm not the only vampire in your life, you know."

Freddy snorted. "None of us is involved in any of that supernatural stuff. *Assolutamente no.*"

I grinned at his misplaced confidence. "Absolutely, yes." I took a long sip from the blood bag and sighed.

The blood tasted a bit different here, but I wasn't yet a skilled connoisseur like my family. They could tell what blood type they were drinking, or even guess at what the donor had eaten that day. I only knew that this blood tasted more…herbal…than the blood back home. More earthy, somehow.

Freddy stood with his fists clenched by his side, tension wafting off him from across the small room. "You do not know what you are talking about." His accent was stronger when he was angry, because I could hardly understand him now.

"Have you met Matteo?" I stuck the straw in my mouth and sipped while I watched him. "He invited me to his house tonight, so I could meet his sire and ask him about the Master." I said it so casually, I might have been talking about a trip to the grocery store. I surprised even myself.

He shook his head, as if not grasping how the one had anything to do with the other. "Bianca's *fidanzato*?"

That eyebrow of mine quirked again. "If that word means 'boyfriend,' then yeah. Her *fidanzato*. Matteo."

Freddy crossed his arms again and narrowed his eyes. He definitely did not want to believe a single thing I said. "You are wrong. I have met Matteo and while I think Bianca could do far better than him, he is no *vampire*." He snorted, and I got the feeling he would have spat, too, if there'd been a way to do it without being completely disgusting.

I shrugged and sipped my breakfast. I felt pretty darn good, even with Freddy and all his resentment and dislike washing over me. "Why don't you ask him?"

"Ask him…"

"If he's a vampire." I watched him while I sipped.

He sputtered a moment, spouting out some stuff in Italian I had no hope of understanding, before finally saying, "I could not do that." I swear I heard his teeth grind.

"Why not? Are you afraid of embarrassing him?"

He sputtered some more and looked wildly around the room. Maybe he was looking for something he could punch.

"We're not embarrassed by what we are, Frederick," I said in the first kind tone I'd used with the guy since we met—though the use of his name might have been a little snarky of me. "Being a vampire is nothing to be ashamed of." I set the bag on top of the cooler and clasped both my hands together.

"Do I wish I'd never been made into a vampire? Yes. Even though there are laws that prohibit the making of vampires against a person's will, it still happens. It happened to me. I didn't ask to be a vampire. But now that I am one, I'm glad that I'm still alive—after a sort. I was only sixteen—and that was just last year." I cocked my head and laughed when I realized it was still September third. "In fact, today's my seventeenth birthday. My real birthday. But I'll be sixteen forever since that's how old I was when I was changed."

I snorted and felt the lightness fade away. "But let's be straight—I wasn't just *changed*. I died. A vampire killed me. And then he brought me back."

"And ya know what? I'm glad. I wasn't ready to leave my friends—or my family, but they didn't want a dead girl as their daughter, so... Anyway, that's a story for another day. The point is, I was just a teenager with big plans for my future. I had people I loved and who loved me. I wasn't ready to give all that up. Now, I have all the time in the world to not only spend with those I love, but to do everything I dreamed of. Now I can do even more than I ever dreamed as a human."

I smiled at Freddy, but though I tried to "sparkle" as my best friend Stacey would say, I felt pretty sure it was a kind of sad smile.

To my surprise, Freddy's whole demeanor changed. He sank onto the edge of Bianca's bed, and dug his hands into his hair.

We sat like that for at least two minutes, each of us deep in thought. I had no idea what Freddy was struggling with, but my own words had brought back some of my own deeper thoughts about my life. I hadn't allowed myself to really think about what I wanted in a long time. Not since Philo died, anyway—or rather, when I thought he'd died. There'd been his loss to deal with, and my parents' rejection. And then there was the whole thing with school and the crisis the supernatural world was in all because of me and Veyo. Really, it was a surprise that the Marinos hadn't recognized me. I would have guessed that just about everyone under twenty years old the world over would have seen the video of us changing into monsters and crashing through the school's cafeteria window.

Since then, I hadn't thought much beyond the next steps I had to take to rescue Philo.

And really, I hadn't needed Siobhan to tell me how impossible that was. It was probably the reason I hadn't even imagined a life with him after he'd been rescued. Did I really think I was going to die trying to get him out? Or was I just that self-assured I would succeed?

I had no idea.

"Were you really changed against your will?" Freddy asked.

I glanced up at him, startled out of my own reverie. I'd forgotten he was even there. The look on his face was awash with anguish, like the idea of my beginnings were horrible to imagine.

I nodded my head slowly.

He opened his mouth and closed it again. Without even questioning it, I let my mind touch his so I could better understand him.

"You want to know how it happened?" I knew he did, but he did that open-mouth-close-mouth thing again before he took a turn at nodding.

And for some reason, right then, I wanted to tell him. So I did. I told him everything—even the part about wanting to get my first kiss over with so I could stop thinking about it. I'm glad I added that part, because it brought out the first genuine smile I'd seen on Freddy's handsome face. He looked a lot more like his brother when his face softened like that.

We ended up talking for at least an hour about how it was to change and what it was like being a vampire. I told him how being a part of David's clan felt like being in a family, but that I suspected most clans were quite different. I didn't tell him how they were different, though. That would probably set him right back to hating on vampires.

"I should let you get back to your, uh, lunch," Freddy said with an embarrassed glance at my cooler. He stood and took the few short steps to the door, then looked back. "And happy birthday, Minnie."

"Thanks!" The smile I gave him would have pleased even Stacey.

He stepped through the doorway and started to pull the pocket door closed. "Oh, hey." He stopped with the door half-closed. "Did you ever get a real first kiss?"

Aw. My heart gave a little squeeze at the blush on his cheeks and the gentle expression in his eyes. I knew there wasn't a spark between us, but that made his question even sweeter. Because it wasn't a question, it was an offer. "I did," I said. "The very best of first kisses."

Freddy smiled and nodded once. "Good, then." And he pulled the door closed.

often accompanied by the senior vampire's personal anecdotes.

Most vampires live very long lives. Have respect for what they have experienced and what they might know. It is certainly more than you.

My Korean culture reveres our elders & ancestors for their wisdom. But I know it's not they way for everyone.

If you can set aside your own pride, what you can learn from older vampires is profound and could greatly bless your eternal life. It's worth taking the time to learn from them, if you can.

13

Remember to be compassionate. Every vampire has a history, and no one can presume to fully understand it. *Like that other statement about respecting what a vamp has gone through.*

You cannot view an individual's history with the eyes of today. Without experiencing it for yourself, you cannot understand the past, not truly. It is completely and utter folly to imagine otherwise.

Similarly, an ancient vampire may have a hard time seeing your own value because of their own life perspective.

14

CHAPTER EIGHT

I DRANK TWO BAGS BEFORE I FELT SATED, BUT THEN I WAS too full to go exploring. And Bianca's bed was so comfy. Besides, tonight I'd get the information I needed to find the Master, and once I had that, I didn't have any intention of lazing around. I might not get time to sleep at all—at least, that's what I told myself when I curled up on Bianca's bed with a narrow shaft of sunlight streaking across the comforter.

I didn't wake until the sounds and smells of a human home woke me. The room was dark, but I couldn't tell if that was because it was late, or just because the sun couldn't get between the buildings anymore. No matter. It's not like I needed the light to find my way about.

After a long, luxurious stretch, I felt like a completely new woman and like I could take on the world—and maybe even the Master. I straightened my clothing and moved through the bathroom and boys' bedroom to the living area.

Here, the bright light had me blinking for a second before I realized the entire room was filled with balloons of every shape and color. Flowers filled the room too, from roses to lilies and everything in between. The scent was overwhelming, especially when combined with cooking meat, but I'd learned some tricks to help me tone down my acute senses, particularly when I was in Korea.

Everyone had their backs to me, and it was only when Luca turned to set something down on the small table that my presence was discovered. "Hey!" he called loudly. "Happy birthday!" Then he, Bianca and even Freddy came at me with their arms outstretched.

"*Buon compleanno amico mio*!" Bianca cried as she elbowed her way past her brothers to get her arms around me first. She gave me a good squeeze before stepping back and letting Luca take her place.

He hugged me much more gently and said, "Happy birthday," before dropping a chaste kiss to my cheek. He stepped away quickly, and I just had time to see Bianco elbow him before Freddy stepped up and drew me into a really good hug.

"Happy birthday, Minnie."

I suddenly realized that he had been the mastermind behind this celebration, and I had to shut my eyes for a long second to will the tears of gratitude away. "You know you didn't have to do all this." His arms tightened around me ever so slightly. Maybe I should have been clearer about that kiss he'd asked about. Maybe he didn't realize that I had a boyfriend. I didn't want him to get the wrong idea. I tried to pull away, but he held on.

"I did. I have treated you…ugh. How do you say *terribile*?"

I laughed. "Terrible?"

He laughed, too. "Sometimes the words are so similar and sometimes not—it is hard to know. Anyway, Bianca has always been a good judge of people, but Luca is usually the one who is slow to come around. I am sorry that it was me, this time, and that I tried to hurt you with my words."

He turned his face so his mouth was right next to my ear, making me shiver despite my efforts to not react to him. "I asked Bianca about Matteo and apparently she has known all along that he is a vampire, but had been afraid to tell me."

I stiffened, but he held me tight. "No, it is all right. She has wanted to tell me, and is glad that now I know. Thank you for talking with me and telling me your story. I hope you can forgive me."

Finally he pulled back, though his hands had drifted down my arms until they clasped my fingers loosely in his. I resisted the urge to tug them back, wanting to be careful not to make the moment awkward. I looked past Freddy to Bianca and Luca, smiling at all three of them. "How is it I am worthy of such kindness and generosity when you have only just met me? I am very grateful."

I let my gaze rest on Freddy and squeezed his fingers. "Of course I forgive you. You had every right to be cautious and careful." Then I purposefully drew my hands from his and took a step away. "What is all this?" I asked in a tone of voice I hoped came off as carefree and joyous. Inside, I was wondering how careful Bianca was being with Matteo. I wasn't sure what I thought of the whole thing. I wasn't at all sure of what I thought of Matteo.

I pulled an armful of balloons down to my chest and peeked above them. "This is crazy! Thank you!"

"When Freddy told me it was your birthday, we just had to throw you a party!" Bianca shimmied forward and gave me a side-hug. Then she picked up the remote control and changed the TV station—which had been muted, but still on the news. She and I both frowned at the scene showing an ambulance at the door of an old Italian home. I couldn't read the caption scrolling by too quickly at the bottom, but the words *soprannaturale* and *vampire* made it pretty clear it was about people like me. *My* people. Bianca changed the channel to an all-music station and turned up the volume just enough to add a fun atmosphere to the room.

"I checked with Matteo and he said you can eat human food—yes?"

I grinned. "Oh, yes! I would have died again if I couldn't eat cake anymore!"

"A woman after my own heart," Lucas cheered from the little galley kitchen.

Bianca looped her arm around mine and led me to the small kitchen table, where she indicated I should sit. "And now that Freddy knows about Matteo—and he is okay with it—he is joining us for dinner for the very first time! *Grazie*, Minnie. It has been killing me trying to figure out how to tell my brothers."

I smiled and accepted her thanks, but I couldn't help but notice the glance her brothers shared. They might know, and maybe they were even sort of okay with it—but they were a long way from accepting their sister's boyfriend was a vampire. And I couldn't blame them. Not at all.

As the food was laid on the tiny table, and then a knock came at the door, I realized that I would have to find out Matteo's intentions, find out exactly what kind of vampire he was, before I could leave the Marinos. If he was on the up and up, I wouldn't say a thing, but if he wasn't, well…Bianca and her brothers deserved to know the truth.

While Bianca greeted Matteo at the door with a passionate embrace that made my own cheeks burn, I dipped into Matteo's mind. He was both more and less the kind of guy I thought he was.

He was eager to drink from Bianca, though I wasn't sure why he hadn't yet. I was pretty sure he hadn't, anyway, based on the way he was imagining what she might taste like. So he was creepy. Just like I thought.

But he also legit cared about her. He worried about scaring her off. He worried about being her boyfriend and what might happen if he ever lost control. He was thinking about getting his own place, because he didn't like taking Bianca back to the lair where every other male vampire there fantasized about sinking their teeth into her.

I shivered, and realized someone was saying my name. I looked up at Bianca and Matteo who stood directly in front of me. I had to get better at mind walking without losing control of myself and my surroundings. I thought I'd gotten better at that, but I guess not.

I stood, forcing the couple to take a step back to give me more room. "Sorry. Just a little wool gathering."

Bianca and Matteo exchanged a glance. "Wool gathering?" he asked.

I waved my hand in the air as if dismissing the question. "Never mind. It's just something one of my brothers says. Hi, Matteo." I made my hand behave in a more reasonable fashion and gave him a friendly wave.

He smiled one of those *don't let the crazy chick know we're on to her* smiles. "Hello."

"Do you two know each other?" Bianca asked, her gaze flicking between us.

Matteo shrugged. "In our world we must connect with others who can help us obtain a reliable—and legal—food source. I was that person for Minnie. We met this morning at Mercure."

"Oh," Bianca breathed, gazing up into Matteo's eyes. They were almost the same height, but Bianca seemed to kind of shrink around Matteo, to curl into him in a way that seemed to diminish her own strength. I glanced at her brothers to see if they saw the same thing I did, and sure enough, they were both scowling as they waited for their introductions to be made.

Matteo must've noticed where my attention went, because he turned and stuck out a hand to Freddy. "*Ciao. Sono Matteo. Sono felice di incontrarti finalmente.*" While he met her brothers, Bianca clung to his arm as if she was afraid to ever let him go, yet I couldn't sense any influence being used on her.

I knew some girls just did that—put themselves aside in favor of their partner. Stacey and I used to make fun of girls like that. I never would have pegged Bianca as one of them. Usually that kind of girl had self-esteem issues, but I didn't think Bianca did. Weird.

"Come," Luca said with a clap of his hands. "Dinner is ready." He smiled and sat, signaling for the rest of us to follow his lead.

I had just put a strip of thinly sliced roast beef into my mouth, and was working hard to keep from moaning in pleasure, when Freddy cleared his throat.

"You came here, with no reservations and no friends, to find the vampire Master."

I quickly swallowed and looked at Freddy. Everyone else looked at him, too.

"Why?" He didn't immediately look up from his plate, but it wasn't hard to guess who he was talking to. I watched him carefully slice his meat into bite-sized pieces while I considered what to say.

My gaze drifted over my new friends' faces. They were quietly going about the actions of eating, but it was clear their attention was fixed on me and my answer. They weren't just nosey, they cared. They wanted to know because it obviously meant something to me—and I wanted to tell them.

I set my knife and fork down on my plate. I was slow to start and when I did, my words were quiet and slow. "In June, my boyfriend, Philo, was summoned by the Master. I guess that's a little different, but not so surprising." I glanced at Matteo, and he nodded.

My thoughts shifted as I reached for them—there was so much from that time, but most of it wasn't important to the story. "He…Well, we were told he had died. That he'd been interrogating a particularly evil, violent vampire and that the effort had killed him."

I looked up, and my gaze immediately found Bianca's. "There wasn't any reason not to believe it was true. They even sent over ashes to prove it." The tears in Bianca's eyes actually helped me, gave me strength to continue. I took a deep breath and she clasped my hand in hers. "But recently, some things happened that made us realize that Philo didn't die at all." This time I had to stop because my own tears threatened to fall, and I couldn't allow that to happen. I'd ruin their whole night if I cried blood all over our dinner.

When I had myself under control, I continued. "I guess the Master has some bone to pick with my sire— David—and he decided to punish him by punishing Philo." My hands shook, so I clasped them together and hid them on my lap, out of view. "David said I could go with him, but he left without me. Everyone said I should stay home and let David deal with it, but it didn't feel right. I just felt so strongly that I needed to come, myself. That Philo needed me."

I let my gaze travel over them. "I know that probably sounds weird, but…well, that's why I'm here. I just got on a plane and came. I don't even really have a plan." I shrugged and tried to give the impression that it would all work out. Since I wasn't at all sure of that myself, I don't know if I was successful.

"Wow," Bianca breathed. She leaned toward Matteo, who put his arm around her and pulled her against him. For his part, I could see the understanding behind his eyes. He could read the subtext in what I'd said, and it was obvious he wasn't at all sure I stood a chance.

Freddy, who'd watched me while I spoke, now stared at his plate. He gave a short nod. "I am sorry for all you have been through. Thank you for trusting us with your story, though." Our eyes met and I sucked in a breath at the fear I saw there. He was worried for me. Very worried.

I smiled at him, at all of them. "So you can see, I really needed a friend right when you guys showed up and instead of just one, I got three—four, counting you, Matteo." I had to grin at the flustered expression on his face, but soon the others were laughing at him, too, and the tension of the moment slipped away.

The dinner was a loud, joyful affair with enough food to feed my family back home. And after we'd stuffed ourselves silly with all the wonderful food, it turned out—there was cake!

I'd been leaning back in my seat, trying not to be too obvious while patting my stomach, when Freddy got up to take some dishes to the kitchen. I started to do the same, but Luca told me to stay put.

Next thing I knew, Freddy was walking back with a beautiful dark chocolate cake piled high with deliciously red strawberries. He started singing, "*Tanti auguri a te, tanti auguri a te*—" and the others joined in with "*tanti auguri a Minnie, tanti auguri a te!*"

I had no idea what the words meant, but since they sung it to the tune of Happy Birthday, I figured that's what it was. They sang the verse twice before ending on a shout and congratulating me again on turning seventeen.

After dinner we took turns playing video games, which wasn't really my thing. After a while it became clear that the real competition lay between Bianca and Freddy, while Luca took turns rooting for each of them. I lay on the floor, my head propped on my elbow while I watched my new friends' happy faces and thought about what I'd say to Demitri. I'd been lost in a fantasy where Demitri took me directly to meet the Master and the Master was like, "Oh, sure. Here're the keys. You don't mind letting him out yourself, do you?" when Matteo sat down just behind me.

"It's really something, isn't it?" His voice sounded right next to my ear and I jumped, inadvertently slapping his face with my flailing hand. "Sorry," he said with hands held in front of him, "I should not have gotten so close."

"No, I'm sorry," I said a bit sheepishly—even though I totally agreed that he'd way overstepped my personal boundaries. Still, I moved beside him and sat cross-legged. "What's really something?"

"This." He waved a hand toward the Marinos. "Them."

I looked at them and smiled, but I had no idea what Matteo was talking about.

"Life," he clarified. "Family. I have my clan, but I don't have anything like this with them. I didn't even with my own family. What they have is very special."

I thought of my parents and our quiet home life before I changed. I thought of Stacey and her fun family—theirs was probably the closest I'd seen to what the Marinos had. And Fearghus and Siobhan were sort of like this. "I think it has a lot to do with culture and personality. Not every family, no matter how much they love each other, will be like this."

Matteo grunted. "I suppose." After a moment of silence, he asked, "Are you close to your clan brothers and sisters?"

I didn't have to think about that one at all. "Yes," I said with conviction. "Very."

Matteo took that in, his eyes glued to Bianca and Luca, who had stepped in for Freddy so Freddy could run to the bathroom, but didn't respond.

"Are you?"

He glanced at me, and I got the feeling he was nervous to be talking to me about this. "I used to think so. Now, I'm not so sure."

I watched him while he spoke, and let my mind touch his. I didn't go deep, just skimmed his conscious thoughts, all the things he wasn't saying. I regretted it immediately.

His family thought that they should be allowed to sample Bianca. That if he ever brought her back to his apartment again, he'd be expected to enthrall her so they could all have a sip. He'd been doing it himself, I saw, and Bianca had no idea.

I hadn't known anyone personally who did this, but I knew it could be done. A human could be enthralled, and a few licks from the vampire could remove any evidence of being bitten. Rage, swift and unfamiliar boiled up inside of me, but I held it back, concealing my extended nails and protruding fangs by looking away over my shoulder. I breathed deeply, in through the nose and out through the mouth, until I regained control.

Matteo couldn't take Bianca to his apartment ever again. In fact, he needed to leave her alone entirely.

"I miss being human," he said wistfully.

I had to fight hard to drag the question, "Why?" out of the basement of my soul and I'm sure I completely failed to hide the vampire in my voice.

But with his attention focused on Bianca, he didn't seem to notice my battle with my inner demons. "Because I think I am falling in love with her."

That got through to me.

"What?"

"I'm almost a hundred years old, and I have had girlfriends before. Women who eventually became my thralls."

And eventually died, I thought with disgust.

"I've always wanted to bring them into my world," Matteo continued, seemingly oblivious to my reaction to his words. "Never until now have I wished with all my soul that I could rejoin hers."

I watched him watching the siblings, and the anger drained out of me. What he'd done to other women…it was awful, but no worse than many other vampires had done. Especially before the Treaty of London. "What's different now?"

He flicked me a glance, love burning clearly for all to see in his amber colored eyes. "Because she is so full of life. They all are. I love her as she is now—right now. I love how alive she is. How full of life. I love the way she lives. I don't know if I am making any sense. But I cannot imagine her in my world. It would take everything she is away from her."

I didn't have anything to say to that, since I got the feeling Matteo's clan was quite a bit different from mine.

As if he read my mind, he half-turned his body so he could face me more easily. "But you're different. You're more human than any vampire I have ever met. By now, I can tell a vamp from across the room, even if I can't smell him. Or her. But you? No. Your scent, your presence, is much more subtle. How have you done it? How have you managed to remain so human despite the beast inside you?"

He was so earnest, so intense, that he made me a little uneasy. I took a calming breath again and forced myself to meet his gaze. And then I was shaking my head, because if I was more human than most young vampires it was because I had tried so hard to hold on to that life. A decision that I was beginning to regret. I'd been so sure it was possible, but all I'd done is hurt my friends and expose the entire supernatural community. I wasn't used to failure and I hated the way it felt.

"I don't think it's reality," I said slowly, my thoughts only then coalescing into something meaningful. "I think I've tried too hard to remain human."

"But maybe that's the key." Matteo's face glowed with hope.

I shook my head. "All it's done for me, anyway, is put my human friends and family in danger." *And left me without the same experience other vampires had.* But I couldn't tell him that, not when I was counting on his help to find the Master. Not when I needed the vampire world to see me as strong and capable. Undeniable.

I glanced away from Matteo, returning my attention once again to the three siblings. Bianca was still competing, but it looked like Luca had lost again and Freddy was taking a go. "Better to leave the human world behind and enjoy the life you have. This is the life that matters. This is the life that lasts."

The words cut me, as if just saying them unleashed a spell of a thousand cuts upon my heart, but I'd said them with all the belief I could muster. I was aware of Matteo's hope fading as he stared at me. I hadn't realized until that moment how much he'd hoped I held some magical key to his future happiness. It made me sad to hurt him, and maybe even Bianca, this way. It went against everything I personally believed. But I needed Matteo to help me tonight and I couldn't have him going all soft and leaving his clan now.

As the game came to a close and Bianca did a silly happy dance while her brothers commiserated together, Matteo murmured, "Thank you. You're right, of course."

I wanted to sink right into the floor, sink all the way down and down until I was so deep in Hell that I'd never get up again. I mean, Hell's where liars go, isn't it?

And because you cannot possibly understand another creature's journey, you must always approach them with care and respect.

Above all, do not underestimate the vampires you meet. **Ha! For realz!**

Assuming you are the young vampire we intended this guide for, any vampire you meet will have more experience than you, so you will not wish to offend them in any way. In a challenge of skills, you cannot hope to prevail.

THE VAMPIRE CLAN

CHAPTER THREE

A "clan" is a family of vampires who all spring from one creator—the dam or sire who stands at the head of the family.

Typically, the name of the clan is taken from the last name of the sire/dam, but we are aware of a handful of clans who have taken names of meaning that are not their maker's last name.

CHAPTER NINE

MATTEO STOOD SMOOTHLY FROM THE FLOOR AND STEPPED up to Bianca where he drew her into a long hug. Meanwhile, I pulled on my boots and toyed with the gorgeous copper bracelet Bianca had given me. Her mother had made it, she'd said, but it seemed so "Bianca" that I thought she must have at least inspired it.

"*Mi dispiace, tesoro, ma devo andare.*" Matteo stepped back, drawing his hands out of Bianca's.

"*Ma io voglio venire con te,*" Bianca said in a slight whine. "Minnie," she angled her body past Matteo's so she could see me. "You want me to come with you, don't you?"

I glanced at Matteo. I did want her to come, but I had to appreciate Matteo for wanting to keep her away from his place. If she came, she might never return.

"This is vampire business, love," Matteo said.

I nodded, unsure if I could trust myself to speak again without spilling the beans. But if I did that, I'd have Freddy and Luca's anger to deal with and at the very least I wouldn't be going to meet Demitri—at the very worst, someone could die.

Neither option was acceptable.

I gave Matteo a meaningful look, then took a chance. *Tell her you'll walk me back so you can spend some more time with her. Tell her I have to go because I need to be sponsored by a clan in order to be in the country.*

Matteo covered his surprise at hearing my voice in his head well, but he didn't respond in kind, which meant he wasn't a mind walker. He gave a tight nod, then started speaking to Bianca in rapid-fire Italian. Little did he know he didn't have to share the gift for me to gain access to his thoughts.

My plan worked, and after a series of thank you's and hugs and kisses, Matteo and I were finally out the door. We didn't speak until we were down on the sidewalk in front of the building, and even then it was just for me to say, "Thank you."

Matteo seemed to be wound tight, but I didn't know why. Was it something in his exchange with Bianca? Or was it my intrusion into his thoughts? Most people weren't too keen on it.

Yup, that's it, I thought as Matteo suddenly drew to a stop and swung to face me. "You know, you're supposed to register your special gifts."

I drew my brows together. "I don't remember that being on the paperwork—sorry."

He rolled his eyes and started walking again. "It's not in the paperwork, but it's common knowledge. It's just good manners, you know?" He glared at me some more, but I was at a loss. Honestly, it came as a surprise to me that David hadn't registered my gifts. I knew he and Thor kept telling me that what I could do was special—was that why he hadn't told the Council? But then, Ying Yue seemed to know. Ugh. Vampires. I'd never understand them.

"I'm sorry," I said quietly. "I really didn't mean to offend—either the Council or you. And I never would have intruded like I did if I hadn't felt like it was necessary."

Matteo strode forward in silence, but I refused to be a meek little mouse. I lengthened my own stride until we were shoulder-to-shoulder again. He sighed. "It's okay. Just—" He glanced at me, then slowed his step. "I don't mind that you did it in that moment. It helped." His lips twitched into an almost smile before immediately dipping into a frown again. "But do not do it at the house, all right? I promise you, it won't go well."

I nodded and hoped my expression was earnest. "Got it."

We walked on, then he added, "For a young vampire, you are quite good."

"Pardon?"

He bobbed his head toward me. "Your mind walking. Your touch was very light and subtle. If you hadn't spoken, I would never have known you were there."

"Oh." I'm sure I blushed—thank goodness it was dark. If only he knew about the times I had skimmed his thoughts that he didn't know about. "Thank you."

The urge to tell him about Philo, and how being apart from him had helped me strengthen my gift, rose up in me, but I tamped it down. Instead I asked, "Have you heard of Thorstein Stringer? I don't know if he's as well-known as he thinks he is but—"

"Yes," Matteo answered. "He's well known to be the most accomplished mind walker among us."

Huh, I thought a little smugly to myself. *Is that so?* I was pretty sure that I'd pulled ahead of Thor in that particular ability, but I wasn't ready to brag about it. "He's been my mentor."

Matteo stopped and turned, gaping at me. "You're serious?"

"Yes," I said on a laugh.

He stared a moment longer, then shook his head as he resumed walking. "That is amazing. No wonder you're so good."

Mentally, I shrugged. Maybe I owed some of it to Thor, but I wasn't willing to give him all the credit.

"Still, best not to mention any of this to the group. Do you have any other abilities?"

"What?"

"You know—most of us have more than one gift."

I had to think about that for a second. Thor and David both had told me it was extremely rare to have all the mind skills, to be a true *imperium protestate*, but from what Matteo had said, I figured it wouldn't be a good idea to list any of those things. Besides, at this point, all he knew was that I could speak in his mind. That was one limited ability within the greater skill.

"In addition to talking in your mind, I am a *memoriae ambulare*—that gift allows me to pick up on specific memories."

"Really?" Matteo grinned at me. "That's amazing. Are you any good?"

I shrugged and decided to downplay it. I didn't know why—part of me worried they wouldn't talk to me if they thought I was a weakling—but for some reason I felt the need to be conservative in what I said about my skills. "I'm still learning."

Matteo slapped my back in a brotherly sort of way and picked up his pace. "Then if he asks you what you can do, just go with that one. It's rare enough that he'll take an interest in you, but you can pretend not to have read anything if you see something that seems…you know…unwise to mention."

That gave me pause, and a nugget of worry blossomed in my chest, but I nodded. I had to move into a sort of walking-jog to keep up with him, and I'd been so caught up by our conversation and my own thoughts that when I looked up from the sidewalk, I realized we'd arrived. Matteo already stood at the building's door, waiting to usher me in.

Night had fallen outside, and night reigned inside the building, too. There weren't even any overhead lights in the entryway. I strained my ears, but I heard nothing. Sensed…nothing. I desperately wanted to reach out with my mind, but didn't dare after what Matteo said.

"Why can't I hear anything?" I asked in a whisper.

He grinned wolfishly and shrugged. "One of my sisters has the ability. It is very rare." He gestured with head to the stairs and I followed him up to the third and final floor. "Wait here," he said, before moving to the left to an unmarked door. None of the doors had numbers on them, I noticed.

He knocked softly on the door, then stepped inside, seemingly without an invitation. Though, whomever was on the other side of the door would surely know him. Just as they knew I was out here, too. When the door closed behind Matteo, I slumped and shook out my arms and legs. It was hard work trying to be a cool vampire when I was just *me*.

It took all my energy to keep from showing my terror and uncertainty. All I wanted was to call Siobhan back and tell her to come help me. To tell Matteo I'd wait until she could get here. Then she could do all the hard work and I'd just follow. Not that I'd ever been afraid of hard work before. *But no,* I reminded myself. As scary as it was, I wanted to do this. I needed to do it.

Look at everything you've been through. At everything you've done. You've got this.

I'd just finished my pep-talk when the door swung open and Matteo leaned out the doorway. He flashed me a quick grin. "Come on in." I stepped up to him, noting that his pupils had gone black as I passed him. By the time I'd stepped fully into the room, my own eyes had gone black, too.

I don't know what I'd been expecting, but whatever it was, it wasn't at all what I got. Despite my best efforts, I still drew to a halt and blinked several times while I took it all in.

From the vibe I'd gotten when I was last in this building, and maybe from my own assumptions about this clan, I'd been expecting something like a squatter's place with random cushions all around and people lying around in various forms of undress. I'd expected something like a Victorian opium den, I realized, and inwardly rolled my eyes at myself.

Once again, I was completely disappointed. The room seemed to take up the entire floor, with two sitting areas divided by an enormous, sparkling kitchen and a domineering table that must seat twenty people at least.

However, the man who lazed in the corner of a pristine white leather sofa was a little closer to what I'd expected. He wore dress slacks and a white tank top, showing off miles of tan, muscled skin. His hair was a deep brown and hung to his shoulders, looking tousled enough to suggest he might have just risen from sleep. He looked like sex on a stick, as Stacey would say, down to his drooping eyelids and wide, full mouth that curved in a seductive smile as he observed me observing him.

"Welcome, Minnie Kim Aristos," he drawled in Italian-accented English. I'd never heard the English language sound so good. He didn't make any move to rise to greet me, but his gaze raked over me and the hair on my arms rose. "Come, join me." He flicked an elegant wrist to broadly indicate the large sectional, but since he sprawled in the corner, it took me a moment to decide where I should sit.

If I sat on the part directly across from him, I'd be closer to his head. And his hands.

If I sat on the other end, the corner closest to me, I'd have his long legs between us which definitely seemed the preferable choice. Except that his position, and that angle, would give me a very clear view of, um—well let's just say I didn't want to sit there.

His smile grew and I swore he'd just read my mind.

I took the corner closest to me, the one with the *view*, and double- and triple-checked on the shields around my mind. I held in a sigh of relief when I was reassured that my mind was as tight as Fort Knox and there was no way anyone would get inside. Demitri's "mind-reading" was probably just born of decades, or centuries, of arrogance.

What he didn't know was that I'd sparred with Thor so many times by now, and I found Thor far more appealing than Demitri. I wasn't tempted—or intimidated—by Demitri in the least.

Okay, maybe I was a little intimidated, but he didn't need to know that.

Leaning back against the rather stiff back of the modern sectional, I crossed one leg over the other and swung my foot, one arm draped over my stomach as I kept my eyes on my host's face.

One of his eyebrows quirked, then without a glance at Matteo, he flicked his wrist again. "You may go."

I didn't look at him either, but kept my gaze locked on Demitri's. Inside, my stomach roiled and my heart threatened to kick up a notch, but I ruthlessly refused to give in to fear. He'd be able to sense it, smell it. I couldn't afford to give anything away.

After a moment, I casually let my gaze travel away from the man and took in the apartment with more care. From where I sat, I could see the entire length of the long room, including the second sitting area which seemed to be done all in black, where this one was done all in white. I inwardly scoffed. Could the guy be any more obvious?

Where the furnishings and fixtures were stark in their simplicity, the walls practically exploded with color. Wild, crazy colored things that reminded me of Salvadore Dalí—all broad, bright strokes with a hint of darkness lurking within—hung on every bit of available wall space.

"Do you like art, Minnie Kim?"

My gaze flicked to my host, then back to the piece hanging on the wall nearest me. I thought for a moment, taking care in how I answered. "I do like art." I gazed at the somewhat violent piece that had a center of darkness and used a lot of deep reds in wild arcs around it. I shifted to look at Demitri. "But not all of it."

I caught the tiniest widening of his eyes, before he bowed his head in a sort of salute. "Well said. It is unusual to find one as young as you, so well versed in their own preferences. Their own desires." He said the last in a deeper tone and I seriously risked rolling my eyes. Was this guy for real?

I shrugged. "I've never been a usual sort of girl." I mean, it was true, right? Even if it was a little melodramatic of me.

Demitri barked a laugh that surprised me, but I'm pretty sure he hadn't seen me jump. "Is that so?" He swiped a finger under his eye, as if to wipe away a tear of mirth, but he hadn't been in tears. Maybe that crap worked with humans who didn't know vamps cried blood, but it was purely affectation as far as I was concerned. "Please, tell me how you are so unusual."

"Ah," I said, dropping my gaze in what I hoped he'd view as self-deprecating and not full-blown embarrassment. "I'm sure you don't want to hear about all that. I'm really quite boring."

Gag. I felt like I'd been plopped directly into a 1940s vampire flick. Stacey was gonna have a field day with this when I told her.

Demitri suddenly leaned forward and pinned me with the first serious expression I'd seen from him. I didn't move a muscle. Not even a twitch. Yay me. "Now, that is not entirely true, is it, Minnie Kim?"

"What? That I'm boring?" I scoffed. "I totally am. Just ask my friends."

His gaze darkened and he drew his heavy brows down, nearly shading his eyes from view. "But what if I were to ask your enemies?"

Inside, I froze. I really, really tried to keep my outsides from betraying me, but inside, I couldn't think. Didn't know *what* to think.

"Oh?" I raised an eyebrow. "What makes you think I have enemies?"

Demitri leaned back, resuming his lounge, but subtle hints in his body revealed his own tension. The way he tapped each of his fingertips to his thumb on his dangling left hand; the way his chest muscles rippled, barely concealed by his tank; and the way a tiny line had appeared between his brows.

He considered me for a long moment without responding. I stared right back. In my mind, I began reciting an old campfire song.

"The other day (the other day), I met a bear (I met a bear). A great big bear (a great big bear), away out there (away out there)." But when I got to the part about shooting the bear, I had to stop because until that moment, I hadn't considered what I'd do if this meeting went bad. I'd planned for him to refuse to help me, I'd planned for Matteo to be here as a sort of buffer, and I'd planned on it being scary and difficult.

And it was scary and difficult.

But I hadn't made any plan for if Demitri knew of me. That he might know my enemies.

I honestly wasn't sure I had enemies anymore, but maybe I did. I suppose it was possible that Ying Yue's people held a grudge against me.

And then, as I pondered who my enemies might be, a terrible feeling of dread came over me.

The video. The unmasking of supernaturals around the world. The *kynigoi*.

I hadn't meant for any of those things to happen, and the video with me and Veyo in our monster forms wasn't my fault at all. But it wasn't hard to imagine how it might be perceived otherwise. Thanks to that video, anyone in the world could know my face. Know my name. Anyone in the world could blame me for revealing them.

As I sat on Demitri's pristine couch, the sudden realization of just how many enemies I might really have came crashing down on me. The answer terrified me, and I waited for Demitri to tell me he was one of them.

Without warning, he moved, and everything about him—his mannerisms, his tone, even the set of his lips and jaw—changed. He stood and drew on a shirt I hadn't noticed draped over the back of the couch. While he buttoned it, he walked around the couch and toward the kitchen. "So, Minnie Kim the Innocent, Matteo tells me you have need of the Master. Is that correct?"

"Yes." I twisted in my seat, drawing one leg onto the couch as I watched him. He took two wine glasses from a cabinet behind him. I really hoped he wouldn't expect me to drink the whole thing because I'd never had a drink before in my life.

He reached into the fridge and drew out a steel carafe. Then plucked a handful of leaves from some sort of plant sitting on the counter. I watched him carefully, even though I had no way of knowing if his actions were nefarious or not. When he began to pour what looked like blood into the glass, I frowned. Cold blood was fine, but it wasn't the norm. Warm blood was preferred by every vampire, I thought.

"And what is it you need him for?" Demitri hadn't looked up once since he'd moved away from the sectional, and I ached with the need to dip into his mind and see what he was thinking. He dropped two leaves into each of the glasses, then used a pepper grinder to spice the blood. The scent of mint reached me.

I waited to respond until he'd returned to the sofa and had handed me the drink. I sniffed it, glanced at him, then took a tentative sip. It was…different.

"Give it a chance—I promise you will like it, but it takes more than one sip to fully appreciate it." He leaned back and crossed one ankle over his knee before drinking deeply from his glass. His eyes didn't leave mine.

I took a long sip, letting the liquid roll over my tongue as I thought about the flavor. It was fresh and sharp—different, but good. Definitely good.

"Thank you," I said honestly. "It's very good."

Demitri raised his glass to me in acknowledgment, but I got the feeling he had no intention of speaking until I'd answered his question. The question I'd been avoiding.

Stalling, I took another sip, then set the drink down on the large glass coffee table. Then I looked directly into Demitri's eyes and told him the truth.

The vampire family, or clan, is essential to a vampire's survival. The blood bonds between you are as strong, or stronger, than those of your human family. However, don't be too concerned if your initial reception is a little frosty. Centuries of hiding their true identities have taught many vampires to be wary of strangers. Just be yourself. You're bound to win them over eventually.

• Good advice & all but I think this statement is belittling. And normally I of humor

Vampire families can be even more in your business than human families. Protect your sanity and

17

your privacy by setting clear boundaries from the beginning. Some quality locks will come in handy, too. *ROFL! So true! ☺*
(I need to get better at locking my door.)

Vampire families typically take every opportunity to celebrate life, as it is the most precious commodity we have. Life sustains us, and our life is extraordinarily long.

• *Other than our family dinners, I'm not sure what they're talking about here.*

The bond between sire and offspring far surpasses that between human parents and their children. Through the bond, a sire or dame can discern

18

CHAPTER TEN

NOON THE NEXT DAY FOUND ME PUTTING THE LAST OF MY things back into my suitcase.

"I don't care if Matteo says you should go with Demitri. I think you should stay. Or let Freddy and I come with you."

I snorted and glanced at Freddy, but his glare told me he agreed with his sister.

Bianca lay sprawled across the bed, her head propped on her elbow and a frown on her face. I smiled at her, a feeling of love swelling up inside of me. She was so easy to love. Kind and generous, funny and easygoing. And even though she was unbelievably beautiful, she was completely guileless. It wasn't even like she didn't know how beautiful she was—she definitely did, and enjoyed looking her best—it was more that she didn't let her beauty go to her head. "Besides, you only just got here."

My gaze flicked to Freddy, who stood in the doorway, leaning his shoulder against the frame with his arms crossed over his chest. I quickly looked back at Bianca.

"I only just got here because we've only just met." I tossed one of her many frothy decorative pillows at her and laughed as she grabbed it and held it tight to her chest.

"But it seems as if we have known each other forever. You cannot go now." She pouted, a look I thought she probably used a lot, and that probably mostly worked given what I'd seen of her family dynamic.

I zipped up my suitcase and hefted it off the bed. I was about to respond, when Freddy spoke with barely controlled anger. "I agree with Bianca. There is no way you will be safe with him."

I gazed steadily back at Freddy. In just the past twenty-four hours, the change between us had been profound and deep. I couldn't explain it, but I knew now that Freddy understood me and cared for me, far more than our brief time together could account for.

"He said he owed the Master a visit, so he might as well take me. He's not gonna do anything to me." My gaze flicked between the two of them. "I'm a vampire. There's not much he could do to me." It was a lie, of course, but I was trying to ease their concern, not blow it up. "Besides, I'm pretty sure the Master knows I'm coming, and Demitri wouldn't dare interfere." Now that—that felt like truth.

I paused while I looked down at my scuffed sneakers, fighting back the fear that filled me at the thought of meeting the Master. "I don't have a choice." I took a deep breath and lifted my chin, forcing myself to meet their gazes. "I have to find Philo. I'm all that he has." Because despite what Siobhan had said, or what David had said, I didn't believe either of them would be doing anything to save him. Siobhan because she would obey David and wait for instructions, David because he would always do what was right for the family, even if that meant sacrificing Philo.

"Even if he is a vampire," Freddy said the word as if it were a curse, "he could still be a - a *stupratore*."

Bianca gasped and sat up. "*Non è uno stupratore! Minnie sarà totalmente al sicuro con lui. L'ha detto Matteo.*" She turned to me and said, "Do not worry, Minnie. Matteo promised you will be safe with Demitri and I believe him. Do not listen to a word Freddy says. He is just jealous." She cast her brother a dark look.

I hadn't used my gift on Demitri last night, but I trusted him. At least I trusted him to get me to the Master and that's all I'd asked him for. Our meeting had lasted all of about five minutes before he'd called Matteo in to collect me, and he'd ushered me out the door with a promise to pick me up this morning. It was pretty much the best scenario I could hope for.

Unsure of what else to do, I left my suitcase and walked around the end of the bed until I stood in front of Freddy. His cheeks were flushed, reminding me that Bianca had accused him of being jealous. I think he actually did like me, which made me sad. Before being reMade no one had been interested in me—now I'd just turned my back on two guys in as many weeks. Maybe there was some truth to that thing I often heard girls say—that boys were only ever interested in you if you already had a boyfriend.

Whatever it was, I was sad I had to hurt another person, even if just a little.

I went to tuck my hands into my front pockets, only to slide them awkwardly around my hips once I remembered I was wearing leggings and there were no pockets. I ended up with my hands on my hips, which felt weird and awkward. I rocked forward a little. If I were Stacey or Bianca, I'd put him and myself at ease with just a hand on his arm. Or even a friendly hug. I sighed inwardly. I'd probably be awkward my whole life. My whole extremely long life.

"I'll be all right, Freddy. Promise."

He eyed me skeptically and I grinned, hoping to ease his mind. "I know I don't look like much, but I promise—I can kick some butt if I have to."

He didn't smile back.

The sound of drumsticks tapping out a beat followed by the unmistakable sound of seventies music began to play, and I searched the bed for my phone. I'd set up this old-timey seventies song called *Time Has Come Today* as my alarm tone because it had the word "cuckoo" in the first couple beats. Plus, if I didn't get to it right away, it was a pretty cool song. I stopped the alarm, then turned to face my friends.

"Time to go." I held up my phone as if it was proof. Slinging my backpack over my shoulder, I extended the handle on my small suitcase and took it and myself out of the bedroom, through the bathroom, through the boys' room and into the living room—with Freddy and Bianca trailing behind. Luca stayed at his boyfriend's house last night, so he wasn't there to see me off, but it was okay. I didn't really love goodbyes, anyway. The prospect of never seeing the Marinos again made me sad. Bianca was like my Italian Stacey and I'd love to introduce them. The fun we'd have? It would be epic. And Freddy…well, maybe it was just as well.

I let go of my suitcase beside the small cooler Matteo had sent over this morning, and turned to face my friends. Bianca immediately put her arms around me and hugged me tight, despite my bulky backpack.

"We must get a selfie!" she said.

"Okay, but we've gotta be quick." I couldn't imagine Demitri being the kind of guy who liked to wait.

We proceeded to take at least a dozen pics of me and Bianca, me and Freddy, and of the three of us. When I'd finally managed to convince them we had enough, I turned toward my luggage.

"*Ce l'ho*," Freddy said, picking up the suitcase and cooler before I had a chance to argue.

We made a little, silent parade down the stairs and out the front door—even Bianca didn't say anything. I stopped short at the sight that greeted me outside and Bianca stumbled against me, which caused me to lose my balance with the backpack tugging me sideways. Great, I thought. So much for giving the impression I was a suave vampire. Then again, I was wearing leggings with an oversized *Drama Llama* T-shirt. Even though I'd dressed it up with a knot in the hem and a jewelry box of costume necklaces hanging around my neck—courtesy of Bianca, of course—I didn't think there was any point in denying who I was.

I'd never had a problem with my wardrobe before; even though Manuella tried to fancy me up, even she had admitted defeat to my K-Pop fashion sense. But now, with me standing there being all…me…I felt incredibly young and silly and not at all like the self-assured vampire I wanted Demitri to perceive me to be. Well, *drama llama whatever.* I squared my shoulders, lifted my chin, and donned my best Popstar demeanor.

Demitri, dressed in dark slacks and a pale blue dress shirt with the sleeves rolled up to his elbows, leaned against some dark chrome space age sports car, his legs crossed at the ankles and his arms folded over his chest, making his biceps bulge. His hair blew artfully in the chill breeze and he smirked at me as I walked toward him. He'd seen every second of my clumsiness and probably saw right through my pretend persona.

"Good morning," he said warmly as I drew nearer. He pushed off from the car and gave a head bow that didn't look at all out of place on him. The ladies probably found it adorable, but I only frowned. I was not here to be seduced by him. *Ew.* He looked behind me and offered Bianca and Freddy a smile and nod that seemed curt and perfunctory.

I couldn't tell what my friends thought of him, though, because they'd both gone to the trunk of Demitri's car and were mostly obscured by the raised lid. Once the luggage had been loaded, my friends and I faced one another again.

To my surprise, Freddy was the one to draw me into a hug first. "I do not like the look of this guy." Behind me, I was aware of Demitri closing the trunk and I could just imagine the glare Freddy had leveled on him.

I squeezed Freddy and reassured him, yet again, that I would be okay.

"Here," he said as he abruptly pulled back. "Get out your phone."

"Why?" I asked, even as I pulled it out.

"Because I want you to have my phone number so you can call me if you need me. If you need anything. *Va bene*?" He looked up from his phone, his gaze intense.

"Okay," I agreed.

"And I want to have your number so I can check up on you. Make sure you are safe."

"Freddy—"

"I know, I know. You have a boyfriend. *Capisco*. Just think of it as me helping the guy out while he is…*indisposto* or whatever."

I entered Freddy's number into my phone and texted him mine.

Demitri said something in Italian, and Freddy threw him a dirty look. But Bianca drew me into one more hug, telling me to stay in touch. Then I whirled around and attempted to throw myself into the front seat of the car but it was a heckuva lot harder than you'd think.

"Take it off and hand it to me," Demitri said with a nod at my backpack. I'd wanted to put it at my feet so I could access all my stuff, but there was literally no leg room. It seemed like a feat of science that he could fit inside with his long legs.

I handed him my pack, and he somehow managed to shove it into what passed as a backseat in that car. I gave my friends a wave, then carefully ducked and sidled into the car. At least I had my phone.

Tucked inside the tiny car, I waved as we drove away, but I doubt they saw me through the darkly tinted windows. Finally I turned to face the road, and tried to put all the bees buzzing around in my stomach to rest.

The leather bucket seat hugged my body as if made for me and I found myself relaxing a lot faster than I thought I would. Some operatic music played softly from the speakers—old stuff, because even though I knew the car and its speakers were probably top notch, it still had that crackly sound of old vinyl—while Demitri navigated the crowded Roman streets with ease.

I'd never been one to do anything reckless. I'd always had a strong stranger danger meter and had never before put myself in the way of danger.

Now, danger sat beside me.

In a very small car on a very long drive.

Because Demitri was dangerous. It practically oozed from his pores—it reminded of a power transformer and how the hairs on your arms would stand on end if you got too close. Not that I needed a reminder not to get too close to Demitri.

Despite all that though, I didn't feel as uncomfortable in his presence as I thought I would. Maybe it was all the time I'd spent with Thor—he gave off the same kind of danger-vibe that Demitri did. I could tell Demitri was old, but his power felt quiet somehow. Reserved. Which is a weird thing to say about a vampire. Then again, he was head of a family, yet he lived in a rundown apartment building. His actual apartment was schnazzy, but I got the feeling that he wasn't all that big on throwing his influence around like Ying Yue. He hadn't made something great of himself like David. Mostly, I felt curious about him, but not enough to actually ask him questions.

I craned my neck, watching as extraordinary historical sites passed me by. What I wouldn't give for a chance to explore Rome instead of just passing through it.

We passed the Santa Maria degli Angeli e dei Martiri, a crowd of people already lined up for a chance to go inside the old basilica. The outside of the church looked kinda weird, with its various add-ons and upgrades over the centuries, but I'd seen photos of the inside in the magazine on the plane and it was *wow*.

We passed the old and the new, villas with lawns and gardens, and hotels, hostels, and apartments, but we were clearly not in the scenic part of town. When we got onto Tangenziale Est, a highway surrounded by warehouses and parking lots, I frowned.

I'd looked up where Demitri said we were going—Otranto, a small coastal town about six hours south-east of Rome. "I thought we'd be going south—not toward the mountains." I turned away from the window so I could see Demitri's face.

He flashed me a quick grin. I couldn't see his eyes behind the dark sunglasses he wore. "This route is only thirty minutes longer but it will take us along the coast. I thought you might enjoy that."

My wayward left eyebrow drew downward. Thirty minutes wasn't a big deal, even though my insides clenched. In just under seven hours, I'd be at the Master's lair. I could finally find Philo. "Okay," I breathed because it was all I could manage. As I faced forward and watched the world pass me by, I thought of Philo and how I'd be with him, finally, *today*.

Without warning, pain lashed through my brain, slicing, cutting, ripping.

It was too much. Too dark. Too powerful. I collapsed under the power of it.

With a jerk, I gasped and sat upright—saved only by Demitri's vampire reflexes from conking my head on his forehead.

"Minnie. Are you all right?" He pressed a damp cloth to my forehead. We were stopped at the side of the road, the car rocking sometimes as another passed by at high speed.

With a hand pressed to my heart, I fought to regain my composure. *Am I all right?* I wasn't certain of the answer. I think my thoughts had wandered to Philo, and I may have reached out to see if I could feel him. I hadn't tried since arriving here. I wanted to tell him I was coming for him, but I didn't want him to worry. If he knew what I planned to do, he'd try to make me promise to stay away.

Even if I had reached for him though, *that*—whatever that was—was not how he would respond. The only time I'd ever felt anything close was when Hashiki attacked me. Except this wasn't an attack on my nervous system, but on my mind. And I still felt it, too. As if an oily slickness had been left behind in its wake.

I squeezed my eyes shut and took a deep breath. "I'm okay," I lied. "Really, it's…nothing."

He leaned back, rolling the wet wipe he'd used on my forehead into a ball. I tried to offer him a reassuring smile, but he didn't respond. Instead, his eyes seemed to glaze before sharpening once more on my face. Then he straightened in his seat and dropped the wet wipe into the pocket on the door.

"Yes, well. Shall we continue?"

I had the distinct impression he'd just had a vision of what was to come and whatever he'd seen had not been good. My aching head and trembling heart were already way ahead of him.

the wellbeing of their child, determine if they are in danger, and ascertain their location. In return, the child will always receive their creator's summons and know where to find their creator.

VAMPIRE GIFTS

CHAPTER FOUR

One of the many benefits of becoming a vampire are the gifts you will acquire.

These gifts are talents are extensions of your natural, human-born abilities—the ones you were born with as opposed to gifts you developed throughout your lifetime.

These gifts range in usefulness, as one might imagine. They might be

20

CHAPTER ELEVEN

WE'D BEEN OUT OF THE CITY FOR ABOUT FORTY-FIVE minutes, when Demitri pulled the car into a dirt parking lot in front of a large house. I sat up straight. "Where are we?"

Demitri smiled. "I am hungry. I think we could do with a little stretch and a snack, don't you?"

I hated that we were stopping so soon, but I couldn't deny that I was super hungry. "Good idea. I haven't eaten since last night."

I got out of the car, and the first thing I noticed was the scent in the air. I drank it in deeply, enjoying the unique flavors on the breeze. It's weird how a whole country can smell different from your own. It was a warm day, with a mellow golden sun shining down on us, and I couldn't help but take a moment to turn my face toward it and enjoy the feel of it on my skin.

"*Tsk, tsk*," Demitri said from just behind me. I jumped and whirled around. "Better not become too enamored of the sun, *sorellina*."

Even though he made me uneasy, I smiled, my face still turned to the warm ball in the sky. "True. But I can't tell you how relieved I was to discover that we could still enjoy the sun for short periods. I might've died all over again if I could never do this again."

Demitri chuckled and pressed a gently guiding hand on the small of my back, directing me toward the front door of the building. I wished he wouldn't touch me, but he was Italian. And old, if I guessed right. It was probably just habit with him. Italian men do have a reputation and all.

It wasn't until we were directly in front of the house that I noticed the sign affixed to the wall beside the door. "*Osteria di Cecilia*" it said. I raised a questioning brow at Demitri.

"You would say bar, I think." Demitri held the door open and I walked inside to a room dominated by gleaming wood and Abba playing loudly from the speakers. "But Cecilia rarely has drinking customers this time of day."

"I thought any time was a good time for Italians to drink," I quipped, earning a smile of appreciation and a chin nod from my companion.

Demitri gestured toward the room full of empty seats. "Sit. I will bring us something."

I started to walk toward a table before calling over my shoulder, "I'll have a Diet Coke, if they have it!" Before I chose a table, I noticed a kitchen garden at the back of the osteria and a small patio surrounded by hedge roses. I passed Demitri, who leaned on the counter talking to an older woman, as I moved toward the back door. "I'll be outside," I said before stepping out into a little piece of heaven.

A clear path led into a small courtyard with four tables. Grape vines heavy with fruit grew over the three arches leading into the courtyard, while the kitchen garden stretched out in organized rows beyond the little wooden gate. I'd only been sitting for a few minutes when I heard Demitri coming my way. I had taken a few pictures of the garden and was looking at them, so I didn't look up as he approached. He pulled another chair to our small table and set it between ours.

Then he and the woman he'd been talking to were there, the woman sitting in the chair between us. She was a little plump and very pretty, with lush dark curly hair and bright blue eyes that stood out against her tan skin. She smiled at me warmly.

"Minnie, this is Cecilia." Demitri and Cecilia shared a private smile, making their relationship immediately clear.

"Oh!" I gave the woman a bright smile and offered my hand. She looked at it a moment before lifting her hand so I could shake it. It was like holding a cold, sticky noodle. "You're the owner?" I asked to cover up my discomfort with her handshake. There was something off about her. Her expression hadn't changed much at all since she'd sat down. I focused on her eyes and noticed they were fully dilated, despite the sunshine. The skin on the back of my neck prickled.

Slowly, I swung my gaze toward Demitri, whose eyes had gone dark. "Where's our drinks? And our snacks?"

"Why, right here, *sorellina*." Demitri smiled and let his fangs drop. They gleamed white against his lips as he shifted his attention from me to Cecilia. Dread sank through my skin and into my blood stream.

"You can't!" I whispered loudly.

"You don't mind, do you *mio caro*?" He lifted Cecilia's chin with one bent finger and drew her attention to himself. "But I will ask you once more, for the benefit of my young friend. May we drink your blood, sweet Cecilia? Just a snack, of course. We've been friends far too long for anything more than that. What do you say?"

Cecilia swayed toward him, then stretched her head away, giving him full access to her neck. Her gaze landed on me, but I don't think she even knew I was there.

"Please," she begged, her breath wafting over my face with a scent that hit me like desire, making me gasp and my stomach clench.

Demitri bit into her neck.

Cecilia moaned and closed her eyes. She even clasped onto the arm Demitri had draped across her chest to stabilize her while he drank.

Holy. Guacamole.

Oh. My. Gosh.

I leaned away from them, but I couldn't tear my gaze away. I couldn't get myself to *leave*. A sudden and intense hunger gripped me, and I wasn't at all sure I wouldn't pounce on the woman if I moved.

Demitri's eyes opened and he looked at me while he drank. He'd caught me staring. With my mouth hanging open. A smile seemed to curl his lips while he bent himself to his task.

A moment later he lifted his face from the crook of her neck, his gaze hot on mine. Demanding. "Join me, *sorellina*. I promise you, she is quite delicious." He licked his lips and I gasped against the roar of hunger inside me. He returned to his task again.

I should leave, I told myself. *I should just get up and go. Go wait in the car. Better yet, just hitch a ride with someone going my way.*

I was still there when Demitri raised his head again.

He flicked a glance at me before kissing Cecilia's shoulder and neck. From his pocket, he produced a black handkerchief and wiped away the small amount of blood that had smeared on her smooth skin. Even though I knew our saliva could heal a bite, it still surprised me to see there wasn't even the tiniest scar remaining. He lounged back in his seat and used the corner of the handkerchief to dab at a small trickle of blood from his lips.

I raised an eyebrow at him. "Finished?" My tone was easy, casual, though I felt anything but.

He waved his handkerchief toward Cecilia. "It would be rude of me to take all she could give. I want to be sure you are able to have your fill."

I fought to ignore Cecilia who sat gently swaying as if moved by a breeze.

"Thanks, but I'm okay."

One elegant brow lifted. "Are you certain? There is not another stop as good as this for at least two hours."

I thought of my cooler in his trunk and nodded. "I'm sure."

"Very well. Let us go." He leaned forward and angled Cecilia's face so he could look into your eyes. "Relax for a few more moments. Enjoy the breeze and lovely smell of fresh basil and mint." He drew in a deep breath as if he was enjoying those scents, and Cecilia copied him. "In ten minutes, you will rise. You may feel a little tired, but it is nothing. You are immensely content. You enjoyed a visit with a handsome man—" Demitri winked at me, "and you will remember he purchased a bottle of red wine and you tucked the money into your pocket."

He let go of her, reached into his pocket and retrieved a silver billfold. It looked old, not tarnished, but well-polished, with a design or symbol etched into one side. After withdrawing several bills that I couldn't recognize, he tucked them into the woman's sweater pocket.

I stood and left the garden, walking on stiff legs that didn't feel like they belonged to me. Demitri followed. I wanted to run. From that place, but mostly from him, but I didn't dare. As much as I hated it, I needed him. Just a few more hours and we'd be in Otranto. I just needed to hang on until then.

"Can you unlock your trunk?" I asked over my shoulder as I marched to the rear of Demitri's car.

"Of course," he said.

It took all my strength not to run to the trunk once it opened, but I couldn't let Demitri know how desperate I was for blood. I sighed with relief when I reached the car—then forgot to breathe at all when I looked inside the trunk.

"Um, Demitri?" I didn't look up from the trunk. "Where did you put my cooler? The small blue one about this size?" I turned to face him, and mimicked the size of the cooler.

"Is it not there?" Demitri leaned past me to peer inside the trunk. "Oh, I am so sorry *sorellina*. We must have left without it."

I stared into the trunk, uncomprehending. "But Freddy put it in here. I saw him do it—we all did."

Demitri's expression was the picture of innocence. "Such a pity."

Panic bloomed in my gut as I considered all the possibilities. "Could it be in the backseat?" I ran to the passenger door and threw it open. I had to climb inside to peer into the back—the backseat was more like a shelf. My backpack dominated the space and there was definitely nothing else there.

I climbed out of the car, stunned and completely confused. "It's not there."

Demitri watched me with sad eyes. "If you are hungry, *sorellina*, we can go back inside." He gestured toward the door to the osteria. "I am sure Cecilia will still be under my thrall and would be happy to ease your hunger."

And then I understood. In fact, it was so obvious I wanted to smack my palm to my forehead. This was his plan. He wanted to weaken me, to demoralize me. *He* had been the one to remove the cooler from the trunk.

He'd known all along that I would grow hungry on this trip and I would have to…have to…

"Shall we go back inside?" he asked gently. He even sounded sincerely concerned for me. Sincerely interested in easing my hunger.

But I refused to be manipulated by him.

I turned on my heel and got back into the car. "No," I said. "I'm fine."

Just before I pulled the door shut, I thought I heard Demitri say, "As you wish," in a distinctly smug tone of voice.

It was a battle to keep my body relaxed and the emotion from my face. Inside, I was fuming and desperate but there was no way I'd let him see.

He'd left my cooler behind. Deliberately. He would have had to take it out of the trunk, and I don't know, left it out of view or else Freddy or Bianca would have seen it and put it back inside. Of course, if they didn't see it until after we drove away, there would have been nothing to do about it. I looked at my phone and checked for a text from Freddy, but there wasn't one. It wasn't until I sent one to him that I realized I didn't have any service. *Figures*.

"I got some really pretty pictures of Cecilia's garden." I wanted to give him some reason besides texting as to why I had my phone out, but I doubted he bought it. Whatever. I'd eaten well last night, and it was just another five or six hours—I could do this. "So. You and Cecilia seemed to be good friends. Or was that the first time you'd met?"

Demitri shot me a pleased smile, then returned his gaze to the road. I took in a deep breath as quietly as I could. I needed to talk and think about anything other than my hunger. Besides, I needed him to talk to me about the Master, but I wasn't sure how to get started. Maybe if we chatted about something else, we could segue into what I really wanted to know.

"Cecilia is a longtime friend. We had a...fling you might say, when she was much younger and the place belonged to her father. Now, I only see her on the rare occasions I travel this way. She has a unique flavor; almost like spiced red wine."

"Like the spiced blood you gave me when we met last night?"

He nodded his approval. "Very much like that, yes. Really, you should have tried her. I am quite sure you would have enjoyed it."

I shrugged noncommittally.

"You are young yet, and have probably existed on a diet of donated blood—am I right?" He cut me a glance, but I didn't respond. "I would expect nothing less, given what I know of the Aristos clan."

That got my attention and I half-turned my body so I could watch him better. "You know my family?"

"I have met David, and a few of his children—but it has been many years. Well before this Treaty of London nonsense. Which, I suppose, David has you all obeying?"

There was a gleam in his eyes, and I suspected there was something more to his question that I couldn't understand. Unwilling to admit my ignorance I shrugged, careful to keep my gaze on him.

"There is no need for you to be so ashamed, *sorellina*. David's betrayal of his kind is well known and you, as his child, cannot be held responsible for the way he has raised you. I certainly do not hold it against you. But—" he shifted his gaze from the road to me, holding me captive in his dark gaze, "the Master will not accept you as you are."

A chilly sense of doom flooded my body, as if someone had dumped ice water into my veins. Though I tried to hide the fear I felt, I'm sure Demitri sensed it. Matteo hadn't told me how old he was, and it was rude to ask, but I was beginning suspect that Demitri was quite a bit older than I had originally guessed. Why he was holed up in a villa-turned-apartment, I had no idea, but there was just something about him that spoke of experience. The kind of experience that can only be acquired over more time than a human's lifetime.

Demitri chuckled. "Do not worry, *sorellina*. I knew what you were the moment we met. There is a certain scent that one exudes when they have been bottle-fed. However, to tangle with the Master, you must be as carnivorous as he—if you will allow me to guide you, you might just be able to fool him when we arrive."

My heart gave a painful, hard thud inside my chest. If what he said was true, then…

Hunger rose up inside me, stronger than I'd felt since the night I was reMade. Stronger even than the time Ying Yue had held me captive. It was as if just the idea of drinking from someone, perhaps from several someones, between now and when I met the Master later this evening, had awoken a monster inside me.

"It is only natural, *sorellina*," Demitri said gently. "You have been living as both a human and a vampire, but that is no life at all. Because you, the human you were, died. You cannot forget that. And though you rose again, it was not as you were. You were never meant to continue as you were. You were reBorn a vampire—a creature so far superior to your human self that as yet you cannot even fathom it. As long as you cling to what you were, you will only ever be half alive. You will never become all that you could. Clinging to your past will only bring you pain." The last was said so softly, it was almost as if he'd said them to himself. But then he drew in a breath and straightened, flexing his hands around the steering wheel.

"You are a vampire, Minnie. A creature of fearsome power and appetite. Give yourself over to my tutelage, and the Master may not crush you beneath his heel. Perhaps he will glory in his own image reflected in your soul."

FOR NEW VAMPIRES

CHAPTER FIVE

Many Clans are eager to welcome new vampires into their families. After being hunted so actively during several generations, the vampire population dwindled quite low.

You may contact us at the email address listed at the back of this pamphlet, but the best way has always been, and remains still, is to ask a friend. Your transition will be

23

much smoother if you have the companionship of a vampire friend.

We are working toward establishing clinics around the world where potential vampires can receive counseling and been a sponsor to help investigators make the best decision for themselves.

In the meantime, we hope people will make every effort to educate themselves and take care with their decision.

CHAPTER
TWELVE

THE LUSH GREEN AND SOFTLY ROLLING HILLS OF THE
Italian landscape passed by while I contemplated the
worth of a soul.

The words *thank you* hovered in my mind, teasing
my tongue, but I couldn't say them. Not yet, anyway.

Stiffly, I straightened in my seat, and while I faced
the window, I wasn't seeing. I had far too much to
think about.

Because in my gut, I knew what Demitri had said
was true.

I hadn't known its cause, but there had been
something very different about Matteo and Demitri
and the other vampires I'd encountered in Rome. A
sense of danger, of barely restrained violence and

sensuality. And they had all smelled of blood. I'd thought that meant they practically bathed in blood, picturing something from the Twilight movies. But was it possible that just drinking "wild" blood as opposed to donated could be the difference?

None of my family felt or smelled like Demitri—with the possible exception of Sang when I'd first met him.

I thought about the other vampires I knew—of the Council members, Ying Yue and Hashiki, and Thor.

Thor definitely had that danger thing going on and I knew he drank straight from peoples' veins. People who willingly gave of themselves, but still…wild versus packaged. Natural versus processed.

For the first time since I became a vampire—not including the time Hashiki had speared my brain with her mental spikes—my head hurt. My heart hurt. But my body was freaking out. In that moment, I literally felt as if I had a monster inside who had just awoken from a long hibernation.

And she was wildly hungry.

"Tell me, what do you know of the Master?" Demitri's voice seemed to come from far away, and I was slow to respond. It was hard to pull myself out of the morass of thoughts that muddled my mind.

"I honestly don't know much," I admitted after a long delay. "Every time I've asked, I think my family omits a lot of the details." *I know he's sadistic and cruel,* I thought. *Considering what he's done to Philo.* I clenched my fists on my thighs, pushing down the anger that was quick to rise at the thought of Philo and his suffering. I only hoped that David hadn't been caught in the same trap. I was kind of counting on him to be there to help me.

"It is as I guessed. No one as innocent as you would be looking for a way into his lair, otherwise."

I bristled at his comment, but he patted my arm and said, "I do not mean to insult you. I suspect you want my respect—and you have it. I admired you before I even met you. Of course, I knew your clan, and I know what Aristos is trying to do. I even respect him for his efforts to bring our kind into the modern age, so to speak. Even I have altered my lifestyle in an effort to comply with the Treaty."

I scoffed, but he pushed on. "It may not seem that way to you, but it is not my habit to go around taking what is not freely given."

"Ha. You just drug them so they don't know what you're doing. You're no better than a rapist." I crossed my arms over my chest and slumped into my seat, which annoyed me but I couldn't change it now. I hated it when I acted my age, especially when I was trying hard to be on equal terms with a vampire. I wanted to ask what he meant about knowing of me before we met, but I'd committed myself to this sulk—I wouldn't allow myself to sink any further.

"See, you have just proven your innocence to me. Your ignorance. I do not enthrall my companions without their permission. It is absolutely no different than having donors on retainer, which many respectable vampires do, and which is entirely legal under the Treaty. Your education has been far too narrow, *sorellina*, and that is no fault of your own. But do you not owe it to yourself and your own future—a very long future, if you are lucky—to examine all the arguments if you will, before setting yourself so thoroughly on a specific course?"

I narrowed my eyes at him. That argument and his appeal to my logical side seemed custom designed for me. Honestly, it surprised me that Thor never tried it on me. Because I began to see the wisdom in Demitri's words. The monster surged and my skin tightened as the veins on my forearms grew darker and more visible. I wasn't sure how long I'd be able to keep it caged.

"We will stop for lunch shortly," Demitri said.

Tense, angry, and completely unsettled, I no longer cared about the polite rules of vampiric company. "Can you read my mind or something?"

Demitri chuckled. "No, *sorellina*. Nothing like that. I am just a very good judge of people."

I opened my mouth, then shut it, unwilling to ask the question burning on my lips: Then what *is* your gift?

"I have the rare, unpredictable, and often useless gift of foresight." He sighed as if the burden was too great to bear. "I spent too long in my youth resenting the gift and wishing for something—almost anything—else, but, well. We all know the fate of wishes."

"You either get what you want and it's not at all what you imagined, or there's no point to them?"

The grin that flashed across his face was bright, almost feral. "Precisely."

I thought about what I knew about foresight. *The Ultimate Guide to Becoming a Vampire* included brief descriptions of the known vampiric gifts, and I'd read about them all. What Demitri said was pretty much the sum total of what had been written about it. It was very rare, and predictions could be made for as few as five minutes into the future or far beyond the known time. However, it was largely viewed as a sub-par gift because the foresight was never 100% accurate. Any number of factors could change the seen future where sentient creatures were involved. The only predictions that were reliable were those about the weather.

"So you're a glorified weatherman?"

Now he turned and gave me the first real, natural smile I think I'd seen on his face. "Exactly. Now you see what a sorry specimen I am."

Hmm. That might be what he wanted me to think, but it was far from the truth. I started to think he might have a second gift he preferred to keep to himself.

"How about you, *sorellina*? I told you mine—will you tell me yours?"

Ha. My turn, I thought.

"Sure, I've got nothing to hide." *Lie.* And we both knew it. "I can sometimes see glimpses of a person's past, and I can..." Why hadn't I planned for this already? What would be the least offensive of my mind gifts? "Dip into someone's mind and catch a glimpse of what they're thinking. But it's a lot like your foresight," I hurried to add. "I often come away knowing what a person had for breakfast, not so much what the password is to their safe—does that make sense?" I mentally crossed my fingers, hoping that I'd made the right choice in what I told him. I would have preferred not to mention either of them, but I'd told Matteo, so it was possible Demitri already knew.

I watched him carefully, but he didn't show any sign of doubting me. He nodded thoughtfully. "Both are strong, useful gifts. The Master will appreciate those. Are you any good?"

My eyebrow twitched. "What do you mean the Master will appreciate them?"

"Well, he isn't inclined to let just anyone into his presence. You have to hold some interest for him, some purpose for being there."

"You know why I'm going," I retorted.

"Yes, but if you are correct and Philo is being held prisoner, it can only be in the catacombs beyond the Master's main chamber. You will have to go through him to find Philo, and he will want something from you. Trust me on this." His gaze flicked to me, but I pretended not to notice.

"Like what?" I couldn't imagine anything I had that the Master of vampires would want.

"Your gifts. He will want to know if you are any good."

"I'm good," I said with a bit more confidence than I felt. "My mind walking is the most reliable—the other is a little more hit and miss."

"That is too bad. It's probably the gift the Master will most like to see demonstrated."

"Demonstrated?" My voice cracked embarrassingly on the word and I had to swallow down the lump in my throat.

"As I said, he does not grant just anyone an audience. You must either be one of his own children, someone he knows, or someone he wishes to know."

I thought about the *kynigoi* and wondered if that would count. At least, I thought they were supposed to bring me in and not just kill me. I couldn't decide if I wanted to play that card, though. No need to remind the Master outright that he'd recently sent his hunters after me.

"Do you know what the Master's gifts are?"

Demitri's bark of laughter held no mirth at all, but it sure made me feel stupid. It took him a beat to regain his control, during which I beat my monster back mercilessly—it wanted to rip Demitri's head off and shove him out onto the highway, which I was both horrified and impressed with.

"The Master has all the gifts, *sorellina*. For where else might we have come by them?"

"But—" Nothing. I didn't have anything at all to say, I was too busy trying to make his words into reality.

"Let me tell you a story, shall I? We have," he glanced at the navigation screen on the dashboard—he hadn't programmed in a route, but presumably he knew where we were. "About twenty minutes until we reach our next stop." He looked at me. "If you can wait that long?"

I wasn't going to "eat" at the next stop, no matter what Demitri thought, so as far as I was concerned, we didn't have to stop at all. I nodded. He didn't need to know just how weak a hold I had on the monster within me and its demanding hunger.

"Before time as we knew it began, there was life on another planet. In fact, life existed on many planets. Life like and unlike our own, on planets like and unlike Earth."

I settled back more comfortably in my seat, already engaged in Demitri's story. I completely believed there had to be life on other planets—it was completely irrational of us to believe otherwise.

"One particular world was far from the sun. A world steeped in cold darkness and strange vegetation and creatures that thrived in a place we would imagine unable to sustain life. But not only was there life, there was sentient life—people, if you will—who lived and ruled that world.

"This species, I cannot say their name, for I have never learned it, lived very long lives yet only mated once—which only produced one offspring. As you can imagine, their world was not heavily populated. Additionally, they were not born to favor peace. They were a violent people, who fought against their base desires in order to see their species multiply and grow. Maybe they were even evolving, their nature overcome by community and a greater sense of what that meant, but there was still violence, despite the leadership's efforts to eradicate it. This violence took place in underground fight clubs, if you will, not at all dissimilar to those you might find on Earth.

"Mankind is surely not unique in their desire to be the best—the smartest, the most desirable, the strongest. Even Darwin saw the truth in this."

Well, I thought. *Darwin wasn't right about everything, we've just closed our eyes to the rest of his writings.* But I kept that thought to myself.

"The leaders of this world had a son who would go on to rule after them. But this son was no ruler. He was nothing at all like what they wished to perpetuate in their species. In fact, he possessed in full every vile desire his parents worked so hard to suppress. Even his appearance was a reminder of the past, and they worried he would never find a mate willing to take him.

"For his part, this son cared nothing for the leadership of his people. He despised them—all of them, even his parents. Even the potential mates they brought to him. Perhaps especially those. He began to spend all his time in the underground dens, unleashing the worst of his character without restraint.

"Soon, even that wasn't enough, and he fought to control his inner beast every moment of every day."

I thought of my own battle with my inner monster and shivered. I'd only felt the struggle for the past hour or so—and maybe just once or twice since I'd been reMade. I couldn't imagine living with it always. Then again, I couldn't imagine giving in in the first place. This story was definitely not going to be a happily ever after, that's for sure. I anxiously awaited the punchline and the reason why Demitri suddenly felt like storytelling.

"During a biannual event meant to bring all the people together to aid in the quest to find suitable mates, the son unleashed his monster." Demitri paused, a shadow lingering in his eyes for a long moment. "He murdered—no, he *devoured* hundreds. Maybe thousands."

"Wha—" I began, unable to suspend my disbelief any longer. But Demitri cut off my response with a raised hand.

"No. I know you don't believe it, but the...this creature was not human. Remember that. And trust that I know of what I speak."

I held my tongue.

"Now, because of the great value they put on life, these people did not tolerate murder. They especially could not allow what this son had done to go unpunished, despite his royal bloodline. The only bloodline to rule the people for as long as they could remember, for as long as their civilization existed. But his parents could not bear to end his life. It was probably the first compassionate thing they had ever done for their son, an evolutionary leap, but the people would not have it. The son must be punished. He could not be allowed to live.

"A compromise was made. This species, like many others you may be surprised to learn, had the ability to travel through space. They had chosen not to, as their focus was on the development of their own kind, but they did have the technology. The son would be sent to another world, they decided. A world that did not possess technology of any kind. A world from which this son could never return—unless or until his people returned for him.

"He was a prince of the people. Their only prince. Yet because of his extreme violence and thirst for blood, he was sent away. Exiled to a primitive world where he could attempt to survive on his own."

I knew where the story was going now. I knew it, but I didn't want to believe it. I couldn't believe it. The roiling hunger in my stomach churned violently, making me nauseous.

"Primitive though it might be, the abandoned son was not, in fact, alone."

"Stop," I gasped. I clung to the door handle, every ounce of concentration fixed on not throwing up. "Pull over!"

Demitri yanked the wheel, driving the car into the dirt at the shoulder, and throwing dirt and rocks into the air. I practically fell out of the car before it had finished moving. I didn't care how I looked or just how much of an innocent his story had proved me to be.

I vomited into the dirt, my tears falling to join the bloody mess that represented what my life had become.

There was no doubt now. Oh, how had I been so wrong? How could I have ever thought I could be both human and vampire? I should never have been allowed to live.

Imagine what you can accomplish if you have several lifetimes to accomplish your goals. Think of all you will see and all you will do.

It's not uncommon for many young vampires to burn bright and hot for a few hundred years, only to lose their way and eventually, their lives. However, successful vampires find meaning in their new life; typically, something larger than themselves. From raising their own vampire family, to developing cities, or researching a cure for cancer.

YES!! I'd love to know what great things vamps have done! This is the one thing I love about being a vamp — the possibility of making a real difference in the word. Even if it takes a long time!

Whatever direction you choose to take, be true to yourself and what you're passionate about.

Try not to change your life too much. The more you can keep it the same—especially in the first few months—the more you will be able to adapt to your new life.

On the other hand, there is something to be said for those that make a clean break from their human life.

CHAPTER THIRTEEN

"UGH," I GROANED. WITH MY HANDS BRACED ON MY knees, I appreciated the weirdness of the moment. Demitri hovered behind me, rubbing soothing circles on my back. Who knew he could be so kind? He demonstrated this latent ability further by offering me one of his black handkerchiefs. I tried to push his hand away. "No. I couldn't. I'll make it all gross."

"It's a handkerchief, *sorellina*. Its sole purpose is to handle the gross things in life."

A laugh burst from me and I shook my head as I took the proffered handkerchief. After wiping my face clean as best I could, I turned to face Demitri. "Ya know, you surprise me."

He quirked an eyebrow. "Truly?"

Embarrassed all of a sudden, I regretted my words. But, whatever. What was done, was done. It's not like I could have hidden all of this from him. "Well," I hedged. "You're a lot nicer than I thought you'd be."

His gaze dropped to the dirt at our feet—thankfully we'd moved a few feet away from my mess. Could he really be embarrassed by the compliment? "Here." He guided me back to the car and helped me inside. "There are wet wipes in the box." Then he shut the door and went around to his side.

It took me a moment to realize the "box" was the glove box, but I was glad for what I found inside—a small container of wet wipes.

Once we were on our way again, Demitri said, "Do you know what *sorellina* means?"

Satisfied my face was clean, I faced him and shook my head. "I've noticed you keep calling me that." I scowled, expecting him to say it meant *innocent* or something else true but somehow offensive.

"It means little sister."

I contemplated that. *Was* he being offensive? I couldn't decide.

"I see something of myself in you—not as I am today, but as I once was, when I was newly Made."

Oh.

"A very long time ago, I was an angry young man. My family worshiped the goddess Demeter, and even named me as a token of their dedication to her. We grew wheat and barley, and enjoyed a handsome living, producing enough for our family and more for barter and sale.

"A blight hit our land and though we weathered the storm for several years, eventually our fields were unable to produce anything edible at all. And then the plague came." Demitri spoke in an even voice, his white knuckles gripping the steering wheel, the only sign that what he said disturbed him.

"It was probably just a common cold, but in those days you couldn't simply run to the local convenience store for remedies. Already weakened with hunger, and with nothing to trade or coin to buy we couldn't have purchased our salvation anyway.

"We did, however, have a boat. I could not sell it, as what little fish I caught each day was all that kept us alive. But I thought I could sail down to the port at Dyrrhachiam or even Buthrotum, where perhaps I could work at the docks for a few days—long enough to earn some coin to buy medicine and food. I thought perhaps I would be gone a few days, a week at most."

He fell silent, a muscle ticking in his jaw. He nodded toward a road sign and said, "We will stop soon, and this time you will eat."

My stomach twisted and turned at the thought, so I pressed him to continue his story. I wanted to know, but I also needed the distraction.

He glanced at me. In a soft voice he said, "I never made it to either of those ports."

"What happened?" I'd seen the dark pain of loss in his eyes, but I couldn't help myself now. There was a reason he'd decided to tell his story—I had to know how it ended. And why it made him think we were alike.

Demitri slowed the car, but didn't speak again for several long moments.

"At first, I thought it was a freak storm. I set out at night, desperate to be at the docks first thing in the morning to find work. I had not seen a storm coming, but the waves roiled beneath my small ship and I was thrust about until I hit something and knew no more.

"Until the dreams came."

I watched as his knuckles clenched and unclenched around the steering wheel, the muscle in his jaw keeping time.

"I dreamt my boat fell apart beneath me, but before I could be lost to the depths of the sea, the devil came for me. I truly believed I had died." His voice was quiet, but his next words were quieter still. "When the pain began, I knew I was in Hades. I believed I was being punished for not being able to save my family—my parents, my wife and our little daughter.

"It wasn't until I awoke that I understood the true horror of what my life had become. It was then that I met the Master—and he is more horrific than any depiction of the devil you have ever seen, though I'm quite certain he is the model that beast was created upon." He flicked me a glance, then released one hand from the wheel to squeeze my knee. "There are no words I can give you to prepare you for meeting him. If you react to his appearance, he will eat you. You must treat him as if his appearance does not frighten you in the least. Can you do that?"

My nod was slow—I was terrified just imagining it. I could still feel the Master's malevolent presence from the time we'd met in my mind place. Drawing in a deep breath to steady myself, I considered Demitri's suggestion. What else could I do but try?

Demitri removed his hand from my knee before guiding the car down an off-ramp. There didn't seem to be anything but farmland nearby, but at this point I trusted him to know where he was going. I wanted him to keep talking because it helped me keep the monster at bay, helped me forget the desperate hunger pulsating beneath my skin.

"It was many months before I was able to return to my farm," Demitri said. "My neighbors were living in my home and farming my land and theirs."

"I'm so sorry." It wasn't unexpected, but I was still sorry. What surprised me most was the depth of his feeling over something that took place so long ago.

"I found the small graveyard they had made for my family," Demitri continued, as if I hadn't spoken. "It was kind of them. Many in that time would have burned the bodies—I mean, they had no reason to expect I would ever return. Yet there they were—three stone markers, for my mother, father and wife."

He paused and I frowned. "But—"

Demitri chuckled. "That's what I thought too, so I returned to my neighbor's house—my house—to confront him. Only he had spoken to me, keeping me outside the little cottage, but this time, I burst inside—and discovered the man's wife, and my daughter.

"But in my anger at his deceit, at his betrayal, I had lost control, and it wasn't her father my daughter saw standing there—it was the monster I had become.

"To this day, no moment has been harder than turning away and disappearing from her life forever. I wanted to devour my neighbors, the imposters. I wanted to end them and be my daughter's father once more. But I was no longer her father. I could not be her father. And I could not take her away from the only normal life she might have."

Demitri pulled up to another house with a dirt parking lot, and I expected he had another Cecilia inside—but there were several more cars in the parking lot, and music could be heard, even inside the tight confines of the fancy sports car. I looked at him, but he still gripped the steering wheel, gazing off into the distance.

"I returned to the Master, not knowing what else to do, and he just laughed. He'd known. I should have guessed he would, but I didn't understand then just how great his power was. In the years since, I have come and gone from his presence many times, and every time I vow I will not return again." He drew in a deep breath and with what seemed like conscious effort, let go of the wheel, and faced me.

"I was once as innocent as you, *sorellina*. Despite what I saw when I first woke in the Master's lair, despite what I thought might be possible as a vampire, I have come to learn that while fragments of our humanity remain, we are no longer innocent. We are born in blood, we live in blood. Over time, your humanity will fade. Over time, you will come to see that you are nothing more than one of the Master's vile offspring."

I felt bad for him, I really did. His centuries-old sorrow and anger were palpable even now. But I knew he had to be wrong. I still felt like me. I felt like a human, with a little vampire. Especially after learning the truth about the Master, that was exactly how I wanted to remain. But before I could tell him, Demitri grabbed my wrist in a tight, painful grip.

"You are young. New. And yet you have a gift more powerful than any other living at this time."

"Wha—"

"Yes, I know more than you told me, but not from Matteo. Good or ill, your name is known. You are an agent of change—we all know it. The question is, what will happen next? Because however circumspect you think you have been in your journey here, the Master is expecting you.

"I know all about Philomon and I know you hope to rescue him. What is being done to him is the most vile thing that can be done to one of us. Whatever Philomon has done, he does not deserve this."

I tried to move, but Demitri's grip remained tight and his gaze just as impossible to resist. "What you have not been told, because it is in opposition to the Treaty of London and every little thing that has been done to humanize us, is that you are weak until you drink from a living being. You are only a shadow of yourself, when you have not felt the life drain out of one body and into your own."

I struggled, hard this time, but Demitri's grip only tightened, holding me firmly in place. "Look at me. *Read* me. I am telling you the truth, *sorellina*. I want you to succeed. I want you to free Philomon. I want you to defy the Master, and I want to be there to spit in his face when you do. But you are not ready. Not yet. You would not be ready if you prepared for centuries, yet tomorrow, or perhaps the next, you will come face-to-face with the devil incarnate. If you are to rescue Philomon before it is too late, you must go to him. Now. It has probably only been your connection that has kept him tethered to his form this long.

"Come. Read me now. And then you may decide if you will be the rescuer Philomon needs, or if you will remain the innocent and flee this place tonight."

He leaned back in his seat and closed his eyes, while I remained rooted to the spot, my wrist throbbing and my mind whirling. There was too much to think about. Too much to consider. And the truth was, I was afraid of discovering that Demitri was right—that the only way I could save Philo would be to cross a line I swore I'd never cross. To become a thing I wholeheartedly believed was as far removed from who I am than, say, the Easter Bunny.

"Tick, tock, *sorellina*."

I flopped back into my own seat, anger and frustration crashing through me. I breathed deeply until I had myself under control, then I lifted my mind, my *self*, from my body so I could sink into Demitri's mind. I wanted to go beyond his current worries, where he might be experienced enough to fool me. I wanted to go somewhere he didn't expect me to go and discover the truth from there.

I'd only done this exercise once before, and it had been on Thor. I'd surprised him with how naturally it came to me, and I crossed my fingers that it hadn't just been a fluke. The mind's memories were like a funnel, going round and round while dropping down and down until you reached the core of a person, the heart of who they really were. I felt drawn to certain points upon the spiral, and from my brief experience with Thor, those points seemed to be the ones of greatest unrest, or the real core memories as I liked to think of them.

I let myself fall deep into the funnel of Demitri's mind, wishing to go far beyond anything contemporary, until I finally let a memory draw me in. It felt dark and sticky, and pulsated with a malevolence that scared me. It was just as possible I was about to observe Demitri committing the most heinous crime of his life as I was to learn anything pertinent to my current situation, yet I dove in anyway.

The path downward is slippery, slick with salt water and lichen, but I've made this journey many times before. It poses no danger to me. Resentment rides me like a beast and I'm practically pulsating with it by the time I crawl through the entrance and stand once more in the Master's lair.

There are no flames within, the cavern as dark as night with no moon, but it is no matter. Thanks to this monster, I can see in the dark. What I cannot tolerate is the stench. I had forgotten, though how I cannot fathom. The filth and decay does not recommend him.

I force myself to ignore the rot and push forward, deeper into the lair. Around me, all around me, vampires lay—as far as I can tell, every one of them has a human companion—a buffet that never ends. These...creatures...hiss and turn away, pulling their food with them as if afraid I will try to steal it from them. There has to be some of them who are capable of more than this—I have never seen the Master without children capable of intelligent conversation.

Could it be he is breaking at last?

I shake my head as I approach him. I need to keep a clear head. I must not give him any more fodder on which to burn my hatred of him than he already has.

Of course, he already knows I am here. Has probably been prying into my mind as soon as I came within his reach. As I step over the last of the bodies lying on the stone floor, to the relatively clear area at the center where the Master resides, I stop, preparing myself for what is to come. I have rehearsed what I must say over and over, and this time—this time I will not falter.

The Master does not acknowledge me.

"Master?" I pull the parchment from my coat pocket, written in blood in the Master's own hand. One glance at it, and my anger burns anew. "I am Demitri Valerius. I have come at your request. Will you not even give me the courtesy of acknowledging my presence?"

I watch the Master's back, wide and malformed, cloaked in a black fabric I have learned not to take for granted. I do not know what it is, but it is as alive as he or I am, and just as deadly. The Master seems larger than when last I saw him, though standing he towers over even the tallest of men. He is not of this Earth, and bile churns in my stomach as I prepare to see the horror of his countenance once more.

"Master!" I practically shout, earning more hisses from his children.

He lifts his head and stillness falls. I imagine him sniffing the air, though he still does not turn to face me.

"Demitri," he purrs as if I am his most precious son, bringing forth a reaction in me that I had hoped to avoid. Still, I had prepared myself for this. Believed I had hardened my mind against this—yet the sound of my name on his lips is like a drug, like manna, like the elixir vitae itself. "Come to me, my precious child."

I lock my knees, willing myself to stand my ground. To force him to face me. Yet even as I do it, I know it is hopeless.

"I have been waiting for you, my child, for I have a most precious gift for you. A gift you will thank me for eternally."

Gift? What gift could he possibly give me? The only thing I want is to return to my family. To find them well and whole. To return to my place by their sides. But I lost them some thirty years ago now. My daughter is married. And I would not want her to see me as I am. I am no one she should know.

"Come, Demitri." Though his voice is as soft as a feather's caress, I feel the command in his tone, and begrudgingly move along the perimeter of the writhing bodies until I come to stand directly in front of the Master. His head is down and I hear him whispering to someone tucked against his side, wrapped within his cloak.

The Master looks up at me and smiles—I fight to keep my features in check, to not let any of my abhorrence for him show on my face. "Look what I have done." And he lifts his arm wide.

Becoming a member of the undead community can be a startling transition for some. Be sure to give yourself lots of time to acclimate to your new life. Avoid stressful situations, starting new jobs or new relationships for at least six months after your rebirth. ROFL!

Omo. This is hysterical. Guess I'm a total fail!

Adjusting to life as a vampire can certainly be a challenge. That's why we encourage all young vampires to explore their talents and gifts. Not only can it be a marvelous distraction from what could otherwise be a terrible time in your life, but gifts can be fun! Take the time necessary to explore and master your gifts.

As you are reMade, your new body craves its prime source of nourishment: human blood. You are now a predator. It's only been in the recent century that vampires have begun to eschew their true nature. I think I've done pretty well but it
(13) a struggle. Plus, I think I generally have more self-control than other ppl.

A young vampire should not be expected to control their hunger. Blood of all varieties should be provided, both fresh and donated,

CHAPTER
FOURTEEN

WHILE I SAT IN THE COMFY LITTLE SPORTS CAR, MY ARMS wrapped around my middle, I tried to keep a grip on reality as the rest of Demitri's memory played out. It was all I could do to stay, when I wanted to rip myself out of his mind and take myself as far away from the Master as possible. But there was Philo to consider, and the grasping fingers of Demitri's terrible memory still wrapped around my own mind, my own soul, as surely as they were around his.

I believe I am prepared for anything. A child. A pregnant mother. A warrior brought to his knees. Any of these and more would please the Master. Any of these could be seen as a "gift" in his twisted mind. I stare at the Master's face—forcing myself to see his too-wide eyes glowing red in the darkness, the black horns that curled from his misshapen forehead, his sharp and jagged cheekbones framing the flat, almost pig-like nose, the wide, thick red lips and the double rows of fangs protruding over them. A horror. But I couldn't keep my gaze from sliding to his powerful naked chest, where a familiar face with madness in her eyes stared up at me.

"Hello, Papa."

I stumble back, feeling as though I have just been kicked in the gut. My knees give out and I fall onto them, barely aware of the pain that ricochets through my bones. I can't take my eyes off her. I want to look away, so desperately, but my gaze is fixed.

She is naked, her body covered in the Master's bites. Bites that never healed, but fester. The impossible woman slides out of the Master's embrace and slowly crawls toward me, her grin wide, her gaze mad. She is no innocent. Not anymore. And she is no human.

Though she is older than when I last saw her, I see her mother in the color of her hair, in the fairness of her skin.

I would know my daughter anywhere.

Chest heaving with air I don't need, but desperately want, I finally yanked myself out of the memory, all the way out, back and back until I cowered like a scared little girl in the corner of my mind. Except the closer we got to the Master's lair, the less safe I felt inside it. I drew my knees up to my chest and wrapped my arms around them, as if by making myself as small as I possibly could, I'd be saved from reliving what I'd seen. But there was no place in my mind that was safe from the horror.

The horrific truth of the Master.

When Demitri put his hand on my shoulder I flinched, and he removed it. Then it landed softly on my head a moment later, and he began to stroke my hair. "I am sorry, *sorellina*. I would not have chosen that memory to share."

"I—" It took several tries before I had myself under control enough to answer. "I know. I—I'm sorry for making you relive it. I wanted to choose a memory at random, something I felt you were less likely to tamper with to sway me."

Stroke, stroke, stroke. Each time he drew his hand down from the top of my head to my shoulders, I sank deeper into myself, returning bit by bit to my own sanity.

"And did I? Tamper with it, I mean?" he asked softly.

I shook my head, then regretted it, because it made him pause his gentle comfort. I held my breath until he resumed. "No."

Stroke, stroke, stroke.

Finally, he asked, "And did it persuade you to give up on this quest of yours? Shall we turn around and return to Rome?"

I jerked my head up so fast, I knocked his hand away. "No! We can't! I just…I don't want…" I shut my eyes and willed myself to calm down and speak clearly. "I'm terrified. You've certainly managed to convince me that the Master is—" my breath caught in my throat, "as horrific as you said. But I just feel all the more like I need to get Philo out of there."

Demitri stared back at me, sadness and resignation warring in his eyes. He nodded slowly, then dropped his gaze to his hands, which he held open as if trying to read the future in his palms. "I understand. Despite all I know, if I had a chance to save my daughter from his clutches, I would do the same."

His voice sounded so forlorn, as if he couldn't imagine anything worse happening—which, of course he didn't have to imagine because he'd lived right through it.

I reached over the center console and gripped one of his hands. Squeezed. "I'm sorry about your daughter, Demitri."

The utter devastation in his eyes surprised me and I snatched my hand away, regretting my inability to deal well with emotions. A moment later, the look in his eyes shifted—no less intense but with a different emotion shining through them. "That day—the memory you saw—I tried to fight the Master. I tried to wrest Nadia away from him. But he had made her dependent upon him in some way I could not give. It is the same with all the creatures he keeps nearest to him. They are not like you and I."

I trembled a little and he stroked my hair again. "They are more like dogs are to humans. I do not know why." He shook his head a little, lost for a moment in his own thoughts. "It is because of Nadia that I know you must be as strong as you possibly can be when you meet him. I was fueled by the heartbreak and rage of a father, and still I may as well have been a kitten. Nothing I did affected him. It only served to entertain him."

He looked away and out through the windshield, for which I was grateful. He took a deep breath and so did I.

"You need blood from the source, Minnie. I know you do not like the idea—I promise you, I do not relish the violence that is inherent in our nature, despite what you might think of me." He flashed me a quick smile, giving me a glimpse of that suave and arrogant man I first found him to be. Now? It seemed so much of what I understood to be true had changed, and it had only been a few hours.

"You have probably not yet had the opportunity to learn that vampires who drink direct from the source, from the vein of a living, breathing human, possess a great many advantages over those who subsist on donated blood.

"I do not know the science behind it, or the why and wherefore—but I do know it is true. I have seen it with my own eyes. Without living blood, you are like a child facing off with a Jedi."

A burst of laughter broke through my clenched teeth. "Wait. Did you just say *Jedi*?"

He actually looked slightly offended that I would think he wouldn't know all about the Jedi. "Of course. *Star Wars* was a most excellent feat of cinematic glory."

I shook my head. "Sorry," I gasped. *Not sorry.*

His own chuckles joined mine, which had become something alive, and it took me several minutes before I could rein it in.

"Sorry," I said again. "I guess I needed that."

"*Sorellina.*" Demitri's gaze was serious with concern and regret once more.

"What?"

A droplet of blood welled from my tongue where my fang had nicked it and all at once I was *vampire*.

A steady rhythmic thump drowned out every other sound—a chorus of heartbeats from inside the tavern, and I could identify each beat unique from another. My gums ached and my fangs seemed to pulse with the need to *bite, rip, tear.*

I clamped a hand over my mouth and shut my eyes even though I knew it was pointless to hide how the hunger raged within me.

"Do not argue with me." Demitri's hard voice had me opening my eyes—only to be pierced by his intense *I mean it* glare. "Wait five minutes, then walk around to the back of the building. You will see a copse of trees—go there and wait for me. I will take care of you, *sorellina*, only give me five minutes."

All I could do was stare at him, as horror for what was to come and the shame it would bring me warred with the monster delighting in possibilities. *Demitri will take care of me. He will feed me.*

Feed me, feed me, feed me.

"Do not let yourself be seen." His last words floated back to me out of the dark as he swiftly exited the car and strode toward the tavern.

With shaking fingers I hardly recognize as my own, I pulled out my phone and set the timer for five minutes. Though it turned out I hardly needed it—I counted the seconds of each minute, focused on those numbers and counting in the exact rhythm so I would not think about my overbearing need.

I turned the timer off just before the alarm sounded, and was out the door a second later. Though it was only late afternoon, no one loitered outside the building, so no one saw me speed from the car to the shadows in the back corner of the building. From there I could see the copse of trees Demitri mentioned, but I paused. I wanted to go inside. I wanted to breathe in the scent of people, to choose my own prey, to experience the hunt, the capture—the kill. The lure was so strong, I took several steps in the direction of the front door before a very dim part of my mind reminded me of Demitri's words, reminded me that I *don't* want this. I don't even want Demitri to take care of me in this way because I shouldn't want this, I always said I didn't want this.

But the heartbeats were so loud, and while someone stood in the doorway, the fragrance of all those people, all that blood, was like manna, drawing me closer, closer, closer.

The door slammed shut and a man walked my way. I hesitated—then ducked into the shadows at the side of the building. I waited, heart thumping in my throat, and hoped he hadn't seen me. The experience was the wakeup call I needed to dash across the sparse yard to the trees at the edge of the property.

I didn't know what I was doing. No, that's not right. I knew, and I was willing to let it happen. Truthfully, I felt I had no other choice. It didn't even have anything to do with finding Philo, or whether I was a human or a Jedi—it had everything to do with the blood rage boiling inside me.

Through the haze of rage, I heard a screen door bang and a woman's easy laughter.

Two women approached. No—three people. A man, two women.

Coming my way.

By the time Demitri stumbled into the little clearing behind the trees, I was trembling like a junkie in withdrawal. He had just opened his mouth to say something, when I lunged forward.

He grabbed me by both shoulders and swung me away as easily as if I were a rag doll. I growled at him. *Growled*!

"Easy," Demitri purred. "Just take it easy. You must be in control, or you will not be able to pace yourself. Do you wish to kill her?"

My gaze fixed on his and muted clarity came to my mind. "No." My voice sounded raspy, as if I'd been screaming, but it was strong. I did not want to kill the woman. But I needed to eat. Now.

"She has agreed to be here, but you must ease her way. Enthrall her. Take care of her. This is our way."

Not *our* way, all vampires' way, I knew, but Demitri's way. Matteo's way. I took a deep breath to steady myself and nodded. If I had to do this, then it would be my way, too. Demitri released my arms and moved aside.

I stood face to face with the woman. She laughed nervously, then stepped toward me. Taking courage from her strength, I moved forward to meet her. She was taller than me, but probably not much older. Of course she was way more beautiful and confident too, but in that moment, my inner monster made up for what I lacked in that arena.

She watched me, wide-eyed, with an expectant smile.

"You know I am a vampire?" I wouldn't enthrall her until I knew she knew what she was doing.

"*Un vampiro. Sì.*" Her smile widened and she bobbed her head. She looked over her shoulder to where Demitri already had his head bent to her friend's neck. "*Sì*," she said again.

I nodded. "Okay, then." Staring into her eyes, I willed her into a sort of waking bliss. The doing of it felt surprisingly easy, like it was what I'd been made to do. A moment later she drew her long hair out of the way and bent her neck in invitation.

Too needy to feel awkward and dumb, I gestured for her to sit on the ground while I knelt behind her. I bit into her soft flesh already exposed by the off-shoulder sweater she wore. She cried out at first, then whimpered, but the sound only made me sink my teeth further, drink deeper.

Soon, she made no sound at all.

사랑해
♥

My awareness swam to the surface of my mind in slow spirals, giving me plenty of time to remember what I'd done. Memories that weren't my own swam with mine—those of the girl whose blood I'd taken. My heart felt heavy with realization that it had been easy. Natural even. And no matter how hard I tried, I couldn't regret it.

I pulled myself up from the slump I'd been lying in, noting the quaint, brightly colored village on one side and the sparkling turquoise blue of the sea passing on the left. The sun seemed so abnormally bright, that I had to pull down the sun visor, though it barely helped. The low-hanging sun lit up the Adriatic Sea with a million brilliant cut diamonds, each one piercing through my eyeballs and into my brain.

Demitri glanced at me, concern evident on his face. "Are you all right?"

I gave him a wan smile and nodded. When did I start to see Demitri as a friend instead of a threat? It would be easy to say it had been when he let me view his memories, but it had started before then. Despite his magic trick with my cooler, I trusted him. Demitri had told me the truth, even when it was difficult to hear. Straight up, undiluted truth—about myself, our kind, and the Master.

"She is not dead," he said softly. "I was able to stop you before it came to that."

I swallowed hard, then closed my eyes in brief relief. I'd assumed I had killed her. Believed it. That she lived didn't exactly change the horror of what I'd done, but it did ease the guilt a little bit.

I cleared my throat. "Where are we?"

"We have just passed through Torre a Mare."

Scrubbing my eyes, I pictured the map in my head. "Torre a Mare. That's like half-way there." That means I'd slept through the past few hours.

"It is like that the first time," Demitri said softly. "It will not always be so."

I thought about the "it" he was talking about, and mentally kicked myself when I started to panic and whine about what I'd done. I *had* done it. And it hadn't been horrible.

"We will need to stop at least one more time before we arrive in Otranto," Demitri said softly.

"What? No!" I angled to face him, ready to argue, but there was nothing but sympathy and understanding in his expression. "I can't."

He patted my knee before saying, "You must. Surely you can see that now. Can feel the difference in your body, and especially in your gift?"

I stared at him for a long moment before I sank back in my seat. I'd noticed the difference the second I woke up. My body felt like a happy cat, coiled and resting but ready to strike, to hunt and kill in a flash. Power thrummed beneath my skin like a drug and I suspected I could do just about anything right about now. My vision seemed to be in HD, my hearing too, seemed maxed out and superhuman. I'd felt something like this that first night after I'd been reMade, when I couldn't stay in my parents' house because of the danger I felt lurking inside my body.

As I watched the white-washed houses with their brightly painted doors and shutters pass by, I went into my mind place to reach for Philo.

The vision I created was so real, I wondered if I'd somehow teleported myself back to Meyers Town. I felt the cool breeze on my cheeks and smelled the scent of autumn as my feet crunched on some of the first fallen leaves of the season. The ground felt soft and loamy beneath my feet, as if it had rained recently—that wasn't a detail I normally included in these little worlds I built in my mind. I felt pretty darn sure teleporting was not an actual vampire gift, so I stepped between that space and my present mind—sure enough, I still sat in Demitri's car, driving slowly down the coast of Italy.

Well alrighty then. Let's do this thing.

I found Philo's mind the moment I reached for it, but though I knew my ability was stronger than ever before, I couldn't draw him to me. Even without the super vamp stuff, being this physically close to him should have made it much easier to connect with him. This felt harder than ever before.

Though I didn't want to do it, I created a new space and stepped through.

The last time, the Master had been the one to draw me here, but I'd dreamt it, too, so it wasn't difficult to recreate Philo's prison in my mind. The smell assaulted me, far stronger than before. Iron first, then rust and water. Before, the smell of blood and decay had been strong...now they were mere notes beneath the others. Fear clenched my gut as I thought of why that might be.

Philo? I picked my way over the gross dirt and stone floor toward the furthest, darkest corner of the cell. I...I couldn't feel him. Had he been moved? Demitri had said the Master would know I was coming—would he also know why? I shook my head. Of course he'd know why. If he knew who I was, like Demitri said, then he knew my relationship with Philo.

Philo, I called more loudly. This time I forced myself to get over the gross floor, the smell and fear, and I walked right up to the shadowed bundle that was the bed, and—no one was there. Just a rotted old blanket and a nest of baby mice huddled beneath.

But where was Philo?

Desperate now, I whirled in that horrible mind space. Could he be dead?

I refused to believe that.

But then, what?

A door to my own mind opened just a crack, and someone began calling me to them.

The tug was gentle at first, barely a thread, a fishing line without a hook. It might have been Philo, weak as he was, drawing me toward him, but it had nothing of his feeling about it. The tug was familiar, but also not. Like something in my family line, but not anyone I knew intimately.

Despite thinking that, I dropped the unknown thread, and took myself to David's office. David should be with the Master—he'd left to meet with him just hours before I did, so he should be with him by now. David would help me. So I called him to his office—it was always easiest to bring people to a space where they felt comfortable.

David! I winced, regretting my forceful call. I didn't want anyone he might be with to be aware that he was in communication with me.

A moment later, David appeared—but once again, it wasn't the same. He glanced around with wide-open eyes, his presence muted as if he were a ghost. He wore his usual trousers and dress shirt, but his tie was gone, his once-white shirt dirty and sweat-stained, and his feet were bare.

David? I prompted again, more softly. Somehow, he hadn't seemed to see me until then.

213

He whipped toward the sound of my voice, and immediately his visage changed—his clothing and personal appearance returned to what I was used to, but his eyes still had that wide, wild quality to them.

Minnie. Get out of here. Go. Now. You can't let—

Pain burst through my brain as sharp and pure as a physician's scalpel. My reaction was to fling myself away, to return to my mind, to my body where I could escape the inexplicable pain. The knife became a hook and this time it was no fine fishing line that drew me inexorably toward a destination I knew I didn't want to go, it was a thick, slick rope made of sinew and muscle.

David's office was gone. David was gone.

This presence—I knew it. I'd stood beside him once before in a mindscape he'd created for us. But I realized now, he'd only hijacked my own abilities, letting his presence be muted like everything else had been before.

But not now. Not now that pure, fresh blood pumped through my system. Not now that I was so close to his location.

Not now that he knew my intent.

Because even as his pull on my mind relented and I was abruptly free to return to myself, I knew the whole of me had been laid bare to the Master.

for optimum health. If food is withheld from a young vampire, he may succumb to blood lust from which they may never return.

> Here's what you need to understand:
> Your friends and family will mourn
> your death. It will hurt and frustrate
> you, but humans don't yet fully
> understand the transformation you
> undergo to become a vampire. Be
> patient with them. Give them a
> second chance. And more when they
> need it. Most importantly, don't try
> to force them to see you as yourself—

[handwritten annotations:]

• There should be a ceremony to help the fam+ new vamp mourn their death. I mourned it, but I was supposed to just ADJUST all of a sudden.

• Maybe if I'd let myself mourn, I wouldn't have kept trying to be my old self & wouldn't have risked going to school.

(scary!)

ALSO. I think new vamps should be prepared for the possibility their friends & family might never accept them. ☹

29

I think my parents / mom saw someone. Wish I could ask her about it. It's a good idea—esp. if it was part of the next vamp ceremony. It's a lot to take in. A lot to deal with.

they will likely see that as some kind of threat and call the authorities.

Changes in your friends' and family's behavior are the most difficult things for a young vampire to endure. Responses may range from grief to hatred, all of which will leave you feeling alone and abandoned. Remember, this transition is difficult on them, as well as you. You will have your Maker and family to help you, but many humans don't have access to proper support systems. Be patient. In most cases, human

CHAPTER
FIFTEEN

DEMITRI DIDN'T ASK WHAT HAPPENED, AND I DIDN'T offer to tell. He seemed to suspect something though, because he squeezed my shoulder and remained silent.

We reached the town of Lecce and I felt the Master near. His pull was an almost tangible thing. All I wanted to do was go straight there, but Demitri's grim announcement that we must eat one more time won.

I hardened my resolve and tamped my morality down as best I could, prepared to accept whatever situation Demitri offered, but instead of a taverna or osteria somewhere in the countryside, he drove to the center of town, past a gorgeous old Catholic church and onto a lovely tree-lined street where a modern apartment building grew amongst the old Italian buildings. When he parked at the side of the road, I looked around. Unless we were going inside the apartment building, there didn't seem a likely spot to find willing donors.

It was mid-morning, and people walked the streets, coming and going from the bank, restaurant and other shops subtly tucked into the buildings. A busy farmers market seemed to be taking place in the park kitty corner from where we'd parked.

"What are we doing here?" I couldn't imagine we'd risk taking anyone in broad daylight like this.

Demitri jutted his chin toward the building on his side. "The *eneteca*."

Only one door had a sign above it, but I still didn't understand. "Wine & More?" I scoffed, slumping back into my seat.

I didn't feel at all easy in my skin. I hadn't since the experience with the Master a couple hours ago. I felt him with every breath, like he was standing too near, breathing down my neck.

Demitri raised his eyebrows and unclipped his seatbelt. "We're here for the *more*. Obviously."

I followed him out of the car, mumbling, "Obviously."

The people on the street seemed ordinary enough, but I felt incredibly young and underdressed in my tights and T-shirt as I walked up to the glass door. Demitri—I narrowed my eyes at him—had somehow changed his shirt between our last stop and now. Despite a few wrinkles in his slacks caused by long hours in the car, he looked perfectly elegant and presentable. I felt like a kid's abused Barbie, with frizzy hair and rumpled clothes.

Hesitantly, I followed Demitri into the shop. The main room was beautiful, narrow and long, with hardwood floors and walls stacked high with wine racks. When a man in a dark suit stepped forward to greet us, I kind of hid behind my large and domineering guide. The man barely spared me a glance, but he shook Demitri's hand as they spoke in rapid fire Italian.

Then the man turned and walked toward the back of the long room and Demitri nodded for me to follow him.

We were led into a room with a sign that said "Tasting Room 4." I've never been in a wine-tasting room, but I was almost one hundred percent certain it shouldn't look anything like this. Four jewel-toned sofas sat at angles from each other, while a large screen TV was affixed to each wall. As we stepped inside, the usher or whatever he was gestured for us to take a seat. He disappeared behind a door at the back of the room, and a moment later a line of people began to parade into the room.

I sat, open-mouthed, as men and women, all scantily dressed, stood before us, waited a beat, then walked away.

"You're to pick someone who appeals to you. They are all willing donors, I assure you, and they are very well compensated."

"But why do they have to be all," I gestured with a flailing hand toward them. One of the guys in the lineup had been close to my age and soooo good looking, I blushed just glancing at his bare chest.

"Ah, *sorellina*," Demitri said in that almost condescending tone he sometimes used, "I forget how innocent you truly are." He'd been examining the handful of people in front of us, but then snapped his head toward me. "You truly do not know?"

I shook my head. "Know what?"

Demitri sighed. "I had heard rumors of Aristos and how he raised his young, but it seemed too far-fetched to believe." He cast me a sidelong look. "I suppose I must believe them, now."

"Argh. Know what?"

He leaned in close and turned his face so he could whisper. "One day you will discover it for yourself, I suspect, but there is a…certain pleasure…that humans derive from our bite. It can…arouse them in a particular fashion, if you get my meaning."

Despite the heat I felt burning on my cheeks, I wasn't completely ignorant of the power of our bite. It was precisely because of the aphrodisiac nature of our bite that vampires had managed to survive so long. I tried to pull away, but Demitri held me still with a hand on my arm.

"It is not unusual—in fact in such a place as this, it may be the norm—for a meal to become…something a little bit more."

I shoved at him. "Ew. I get it, okay? Gosh." Demitri chuckled and I gave him the side-eye. "You better not be doing," I gestured wildly again, "all that. Not while I'm here."

At least he had the good sense to appear affronted at the suggestion. He placed a hand over his heart. "You wound me. That you should imagine I—"

"Ugh," I interrupted, rolling my eyes and half-turning my back to him. "Let's just get this over with, okay?" My nerves literally felt frayed and worn, threatening to break any second.

"*Come dici tu, sorellina.*" He nodded toward a long-legged woman with glorious, thick blonde hair and she sunk down on the sofa next to him.

I pointedly looked away—I did not want to see what was going on over there—just in time to see the line of donors move away and another group step in. There weren't as many as I first thought, as I'd seen the people in this group before. My knee bounced with nervous energy. I did not want to be there. The whole thing just felt so creepy and weird, but I knew I'd much prefer this situation than what happened last night.

I hadn't asked Demitri what happened last night. I hadn't asked the hard questions like How far did I go?

and Did I hurt her? I hadn't asked because a part of me didn't want to know, while the other part of me already knew. I still didn't know how to be *myself*, and also a vampire. I had to shove everything down deep just to get through these terrible days.

With a lump in my throat, I looked up at the potential donors. All of them gazed at me. All of them begged with their eyes for me to choose them. A petite dark-haired girl who looked my age, a man about Demitri's age but somehow even more handsome, a somewhat plump woman with shockingly red hair, and a young man a few years older than me with humor twinkling in his eyes.

I shut my eyes, trying for calm, then chose the guy with the smiling eyes. I felt so weird, so *ick* and *yuck*, but he'd been the only one to look at me with humor as opposed to icky seduction.

The guy grinned while the others left the room, then reached down to take my hand. "*Andiamo a sederci lì.*" He had a dimple in his right cheek. I tried to swallow past the boulder in my throat.

"Uh, what?" I stood when he drew me to my feet, but I felt as stupid as a piece of rock.

"Come," he said. He tugged and I followed to the sofa furthest away from Demitri and his, um, companion. "*Pensavo volessi un po 'più di privacy.*" I guessed the word privacy meant what it sounded like, so I smiled and took the seat he gestured to.

"I've never done this before," I said as he sat beside me, his bare chest touching my shoulder. *Omo.* I felt like I was cheating on Philo. The monster inside me shifted, making me feel nauseous, but it didn't rise up and take over like it had before.

"*Rilassati, bella ragazza,*" the guy whispered as he drew himself even closer. He reached up and pulled the elastic out of my messy bun with expert fingers, letting my long thick hair fall around my shoulders. He drew his fingers through it. "*Bellissima.*" Then his fingers grazed the underside of my jaw as he gently lifted my face.

He leaned down to kiss me, I'm sure, but I put both hands on his shoulders and shook my head. I got that it was probably easier for most people to start with a little kissing before the biting. I wished there was something to ease me into it, for sure. But I was here for Philo. He was the only one I wanted kissing me for any reason.

Thankfully, Monster Minnie rose from the darkness of my being—strong, confident, and utterly in command of what she wanted. The guy licked his lips and his eyes dilated as Monster Minnie stroked one finger down his neck, stopping at the rapid thrum of his carotid artery.

This is what we must do, she said. *This is what has always been done. Relax. This is natural. Only natural. It will make us strong; it will make us the best we can be. This is what must be done.*

The voice in my mind enthralled me as much as I naturally enthralled the young man.

I was beginning to understand the reality of what I was. And I knew I needed every possible advantage when I went in to meet the Master. I could view it as practical and logical.

But I vowed I would never do this for pleasure, and I would never lose myself enough that I killed.

I sank my fangs into his neck while he gripped me tightly to him and moaned. The sound and feel of him almost made me stop, but my monster refused to be so weak. We would do what we needed to do. For Philo.

While the boy's own thoughts swirled with my own, I thought of Philo. I had less of a plan now than I had before. I now knew that sneaking into the Master's lair unnoticed would be impossible—he already knew I was in the vicinity, he'd totally know when I arrived. Which meant I would have to face him and hope I could convince him to let Philo go. And David, too, if he was holding him there against his will, too.

I knew David had gone to meet with him, but I'd imagined something akin to a lunch meeting while David stayed safe in a five-star hotel. All this time, I'd assumed the luxury and humanity of the vampires' lives I'd seen so far were indications of what I might expect from the Master. He'd be elegant and urbane, more even than David. He'd live in some vast estate on the coast.

Sure, I pictured hoards of thralls who lived to serve him—like Ying Yue had had—but still, the Master of my imagination would be a businessman and conscious of the public place his people now possessed.

Never in a million years had I pictured a damp sea cave with no luxuries at all. I hadn't expected the truth of the Master to be anything at all as Demitri said it was.

The guy in my arms sagged into unconsciousness and I withdrew my fangs slowly, gently sealing the wounds they'd left with my tongue. I eased him back against the couch, then glanced over to Demitri. He still had his head bent over his donor, but he seemed to feel me looking at him because he glanced up and managed a sort of nod.

I took the time to go into the adjoining washroom to tidy up. Our seven-hour drive had taken almost twelve and I felt grungy and unkempt. In the mirror, I saw the girl I'd seen that first day after I changed, everything about my features appearing their very best. But my eyes were unnaturally dark, no longer deep brown but an endless black. And there was something else, too. Something unseen.

I didn't feel like myself.

Or rather, I didn't feel like the human girl I'd been. Or even the human/vampire hybrid I'd imagined myself to be just days ago.

The monster inside moved like a snake, a giant snake that filled up the entirety of my being, sliding and roiling within me. It seemed to be too large to inhabit the space inside me; I expected it to crush my *self*. Instead, it had somehow assimilated me.

This was what I was now. Who I was.

As I straightened my T-shirt, I wondered what David and Philo would think of me. Would they be ashamed? Or disgusted? Would they turn me away? I honestly thought Philo would understand—and not just because I rescued him, but because I think he lived just on the edge of the restrictions the Treaty put on him.

But David wouldn't approve.

That nugget of worry gained grit and debris as the coils of my monster clutched it within its body and rolled it around. It would hurt to have him disappointed in me. The loss of his faith in me would be hard to take. All I could do now was hope that he'd understand why I had to do it. Surely he, more than anyone, would know what it would take for me to even have the strength to stand in front of the Master and ask for his favor.

When I left the washroom, both our donors were gone, and Demitri stood by the exit, his phone pressed to his ear. I startled when I heard Manuella's voice through the phone, and I hurried over to him.

"What are you doing?" I hissed as betrayal bloomed in my chest. Was he selling me out? After all of this?

He shook his head sharply and held a finger up to his lips. They spoke in rapid-fire Spanish, I thought, so I couldn't understand what they were saying—other than it was about me, Philo and David.

A moment later, he was done and ushering me through the door he'd pushed open, guiding me with a hand on the small of my back.

"Ready?" he asked once we were outside the building.

"You mean you didn't just promise Manuella to have me on the first plane or ship out of here?"

With a beep, the car's doors unlocked, and Demitri joined me at the passenger side where he opened the door for me. "Of course not. I would not have brought you this far and insisted on, well…" he gestured toward Wine & More.

I cast him a skeptical glance before sliding into the dim interior of the car.

"Okay," I said once he'd joined me inside. "I just assumed…"

After pressing the button to start the engine, Demitri patted my hand which lay on top of my thigh. "I only called to tell her I had you, and that I would remain with you while we went to visit the Master. I assumed she would want to know you were safe."

"Oh."

I didn't say anything else until we'd wound our way out of the city proper and were once again traveling southward along the coast.

"I didn't know you knew Manuella."

"I have never met her, but as I said, I know David, though it has been a very long time since we last spoke. Our community is larger than humans realize, and small at the same time. It is difficult to live for centuries and not cross each others' paths at least once or twice. And we often know of the more powerful or more interesting members of our kind." He cast me a sparkling sidelong glance, a slight smile on his lips.

"Well, that was nice of you. To tell her I was okay."

"I know if it was my daught—" he stopped and cleared his throat, his gaze resolutely forward. "If it were my little sister in your situation, I would want someone to be there for her. I would want to know she wouldn't have to face this trial alone."

My thoughts curled around what he'd almost said. If he meant to protect me because he had not been there to protect his daughter, then it explained so much. I wondered if she was still alive—I'd left his mind before I'd found out. My guess was no, though.

"I didn't mean for you to come in there with me," I said softly. "I don't want you to think you have to, regardless of what you told Manuella."

This time when he glanced at me, his smile was sincere and there was no sign of his thoughts from a moment before. "As I told your mother, I will not let you go in there alone."

I held his gaze as long as I dared, considering he was operating a car, before telling him, "Thank you."

An odd sort of energy buzzed within my brain, in my heart, in a way I couldn't put my finger on. It wasn't painful, but it couldn't be ignored. I found myself leaning forward, straining against the seatbelt as I scoured the scenery for...something.

"I feel weird. Is it because we're close?" It felt a little like when David had Called the family to him when the *kynigoi* were after us—like an itch under my skin.

Demitri's face was set in firm determination and he nodded. "It is similar to our ability to enthrall people. It works as a lure for everyone, vampires and humans alike."

"You mean humans can feel this, too? And it makes them...go to him?"

"Exactly. The Master rarely leaves his cave, yet he must survive somehow."

"You mean humans actually want him to drink their blood?" I'm sure the horror was plain to see on my face, but I no longer felt like I had to hide myself from Demitri.

"Yes. Sometimes his creatures will bring others with them, but for the most part, he calls people to him."

"But this isn't a very populated area, how can he get away with it? Why is it people still live here when people must go missing all the time?"

"They do not go missing," Demitri said. "The Master has survived for thousands of years because he knows how to preserve his resources. He takes what he needs to survive, then sends the people home. They return from their sojourn to the cave a little tired, but with a euphoric feeling that makes them believe the cave is the source of eternal happiness or peace. They stand fiercely by their legends that say the caves beneath their farmlands are a blessing, filled with magic that grants them bounty."

"Wow." I rubbed at my chest, fascinated by the way my whole body buzzed with restrained excitement. "But what about offspring? How did he manage that without leaving his cave? And why does he even bother?"

Demitri slowed as he exited the main road, taking a gravel one that took us even closer toward the cliffs. "In the early days he came out more often. Maybe because there were fewer people to see him, or maybe because today's modern technology would expose him should he reveal himself now. I am honestly not sure, as I have never asked him.

"I have also never asked why he made so many vampires when he seems to feel no real love for us. I suppose when you have come from a place where even producing one offspring is a miracle, coming here and finding that his bite could make numerous 'children' must have felt a little like being a god." He pulled into a gravel lot, with nothing but the deep blue sea and endless sky before us.

"Wait. I thought he'd only made a few children. David told me—there was Ying Yue, and some guy from South America or something. But you're saying he made many? I didn't know about you, for instance."

Demitri undid his seatbelt, so I did the same. My knee bounced impatiently and my hand was on the door handle ready to burst from the car, but another part of me wanted to stay right where I was. The next step in my journey terrified me.

"Perhaps what David meant to say, is that there were only those few, plus another one or two, that the Master made in the beginning. The truly ancient ones. His original children. It is possible he gave to them something more essential from his being, for they have always been revered as greater than the rest of us. They are certainly more powerful.

"But the Master has made other children throughout the centuries, though still not many. I think the process is too exhausting for him, and puts too much risk on his own survival. But there are others beyond those few ancient ones. I actually think he cares something for them."

He stared out at the sea for a moment, then rotated a little to face me. "And you killed one of them."

I held my breath for a moment. I wanted to deny it, to tell him how Hanjo, the dragon I'd befriended, had actually been the one to end her, but it was pointless. She had died *because* of me. Whatever the reason or the exact details.

Demitri patted my hand as if to say, it is what it is, then he got out of the car. He leaned down and said, "Do you mind if I take just a moment? To collect my thoughts?" I shook my head and he shut the door.

I felt a gentle nudge on my mind and my heart leapt. Philo? But when I turned my attention to it, I found not Philo, but Hanjo.

My child, he said as soon as the way was open between us.

I was just thinking about you. I gave him a mental glare. *Have you been spying on me?* With everything that had happened, and what was about to happen, his presence in my mind was like a hug from an old friend.

I know. I have been speaking with Master Yi about your situation, and when you thought of me, I felt it. I decided it was time we spoke.

But—how? I only just thought of you. How can you possibly feel or know that from thousands of miles away? And what do you mean my situation?

Why, your quest to save your love from the clutches of the evil vampire Master, of course. And of course I know when you think of me—I am a dragon. My power is endless and supreme, and you and I have a very special connection.

I chuckled. I could just imagine him swinging his great head from side to side at my ignorance of his power. *Wait. What do you mean we have a special connection? How can you possibly pick up on a single thought?* I didn't know how to feel—honored or annoyed.

His sigh echoed in my mind with all the weariness of the ages. He *tsked. Of course. I would not have ascended as quickly as I did had you not agreed to help me. Few humans in our history have ever bonded with a dragon as you have done.*

Oh. I don't know what to say. I glanced at Demitri, but he was lost in his own thoughts. I squeezed my eyes shut and focused on this moment with Hanjo.

Words are frivolous things, he said in his deep, rumbling voice. Say nothing. Now, as for your situation, I believe it would be wise for you to wait until I can come to your aide.

Oh, no. It's okay. I couldn't ask that of you. Besides, I'm already here. As soon as I'm done talking to you, well…I guess I'll be going to meet the Master.

I watched Demitri wander along the short guardrail separating the cliff from the sea.

Hmph, Hanjo snorted. *Master Yi will not be happy if you take such a risk by yourself. He has told me of your tendency to do things alone.*

But I'm not alone, I responded as I watched Demitri. I realized his body was angled just so, to where a distant coastline was just visible. I wondered if that was where his boat had capsized. Or if it was his homeland he was thinking of. *I'm with another vampire. He's become my...mentor...of sorts.*

I see, Hanjo said. *And he has facilitated your journey into becoming a true blood eater.*

I bristled at his words, but suppressed the reaction when I realized he wasn't wrong. *Yes,* I offered softly.

A long silence followed, in which I felt Hanjo's presence, but neither of us spoke. I wondered if he thought less of me now.

It is good you embrace your true nature, little one. I am glad you found this guide to help you become stronger. You will need all your strength to reach a favorable outcome with your opponent.

But...aren't you disappointed in me?

How could I be? When any other might have fled, or have been unworthy of helping me at all, you stood by me. Junu, Master Yi, we all know and honor the strength within you.

Yeah but, the whole vampire thing...

Dda-nim. You have become a powerful creature with the ability to do much good and much evil in the world. I know your soul. I trust who you are to determine your path as a vampire. What you are does not define who you are. Neither does being a powerful, fearsome creature relegate you to eternal misery and woe. If such were the case, I should not have desired so greatly to fulfill my own destiny and become a dragon, for there is none more feared in the world.

Tears welled in my eyes, and I pulled out a handful of wet wipes to dab at them when Demitri turned to face the car and nodded. Hanjo had called me *daughter* and the honor I felt resonated within me so strongly I couldn't find the right words.

So of course I was my typical lame self and ignored the kindness. *I've gotta go now, Sun-bae. Wish me luck?*

You have no need of my wishes, for you will have my strength within you. Master Yi also wished for me to tell you to remember you are not alone in the universe and that there is a purpose in this moment. Remember your ancestors. Reach for them and they will grant you power.

I took a shaky breath. I wanted to believe that I could have help from the universe, from the gods, my ancestors, and even Hanjo, but at the moment I felt like all I'd done is come here to die. I probably wouldn't even get to see Philo before the Master laughed in my face and ended me right there and then.

Remember you are the friend of a dragon, little one, Hanjo said before I felt his presence withdraw.

Unable to delay any longer, I pushed open the door and stepped outside. I thought about telling Demitri what I'd been doing, but decided against it. Even I wouldn't believe I had a dragon friend who could speak telepathically.

Because despite Hanjo's words, I didn't think being his friend could possibly be of any use in this situation. I was on my own, that's all there was to it.

"Ready?" Demitri asked when I stood before him.

I nodded. "Ye—" my voice broke, and I had to clear my throat. I straightened my shoulders and tried again. "I'm ready."

I think my parents saw someone — or Mom did. It's a good idea — especially if it was part of the ceremony we had when a person DIES, then rises again. It's a lot to take in. A lot to deal with.

relationships are repairable, though how long it takes varies from individual to individual.

There is no set standard for how one should deal with becoming a vampire. For some, it's necessary to start their life anew, with new friends, new lifestyle, new location. For others, the desire to remain as they were is strong. In those rare cases it's important to constantly assess one's state of hunger — or risk eating one's best friend. *Omg! I'm glad that didn't happen to me! Otherwise, I did everything else wrong.* :/

This was so not my experience.

THE COUNCIL OF VAMPIRES

Plus — this info shouldn't just be out there!

Diet and nutrition are especially important to your health as a newborn vampire. Your Maker will ensure you receive your fill upon your rebirth, usually letting you drink from his- or herself. This is ideal since it strengthens the paternal bond and provides the newborn with the very best nutrition from the start. That first feeding will ease the feeding frenzy most newborns experience upon rebirth. Once satiated, the newborn can then decide if they'll hunt

CHAPTER SIXTEEN

DEMITRI LED ME TO THE EDGE OF THE GUARDRAIL, AND I noticed he'd changed his shoes from the shiny black dress ones to a pair of sturdy hiking boots. I glanced down at my own shoes—the wimpy soles of my Converse sneakers not likely to offer me much help on the climb down. Oh well. It wasn't like there was anything I could do about it now.

"Don't worry," Demitri said, throwing a look over his shoulder. "I'll go down before you, so if you fall, I'll be there to catch you."

He doesn't see my wan smile of thanks.

Suddenly, I wish I'd asked so many more questions. That we had an actual plan. Why didn't I? Why didn't I revise my plan once I better understood what I was about to face? I don't know the answers to these questions, or any of the other things that clamor for my attention. Like how I've come to trust Demitri so thoroughly, that watching him descend the steep path causes my heart to flutter with worry. In just the last few hours I've come to rely on him. To trust him implicitly. Now I wonder why he came with me.

And what happened to his daughter.

I dread the climb. I dread what we might find in the Master's lair—both for myself and for Demitri.

The afternoon sun beat down on my shoulders, but despite the warmth, goosebumps rose on my arms where the fine mist from the ocean below cooled me. The first step was like a leap of faith, requiring me to step out and down without a good view of where I'd put my foot. Demitri guided my hand to a rope stretched down from an iron ring anchored in the stone above me. I wondered how long this rope, or one like it, had been here—probably for as long as the Master had been here. Without it, I couldn't imagine any human making their way down to him, especially in the dark. I wondered how many fell straight to their deaths even with the rope guide.

Slick with water and unevenly spaced, the steps barely provided somewhere to set your feet. If it hadn't been for the rope—thick and black from the grime of the sea—anchored somewhere below, the way would be utterly impossible. Each downward step felt like it could be my last. I tried not to look out at the ocean, but I couldn't help but wonder what would happen to me if I fell. Because I wouldn't die—I'd just be incredibly broken and bruised and I'd still have to fight the currents to make my way to the shore. A shore that was nowhere in sight, unless you wanted to cling to the rocks. Or take your chances in one of the sea caves—and hope there wasn't an alien vampire master inside waiting to devour you. Except he wouldn't devour me, he'd just…what? Make me his slave? Use me as a pawn in some game like he seemed to be doing with Philo?

I wanted to ask Demitri all my questions, but the surf was so loud, even my superior hearing had trouble picking out anything beyond it.

Down and down we went while my body quivered with tension, every single muscle and tendon engaged to keep me upright. When I was mere feet above the roiling, battering crash of the ocean, I saw Demitri move to my right and look up. He called something to me, but his words were lost to the tumult. He raised his hand and on the next step I was able to grasp it. I sagged into his arms, mentally exhausted from the harrowing climb.

When I felt sturdy enough to stand, he helped me find my footing, and we turned to face the last part of our journey.

Power resonated from within the dark, yawning cave we stood before. I wanted to run—both toward the

Master and far, far away. But inside that cave were two people I loved, and I wouldn't turn away for anything.

Demitri led me toward the entrance, sliding along a narrow rock ledge worn smooth from the passage of time. Tendrils of hair, which had fallen from my top knot, stuck to my cheek and neck, while my T-shirt and leggings clung to me, dry in some places, soaked through in others. At least my feet felt dry, surprisingly.

Once inside the cave, the temperature dropped. Even though I didn't feel the cold the way a human would, I still shivered, my body mourning the loss of the warm sun.

This was it. In moments, I'd meet the Master and…what?

I still had no idea.

I knew what I wanted to happen—what I needed to happen—but with every step forward I cursed my own hubris.

How would I convince the Master to let Philo go? If he refused, how would I get him out even if I did manage to free him myself?

And what about David? I couldn't leave him behind, either.

Before, when I thought Philo was in some prison, I imagined slipping in unnoticed and sneaking him out.

I'd never once even considered that the Master might have a blood tie to me like David did, and that frustrated the heck out of me. The Master was David's Maker, and David's blood ran in my body. Of course the bond would extend to me.

I'd had basically a whole day to come to terms with the truth, and I hadn't come up with anything helpful at all. All I had was a question—would he allow them to leave with me?

Even as I shuffled closer and closer to my goal, I scoffed at myself.

Sometimes it felt as if I allowed myself to be deliberately obtuse. That I leaned into this *gullible girl* mentality. I blamed it on too many K-dramas. But not all the heroines in those stories were gullible. Or if they started out that way, they quickly got over it and became strong and capable. When would I?

As the monster inside of me, the monster that *was* me, responded to the nearness of the Master, I knew this was my moment. It was way too little way too late, but I was here now and however misguided or hopeless, I would give it all I had.

I felt the flicker of a presence in the back of my mind and a rush of gratitude filled me. At least I wasn't going in to meet the Master alone. I had Demitri, true, but I also had Hanjo. Even though he was half a world away, just knowing he was thinking of me and lending me his strength in a way only a dragon could, gave me courage.

The smell hit me first. Outside the lair had been fresh and salty with the tang of wet limestone. Inside, the cave smelled of dying and dead things—and not just fish. I wished I could cover my nose, but I knew that would be useless. I had no choice but to get used to the stench and do my best to ignore it.

A few yards further in and I was able to identify the smell precisely.

The rot and decay of human remains.

I'd seen it in Demitri's mind, but it had seemed so unreal that I'd subconsciously decided it couldn't be the same now as it had been so long ago. And it wasn't—not exactly.

The narrow ledge we'd followed into the cave gradually opened up to solid ground, revealing just how naïve my assumptions were.

Bodies lay everywhere.

In the shallows of an underwater bench where the sea and sea life ate away at them.

Piled against both walls, all the way up to the high ceiling, like bricks.

The burial wall was at least three deep, the layers a kind of strata marking the passage of time with bones on the lowest level of the first and second wall, while the top of the third wall only reached my shoulders with corpses that seemed to have died relatively recently stacked on the top level.

So much for the Master not killing his victims.

The stone floor was littered with personal belongings, from old rusted weapons to cameras, backpacks and so many phones and shoes I shuddered to think of the number of people who had died down here.

Demitri took my hand and squeezed it.

Inside my head, the Master beckoned. Not with words, but with *feeling*. Even if I'd wanted to turn back now, I wouldn't have been able to. My feet moved forward of their own accord.

And with every step, the cave grew darker. Even after Demitri's vision, I still imagined this place with torches or fire pits, but there was nothing. The darkness and cold were unrelenting, becoming thicker and more complete until I was forced to rely entirely on my vampiric night vision. The ability to see in the dark worked well when finding your way among people, as they lit up like torches to my eyes. Otherwise, it was less the ability to see than it was to recognize the depth of darkness around me. Things were black, blacker, and blackest. I figured it was a talent like everything else, and one that I had very little skill in. While Demitri seemed to move forward with ease, I watched my feet.

I still managed to kick something, sending it skidding across the floor until it hit something hard, causing it to ricochet away.

I stopped, utterly still and frozen.

At first there was no reaction, even though I knew we were not alone. Using my senses, I found Demitri and pressed against his side.

A low, grinding hiss emanated from the darkness, but I couldn't tell if it was in my head or in the cavern—or both.

I searched the darkness until shapes, blacker than black, began to emerge, some moving, some still.

There were no humans among them. At least I could be grateful for that.

"Come forward, my little daughter," said a voice from inside my mind and without. I turned toward it and watched as a black lump shifted—and red eyes peered at me from the dark. I gasped, and took a half-step back, but Demitri kept me from running away. The Master— for the creature could be nothing else—laughed.

"You have been so brave, do not give into fear now, little daughter. Come. Your loved ones are waiting."

I lunged forward, my gaze fixed on the Master's steady red gaze. I couldn't feel Philo or David, only the Master's presence so large within me that I feared there was no room even for myself.

Vampire-like creatures hissed and scuttled out of my way as I moved. I couldn't see them with any kind of detail, but they reminded me of Gollum from *The Lord of the Rings*. What made them become like that instead of a regular vampire? I wished I'd asked Demitri more about them when he'd mentioned them before.

Distantly, my brain cataloged and categorized, demanding answers for all the unknowns.

With brutal efficiency, I ignored my natural desire to study and learn.

The Master chuckled. Probably reading my mind. *Great.*

"You can do this," Demitri said softly behind me.

I could. I *could* do this. I'd spoken in debates, participated in fake trials, and met with Ivy League deans of admissions. And I did all of that before I had a vampire's power within me. I'd been an awesome girl. Now it was time be an awesome vampire.

"Yes, yes," the Master encouraged. "So very brave."

A tendril of darkness snaked out from his form and grasped my wrist, pulling me forward until I stood directly in front of the creature called *Master.* Instinctively I fell to my knees and bowed my head— and noticed the thing wrapped around my wrist was part of his cloak. I think. It released me, slipping back and away until it sank into shadow.

"You may look at me, child. I know Demitrius has already shown you my face, so what more have you to fear?"

Oh, only everything, I thought. But I lifted my chin anyway. His white face seemed to glow in the dark and I noticed his eyes weren't the pale red of an albino mouse but the deep blood-red of a nocturnal predator. Was it our own human DNA that kept us from developing that trait? The ridges of his cheek bones created a sharp hourglass shape on each cheek, and his nostrils fluttered, almost like fish gills. It was so fascinating, that I almost forgot I should be afraid or repulsed.

"Do you know," the Master said, the slash of his red, red mouth moving in an awkward way that suggested he hadn't been born to speak with his mouth, "I find you just as fascinating as you find me. Never before have I met a human with a mind so free of fear."

My eyes went wide and wider still when a burst of laughter came from my mouth. "*Omo*. I'm not at all free of fear. But I'm not just human, I'm vampire, which means you created me in a roundabout way. And I can't help the way my brain works—when I get nervous, logic and science help me stay calm."

The Master laughed, too, and bowed his head as if in concession. "Regardless, I can see now why you have created such a stir."

He angled himself, and his cloak slithered and shifted to reveal David. He knelt, though it seemed like some of the wraith-like ribbons of the cloak wound around his chest, kept him upright.

The ones that covered his mouth and eyes made me burn inside.

"Is this why you chose her, David? Because of her unique mind?"

The cloak covering his mouth and eyes slipped away, and David blinked until his eyes regained focus and came to rest on me. They peered at me with such intense sorrow, it seemed as if he hadn't realized until this moment that I was here.

"Speak, David. It is rude to stare."

David blinked, then turned his attention to the Master. "I-I'm sorry, my lord. But what is it you would like me to say?"

My monster roiled within me. I hated seeing David this way; meek and utterly without control.

"I asked," the Master said in a near-whisper that seemed to convey even more danger, "if you chose her because of her unique mind."

David's gaze flicked to me, then returned to the Master. He hung his head. "I did not choose her, Master. She was the unfortunate result of my grandchild Tim's inability to restrain himself."

Something about the Master's demeanor seemed to harden, but nothing happened, so I tried to ignore it. He made a sound between a scoff and a spit. "Tim. That he lives does you and your family no service. He should never have been allowed to live."

David's chin ticked upward imperceptibly. "If he had been destroyed, Minnie would not be here."

The Master's gaze shifted to me once more, no longer angry but contemplative. "Indeed."

He flicked a hand at me, startling me with its appearance. "Make yourself comfortable, child." I did as he asked, and sat on my bottom, my legs crossed—not that it was all that comfortable given the stone floor was so cold and damp. Demitri remained standing, but I guess he hadn't been invited to sit. My gaze roamed everywhere. Where was Philo? Was he behind the Master? The shadows were the deepest and darkest there. I reached for him with my mind, over and over, but I couldn't feel him. I clenched my fists in my lap and refused to think what that might mean.

The Master shifted, too, as if copying my pose, but something seemed wrong beneath his cloak. Like there were too many limbs, like his shape wasn't exactly humanoid. I hadn't seen that in Demitri's mind, so either I was wrong, or there was more to the Master than even Demitri knew.

"So. Make your request." The Master flicked a hand at me again, and this time I saw that he only had three fingers on that hand—long, sausage-thick fingers with black nails. *Fascinating*.

I stared at him, trying to get a handle on the game he was playing. Because he was playing at something. He seemed too friendly, too chipper. Like he was making fun of me or something, but I couldn't decide why.

"Well," I hedged. I really wished I could see. That I knew where Philo was. That I didn't feel like the Master was toying with me. "I've come in hopes of bringing Philo, and David, home."

"Ah." He stared at me for a long time, his red eyes narrowed to slits. "That isn't exactly what you came here to do, is it?"

"Um…"

"You came to end me. To rid the world of my *evil*."

"What? No! I only want Philo back. And David."

"But you came to deceive me. Tell me at least that much is true."

I stared at him, wishing I could read some meaning in his gaze or expression, but his eyes were unreadable and his face so foreign, I had no way of understanding. I let out a sigh. This chatting was just a game—he already knew my mind. "I thought Philo was in your prison, so I thought I would sneak in and rescue him."

"There it is." The Master rocked as if laughing, but I didn't hear it. "That is the truth I was looking for. You *would* steal him from me. You would take what is mine."

My mouth dropped open. "No. I—" My mind whirled, thinking of responses, then discarding them. "I'm sorry," I finally said. "I hadn't thought of Philo as belonging to you. He belongs to himself. And as his own man, he has the right to his freedom. And his life— because he was dying in that cell you put him in."

I felt Demitri shift behind me, but I couldn't second-guess myself now, the words were already out. Besides, he'd have read them in my mind anyway.

"Ah, but there is the error in your logic, child," the Master cooed. "Philomon is not his own man, as you said. He is mine."

My brows drew together. "How do you figure that?"

"Why, I created him."

"No, you didn't. You created David, who created Philo. So even if the child belongs to the father, then Philo belongs to David, not you. But I don't believe that thinking is logical to begin with."

The atmosphere around me had changed while I spoke. Like an approaching thunderstorm, the air snapped with tension, but I couldn't let myself be distracted by it. I was aware of Demitri, of David, but I couldn't think about them, either. I had to be *here*, in this moment with the Master. No one else mattered but him and me.

"Tell me, child." The Master's voice was tight and dangerous, and I didn't like his emphasis on the world *child*. "Where is the error in my logic?"

"Well," I began, feeling my way as I went, "human beings are no longer considered possessions. Once upon a time one person could own another person, but that's been over for a long time now. There are still some places that allow slavery, but there are numerous human rights organizations bent on seeking out these places and eradicating slavery—or possession—in all its forms. People don't like human ownership in that way. And it's particularly heinous for a parent to own a child.

"Additionally, as I said, you would only be the grandparent in this scenario, so your right to Philo would be slimmer still."

A ribbon of darkness moved across the floor, wrapping around me, but not touching me. I shivered, but forced myself to ignore the shadow circling me.

"Ah, but your reasoning is faulty, child. You speak of humans and human law. I care nothing for these things, and none of us are human here." He laughed, and I heard it echoed through the voices of the other creatures in the cavern. I realized I had no idea how large the space was. In my mind, I imagined it to be like a large living room, or even a ballroom—but the way the laughter echoed I began to think the space might be far, far larger than I ever imagined.

"You're right," I said in a thoughtful sing-song voice, like I actually was just having a friendly debate, "we aren't human. But neither are we like you. We don't have red eyes like you do and none of us look like you. While we possess some attributes, or qualities, similar to yours, we can leave this place. We can exist in the human world, but you can't. I wonder, if we were to submit to a study, you and I, how different we would actually be observed to be. I wouldn't be surprised to discover we are more different than alike."

It was only after I'd finished speaking that I realized how much the tension had increased, how hisses sounded throughout the room, and the Master's presence in my mind pressed against my brain as if it would push it out.

The Master moved, crawling across the short distance between us in a completely unnatural way. Beside me, Demitri dropped to his knees, his hand coming to press reassuringly on my shoulder.

The Master's face loomed large and terrifying before me, but I had no choice but to remain still as he sniffed up my neck. I thought for sure he was about to bite me, but he didn't. Instead he said, "You smell like me."

Behind him, maybe forgotten because of our discussion, his cloak or shadows or whatever it was that had covered David released him and he slumped forward, though his gaze, wild and fearful remained on me. And beside him lay a figure that had been hidden from me until now. My heart leapt into my throat, and if it hadn't been for Demitri's hand on my shoulder, I would have thrown myself at him. Because the body, little more than a skeleton with empty, saggy skin clinging to his bones, was Philo. I gasped and the Master chuckled, as if it had been him that had caused me distress.

He licked my cheek and I shut my eyes, wincing away from the contact. *Ew, ew, ew!*

"You taste like me," he said. He rose above me, making me lift my gaze to meet his. "So you are mine."

"Really?" I said without thinking. "Because I'm smelling you right now and I can honestly say, since it's such a unique smell, that I haven't smelled anything like it in my whole life." I sniffed my arm, which despite not having had a shower in over twenty-four hours, still had the faint scent of strawberries and cream courtesy of my Bath and Body Works body wash and lotion. "I don't smell anything at all like you. And I'm almost positive that I don't taste like you, either."

Demitri's grip on my shoulder tightened and he murmured, "Minnie," in a warning tone.

But while the Master swayed back and forth like a robot having a meltdown, I spied David just beyond him. He met my gaze and smiled. In that moment I felt everything come together inside of me, just like it did when I was solving a particularly hard mathematical equation. I felt seen and known, strengthened by David's trust in me. In who I was.

I'd never be able to beat the Master—that had never been within my reach. But I had a good brain, and excellent reasoning skills. My only chance here at getting what I wanted, was to be *me*. The very best, boldest and badass version of me.

reserve animals, or drink donated or synthetic blood.

It can be hard to adapt to your new diet, but you'll soon come to appreciate it. Be sure you try blood pudding! *FTW!!* Many young vampires eschew this delicious treat, but with so many flavors and textures available, it really is an excellent on-the-go snack. *Reminder: thank Manuella for always taking care of me so I never go hungry around humans.*

Relationships between family members are highly encouraged. You might be surprised by that fact, but the truth is, vampires are quite territorial, so inviting a member from another clan into your family home can be a tricky—and deadly—business. *There's me + P & D+M, but I don't know of any other couples.*

Remember, you are never alone. Your vampire family understands what you're going through and will stand by you, no matter what. *→ it probably just depends on your clan.*

You have eternity before you and we urge you to not waste a minute of it. ❦

CHAPTER
SEVENTEEN

MOVED BY A DESIRE I COULDN'T—AND DIDN'T—
question, I shuffled forward, closing the distance
between myself and the Master. Though everything
about him repelled me, I forced myself to place a hand
on his arm. Immediately, his whole body calmed and he
faced me. I dropped my chin to my chest.

"I honor you, my Master. You are my ancestor, and
I honor all who have helped make me who I am today. I
honor your strength that runs within my veins. I honor
the skills and abilities I now possess because of the
power of your blood. Because of you, I will live
forever—or as long as I am useful on this Earth."

He made a growling sound that I chose to take as
approval. I took a chance and looked up, meeting his
gaze straight on.

"I also honor my human ancestors. Because of them, I have the intelligence and ability to think for myself. The ability to feel compassion and love for my family and for all creatures that roam this Earth. They taught me that this world, and everything that lives within it, has the same right to life as I do. The same right to explore their purpose for living and to find a way to contribute to the world at large.

"I honor my mother and father, who raised me to work hard and to expect the best from myself and others. They taught me that when I raise myself up, others rise to meet me, and when I help others rise, I am lifted up with them.

"My father often told me the purpose of life was for your child to grow stronger and more capable than yourself. And I am meant to remain in tune with the ancestors—so they may see what their generational line has wrought.

"I thank you, Master, for your contribution to who I am today. I will strive, in all I do, to make you proud."

I held his eyes a moment longer, then bowed my head in respect and deference.

I felt…good. I could only hope and pray that my words found purchase in the Master's mind and heart.

For a long time there was only silence. I wanted to look up, but something told me I should let the Master make the first move. Maybe his move would be to lob off my head, but I really didn't think so. And so I waited.

I felt him move, but I kept my gaze down. It seemed he stood, rising far above me, but still I held my ground.

Look at me, child, he said in my mind. Though it was a command, he didn't compel me, which was a surprise. Hope blossomed within me.

I looked up.

He did stand tall. Taller than any man and twice as wide, too. I'd gotten the impression of him moving on more than just two legs and two arms, but if he had any other appendages, they weren't visible now. He stood regal and proud, his cloak wrapped around him in undulating waves, sometimes appearing like actual material, other times as ephemeral as smoke. He looked every bit the royal prince he once had been.

Stand.

And I did. I only reached mid-chest on him, so I still had to tilt my head back to look up at him.

"Minnie?" David whispered, our view of each other now uninhibited. "What's happening?" But there was no chance to answer or explain.

Tell me what you see, the Master commanded.

As I spoke, I let him see what I saw. *You are regal and powerful. Astonishing in your strangeness, yet I feel your power and it is the same power that lives within me. I am honored not only to be one of your progeny, but also to count you as my most honored ancestor.* I let him see my ancestors, picturing in my mind my parents and grandparents—everyone I could remember seeing in photographs.

We looked at one another for a long time, my mind wide open to him, as he contemplated what he saw there. I didn't get the impression at all that he was sifting around in my brain—it seemed like he was only looking at my ancestors, simple farmers though they'd been, simple people as they were now.

After a long while—during which I became very grateful for my vampiric stamina because if I were still only human, my neck would've been killing me by now—I felt his awareness shift within me before he withdrew and rejoined our conversation.

Your father and mother have rejected you.

I don't know why, but tears immediately sprang to my eyes. I swiped at them, not wanting to show weakness before him. *Yes,* I said. *I think that's pretty common among vampires. Most of them haven't been able to stay with their human families because they haven't been accepted. I know I'm not alone in that, anyway.*

But you miss them. Their rejection has been…painful for you.

I felt something then, like a tiny crack had opened within him and his own sorrow and his parents' rejection seeped through.

Yes. But I'm not without family. David and Manuella love me and have taken such good care of me.

A slight frown appeared on his harsh mouth as I showed him a few of my favorite memories of David and Manuella.

One of those memories included Philo, and the Master grunted. I tried to pull back from it, but he yanked the memory closer to himself, then plunged deep into my mind, plundering all my memories of Philo—even those most precious to me. I gasped and cried out. I tried to wrap a shield around them, but I was too late.

Just as suddenly as it had begun, it was over, and the Master almost entirely left my mind.

I stared at my dirty sneakers as I fought to hold onto my hope. It frightened and worried me that he responded so badly to me trying to keep some things private. "You shouldn't have done that," I said aloud as I swiped at the tears on my cheeks. I glanced up at him, but his face was an unreadable mask. "It's rude to go looking at things people want to keep private."

What the heck was even happening? This Master seemed so different from the one I'd seen moments before—changed from a cruel overlord to a being of curiosity and a certain kind of tenderness.

You are a family, he finally said. He ignored my reproachful comments, but his mind voice was softer than before. Soft and full of…wonder? *But what you feel for Philo is something more. Something different. Explain it to me.*

I swiped at my eyes again and looked upward. Surprising me again, the Master reached down and pulled his long-nailed thumb over my cheek, smearing my tears.

Why do you cry?

I fought down the sobs that begged to be heard, and said, *I'm sad.* Even my mind voice sounded broken with tears.

He swiveled to look at where Philo lay on the ground. His body didn't seem to move, though. *Can he rotate his head like an owl?* I had no idea, except that he was an alien—an *alien!*—so who knew what he might be capable of.

I followed his gaze to where Philo lay unmoving on the ground. David sat beside him, his hand resting on Philo's body. Sorrow and fear raged within me and I wanted to run to them and throw my arms around them. Around Philo. I needed to see him, to touch him and know he was real. I hadn't felt him stir in my mind at all and it scared me to think of what that might mean.

I know a great deal about love, the Master said. *It is love that most of my victims have thought of as the last of their life source left their bodies. I have felt love through them, but I have never felt it for myself.* He returned his gaze to me, and instead of the softening I had hoped for, his gaze seemed as cold as steel. *It seems to be a pointless, meaningless human construct.*

My heart sank, but I held tight to my hope and marshalled myself as best I could.

"Why did you punish Philo, my lord?" I asked aloud, so my friends would be able to follow the conversation. I also really hoped that 'my lord' had been correct and didn't seem like I was trying too hard to impress him.

He cocked his head in Philo's direction as if tempted to turn and look at him again. He seemed unsure of how to answer the question, his expressive brow forming what appeared to be a frown. "He…he killed one of my children. One of my dearest children."

"Hashiki? Is that who he killed?"

His eyes narrowed. "Yes. She was brilliant and fearless, and very young. She should have lived for many more years."

"Master." I mentally crossed my fingers. "What do you think of me? Would you be as upset by my death as you were over Hashiki's?"

He inched closer to me until I felt his strange cloak moving and shifting around my legs, waist and torso. I fervently hoped and prayed he didn't mean to crush me with it.

"Many of my children die. I have lost more than I can count."

"Does that mean you care for all of us?"

He sighed, and his breath blew over me while his cloak slithered around my arms. I fought hard to resist trembling, but it was impossible.

"Yes." His "s" continued in a long hiss, and many of the creatures around us echoed the sound. "I do care for my children. All of them. But some—a precious few—have potential to be something more."

"Maybe you see more of yourself in them, and that's why you care about them?"

He quirked his head, regarding me with fathomless eyes that seemed to swirl with flowing blood. "Perhaps. But I see little of myself in you."

The trembling in my limbs grew and I was suddenly glad for the wrapping tendrils because maybe they would hide my true state from him. "Is that a bad thing?" I asked very quietly.

The Master seemed to consider this for a long stretch of time. "You are refreshing. You are also a frustrating contradiction. On one hand, you reverence me, and on the other you refuse to bow to my demands. You stand here before me, having perhaps the longest conversation with me than I have had with any human since..." he glanced toward David, "since a very long time ago."

When he didn't continue, I asked again, "And is that bad?"

A grating, ripping sound seemed to come from the Master and it took me a moment to realize he was laughing.

"My life is far too redundant to keep me occupied, I am afraid. You have provided an interesting distraction from the sameness of my existence."

"Well," I hedged, still not entirely sure whether being a distraction was a good thing or not, "Hashiki tried to kill me. Several times. If she hadn't been captured, I'm sure she would have succeeded. She was incredibly stubborn and used her gifts to keep me away from Philo. I know Philo didn't mean to kill her. I bet she died because she was unwilling to share her information with him."

The Master scoffed. "Why would she do such a thing? It is illogical."

"It was," I agreed. "But love can make us do crazy things—like come down here to beg the scariest creature on any planet."

He seemed to startle a little at that, and leaned back and away while turning to face the people I loved.

"You love them?" he asked wistfully.

"I do. With all my heart." I stepped closer still, until I was definitely well inside the Master's personal space. The scent of him—old rot and decay, blood and dust and stone—was so strong it made my knees wobble, but I held myself straight. "Will you allow me to take them home now?"

"Why does love make you do crazy things, as you said?" He returned his gaze to mine, but I stayed true.

"Because our heart is our most powerful muscle. Not only does it pump blood through our veins, but it somehow makes magical connections between people. That's how you become a family. Family's about a lot more than blood."

"Do you love me?" he asked suddenly.

I jerked back a little. I knew I had to say yes or else he'd be angry, and all my efforts would be lost. But another part whispered that I had followed my heart until this point, so I may as well continue. My words were all I had.

"No, my lord." The vampires around us hissed, while David and Demitri made noises of protest, but I ignored them. "Love isn't arbitrary. It's earned. It's shared. For instance, my parents refused to accept me as I am, which has made me question their love for me. I have to assume they have some love for me, as their daughter, and I'll always honor them for bringing me into this world and raising me. But my friend Stacey has loved me since I was a little girl. We grew up together, and even though it's sometimes a struggle to reconcile our differences since I was reMade, she still loves me. She's still there for me, to be my friend, to be my helper, to encourage me and to help me be my best. I think *that* is real love.

"I have not met you before now. You haven't been part of my life, except in an abstract sort of way. And then, when I discovered you were holding Philo prisoner, starving him of his life—then you became someone to hate, someone to fight against. Does that make sense?"

I held my breath, my whole body still, while I waited for the Master's response.

He was no longer looking at me. He seemed to be staring off into the distance, his arms crossed over his chest and his cloak wrapping around me, encasing me, then slipping away, only to resume again.

"Love is not a concept known to my people," he said. "But family…"

He continued to stare off, his silence so long the creatures around us grew restless. I got the sense that David and Demitri were trying to get my attention, but I still ignored them. This was between me and the Master. This was *our* debate. I couldn't lose focus now.

"Family is everything to my people."

The Master's mind opened into mine, sending tidal waves of impressions, feelings and thoughts, so overwhelming, so powerful, that I fell to my knees, then curled in on myself. His emotions were different from a human's—more intense and visceral. I'd expected him to be more logical, more intellectual, but now I wondered why I ever thought that because while there was intelligence here, and power beyond imagining, he seemed entirely made of emotion. So much that it became hard to think rationally beyond the emotion that rode him.

My tears fell to the stone ground, mingling with the old blood stains of who knew how many victims. Yet it wasn't for them that I cried, but for the Master. "I'm so sorry," I gasped between sobs. "It must have been terrifying to be left here. To have to leave your people. Your—your parents."

Deeper darkness fell over me, and cold engulfed me. Dimly, I heard Demitri, then David scream my name, but I wasn't frightened. I was feeling too much, too lost to the Master's emotions to feel any fear for myself.

His arms were around me, his body curling around me as he pulled me close. His cloak fell over us both, creating the sensation of complete isolation.

Why do you cry now?

For you, I said, and I wrapped my arms around his large body as best I could. I felt no disgust, no fear, only empathy.

But…why?

Because of what you suffered. Because your parents loved you so, so much and you hurt their hearts when you couldn't find someone to love. And I know it hurt you, too. I felt it. And I felt your…your sorrow and loss and your utter…loneliness.

His arms tightened slightly around me. *My people are passionate and…extreme…compared to yours.*

Somehow, I felt a laugh bubble up inside of me. *I've noticed.* I pulled back a bit, wanting to look at him.

269

He met my gaze, and this time I was able to see inside *him*, to his soul and, maybe, into his heart.

I can see now how, in the rage and sorrow you felt when you were left here, you sought to fill your loneliness. How your need for blood, and the hatred you felt for the species you found here, drove you to seek their deaths.

He stared back at me, and I tried to allow myself to be as open with him as he was with me.

But…can you see how the children you created were made in that rage, and were given none of your…well, we'd call it love, but it feels like it was your familial bond or something.

Hirew, he whispered in my mind. *It has no place here.*

You're right. Humans don't have that exact feeling. Possession and belonging are different. Love can be earned and lost.

He lifted a hand and stroked my ponytail. *I would like to be loved. And to give…love.*

I smiled then. A big, goofy smile that startled him. When I started to sing "All you need is love," by the Beatles, he rocked back on his heels and smiled right back.

I will return your Philo to you. He will survive, the boy is strong. And David, too, whomever you wish. I do not wish to possess, *I wish for belonging.*

We all want that. To belong. To be loved.

Will you love me, then?

We gazed at each other, each of us taking this last final measure of each other. *I would like to come to love you, but we'll need to work on it. Releasing the people you've held against their will is a great start. Thank you for that.*

Something passed over his expression then that I hadn't seen before. I wasn't sure if I was imagining things, or if the Master really could feel shame or embarrassment. Whatever it was, was there and gone, and then he rose, the tendrils of his cloak becoming firm around my arms and lifting me to my feet. When they released me, I nearly stumbled, but Demitri caught me and held me close to his side.

"And you, Demitrius? Do you love me?"

ON BEING A VAMPIRE

CHAPTER SIX

So you've decided to become a vampire and you survived your remaking. Congratulations! We're happy to have you.

Here are just a few things we felt you should know at the outset:

Tears are a normal part of human life, however as a vampire, you might want to find a different way to express your feelings. It's especially

Vamps need a financial training course — like estate planning, but for our long life, not our death.

important to avoid crying in front of humans; they find it extremely disturbing to watch blood leaking from your eyes. Also, instead of packing tissues in your bag, you might want to keep wet wipes on hand — they're much handier at cleaning up bloody messes. *Ugh. SO so true.*

Contrary to popular belief, there are financially challenged vampires. However, over a long lifetime even the most inept investors can usually reap a profit. *Demitri's clan?*

• I want to be able to live well for a long time.
• Also want to provide for my parents (secretly of course.)

36

CHAPTER
EIGHTEEN

DEMITRI STIFFENED BEHIND ME AND I BEGAN TO PANIC. I didn't exactly know what, if any, kind of progress I'd made with the Master, but I knew it was tenuous. His mind still lay bare to me, and it was a whirling chaos of emotion that I couldn't grasp. It was like standing in the middle of a whirlpool, trying to grab one tiny leaf. Impossible.

I leaned toward the Master, trying to send him soothing vibes, but I didn't have much to offer since I didn't feel too calm myself. My gut told me the Master needed to believe that letting us go was the key to securing our love, but he was still so full of turmoil and need and confusion that one wrong word could ruin it all.

And Demitri held no love for the Master.

I shuffled to my right so I could see Demitri, but David caught my eye. He stood over Philo's prone body, very tense, very alert. I couldn't remember ever seeing David this dangerous looking—and I'd seen him in battle before. His eyes were black, and his skin had gone that ashy white that we seemed to get when we were in vamp mode. Another time I would have to see if I could determine what sort of physiological change went on in our bodies, but I shoved that inopportune thought aside as I considered the man I'd come to love like a father. His body hunched around Philo, every bit of revealed skin pulsing with black veins. He looked every bit the predator he was, but I couldn't understand the change in him. Who did he consider a threat? The Master? Or me?

Unable to look at him anymore, my gaze dropped to Philo, and my whole world crashed down around me.

His head was turned toward me, almost indiscernible from the corpses and vampires lying all around. Except even like this, even beyond death the way he was, I'd know those eyes anywhere. They were faded, more like an old pair of blue jeans than the bright blue of the sea he'd known as a child, but as soon as my gaze met his, my fear and worry melted away. This was the boy I loved with a purer love than I'd loved anyone before.

I reached for his mind, and though it was weak and his thoughts were a jumble of mis-matched thoughts, I heard one word loud and clear: *Love*.

Minnie. The harsh guttural growl of my name jerked my gaze upward to see David, his being still as intense as before. His gaze flicked to the side, then back to me.

The Master and Demitri stood very close together, neither paying me, David or Philo any attention.

Get ready to run, I told David. His nod was so tight I would have missed it if I hadn't been watching so closely. *Can you carry Philo?*

Yes, he hissed in my mind.

Then be ready.

I turned away without waiting for a reply. In the back of my mind I wondered at my nerve in presuming to give David orders, but just then it all felt natural. I'd come here to rescue, so rescue I would.

Taking a step closer to Demitri, I let my mind drift over the Master's. I wasn't sure whether to be worried that the rush and whirl of emotions that had been riding him had settled down from tornado to thunderstorm.

"Ah, my precious child," the Master said as I stepped close. He held his arm out and I felt I had no choice but to allow him to wrap it around my shoulders and pull me close to him. Demitri stared at us, horrified. "Demitri and I have just been discussing the nature of love and I begin to suspect you have lied to me, my little doll. That you have manipulated me." He turned his gaze on me and the blood red of his eyes seemed to darken and swirl. *Mesmerizing.*

"I haven't, Master. But because we are human first, we each see love differently. Value it differently. Like I said before, love isn't a given. It has to be earned. But the way that love is earned is different for everyone." I no longer felt as confident in those words as I had before. They sounded empty and far too simple for this creature. The first rule of debate is to never let the competition diminish your confidence. You could make anyone believe anything so long as you were confident. Now, I literally felt my world fraying around me as I waited for the Master to tear it all away from me.

"Yes, yes. You and your human sensibilities. But I am not human and I care nothing for them. I have made you—all of you—and you are mine." See now, the Master—he spoke with such confidence that even I believed his words. At least for a minute. I 100% knew he believed them and believing them that powerfully just might make them reality.

Demitri looked as if he might be sick, but I struggled on, despite my own growing fear. "It might be harder for Demitri since you took his daughter." It was a risk, but I had to play every card I had or risk losing the entire game.

The Master grinned at Demitri and there was nothing at all soft or repentant about it. But man, Demitri was amazing—he squared his shoulders as he lifted his chin.

The Master's strange cloak dissolved into shadow again, rising and coiling around Demitri. "I believed it would please you, to share this life with her. And yet you rejected her. You cannot love her overly much or you would not have left her with the one you despise the most."

Demitri's mouth worked, but no sound came out his first few tries. When he did speak, his voice sounded harsh and broken. "I do not despise you, but I do despise the creature I have become."

The Master seemed to sway back and up, rising high again. I wondered if he could extend his legs somehow? Because sometimes he seemed man-sized, and others...not. Was it his cloak? "But I gave you life! I rescued you from certain death!" His voice fell short of a roar, but I felt the pain in it. He truly did not seem to understand why we weren't all falling down in gratitude to him.

Demitri sighed and dropped his gaze to the floor. He shook his head before returning his gaze to the Master. "This is no life," he said. "This is just another kind of death."

The Master dropped down and drew his face close to Demitri's. "You would have preferred your sorry human life? Your puny lifespan? Your fragility and ignorance?"

They stared at each other for a long, long moment. Finally, quietly, Demitri said, "Yes."

The Master flew into action, moving around the cavern like a shadow, somehow encompassed by—or turning into?—his cloak of mist. I didn't have to search his mind for what he was thinking or feeling, it spilled out of him, falling like torrential rain and drenching me. So many emotions, too many to name, let alone process.

Now! I shouted at David. *Go, now!*

I rushed to him, but he already had Philo in his arms and was speeding toward the cavern entrance. I turned to follow him, but stopped short at the stricken expression on Demitri's face.

"I can't." He moaned, his gaze sweeping rapidly over the crowd of hissing vampires before turning, beseeching to me. "I can't leave without her. I have to find her."

"We'll come back for her." I grabbed his arm and tried to pull him with me, but he stood as still as a stone. "We will. But for right now, we need to go!" I tugged him again, and this time his body loosened and he stumbled after me.

"Nadia!" he called. "My daughter, come! Come with me!"

I cringed as his words echoed around us, desperately afraid they'd be enough to draw the Master out of his fugue. His shadowy self was nowhere in sight, having disappeared into the deep darkness at the very top of the cavern. His emotions still pulsed around me, but I knew he'd gain control over them any minute. And when he did, he'd realize we were on the run.

We'd reached the narrow ledge where the sea had worn away the cavern floor, when I heard a whisper. I ignored it, praying Demitri would, too. I held my hands out toward his back, ready to nudge him forward should he falter.

But when he did, I didn't stand a chance against him.

He stopped short and whirled, nearly causing me to fall backward on my butt, but he grabbed me and basically lifted me and set me on the path behind him. What I wouldn't have given to be as big and brutish as Fearghus in that moment.

"Papa," the whispered voice said again. The word floated in the air, impossible to tell who had spoken it or where it had come from.

"Nadia?" Demitri called into the darkness. "Nadia, my child, where are you?"

"We've gotta go!" I shouted. "Now! Come on!"

I yanked on his arm, but he didn't budge. Instead, he took a step away from me, back toward the mass of vampires or creatures that roiled on the floor.

The Master went silent in my mind.

"Demitri!" Tears welled in my eyes now, clogging my throat and making it hard for me to speak. "Come on!"

He took another step away. "Nadia?"

A blur rushed by me, nearly knocking me to the ground. David appeared just long enough to sweep Demitri into his arms. "Run!" he roared at me.

Turning away from the brutal expression on his face as he struggled with Demitri, I focused on the light of day ahead. On freedom.

And man, did I run. The rest of the cavern passed in a blur, and then I was outside, standing on the narrow dirt path, Philo curled in on himself in the dirt. I picked him up, refusing to allow myself to notice the feel of his bones grinding together in my arms or his weight, which couldn't have been more than seventy pounds.

Just as my foot hit the rough-hewn stairs up the cliff side, the roar reached me. I wanted to turn, to make sure David and Demitri made it out, but the stair was too narrow and I needed to get Philo up and to safety. "David!" I yelled. "Come on, David! You can do it! Come on, Demitri!"

What have you done? The Master roared in my mind. *Why are you leaving me?*

I trembled with fear and had to lean my whole body forward against the cliff before attempting the next step. I couldn't look back. I couldn't look down.

I had to keep moving upward.

I'm sorry, Master. I'm so sorry. And I was. Truly. I'd felt his loneliness, known he needed us—me, for whatever reason. *But I love him. Please understand. I need to save him.*

You know nothing of love! You know nothing!

His roar, sent with the intensity of a hundred atomic bombs, shattered me inside until I was gasping for breath, fighting to keep my forward and upward progression when every particle of my being was being flayed from within.

"I'll come back," I whispered. *I'll come back. When Philo is well. When he is strong again. But please let my friends go. Please. I need them. I love them. Just as I love you. And I want all of you to be safe and well.*

You are a liar, he growled in my mind, and he shoved an image at me of what he did to liars, what he did to punish those who betrayed him.

The shock of it, the utter violence and evil of what he showed me shut my brain down for a second, and I lost my balance. Bits of grit and sand slipped beneath my feet and I fell forward, smacking first Philo's head and then my own, against a step. Blood rushed in my ears as I half-lay against the steps and half-clung to the rocks with my body, trying to find the courage and strength to keep going.

"You can do this, Minnie," David said from just below me. He'd caught up to me, but we were only going to escape now at whatever speed I could manage.

I straightened and took another step upward.

I'm sorry, I told the Master. *I meant everything I said. You can see in my mind I meant it. I am leaving with my family and with my friend. You know the value of those things more than anything. I know you do.* I pushed back to him some of the emotion I'd gleaned from him when he allowed me to view his own mind. They were rich with sorrow and regret and a desperate desire to not be parted from those he loved.

I reached the top of the cliff, and basically shoved Philo onto the flat, dirt top. I thought he would roll, but his skeletal body just skidded over the dirt. I winced, knowing his skin, concealed by rags as thin as tissues, would tear from the abrasion.

David pushed up on my butt, but I didn't care. He was like my dad, and getting from the top stair to the flat ground was hard. A moment later, he lay on the ground beside me, him staring up at the sky, me staring at Philo, who wore a pained expression on his pale, pale face, his eyes squeezed tightly shut.

On my hands and knees, I crawled toward the edge. "Come on, Demitri! Hurry!" He was still several steps down, but pressure was building in my mind, a storm of rage and hatred so potent, that I knew the Master wasn't done with us yet. "You have to get away from there!"

Demitri paused and looked up. His eyes widened as he looked at me, but I don't know why. Whatever it was, it made him look down—just in time to see Nadia stumble from the cave.

She wore the remains of what had probably been a man's suit jacket, and nothing else. Her long, black hair draped over her shoulders and hung below her bum as she stood there, one arm wrapped around herself while she held the other up to hide her eyes from the light. I wondered just how long it had been since she'd seen the sun.

"Papa?" she called in a trembling voice.

It was a trap. Of course it was a trap. Even if I hadn't felt the Master's building rage, anyone could see it was a trap.

But trap or not, Demitri had to return for her. I knew he had to. Knew he would. He stared down at his daughter before looking back at me. Hope flared bright in his eyes and he smiled, quick and brilliant, before climbing downward.

"No!" I called. "It's a trap!"

But he had to go. His daughter was calling him.

I watched, one hand digging into the rocky dirt and sparse grass at the edge of the plateau, the other pressed to my heart. My heart felt like it was literally breaking as I watched my friend go to his daughter, knowing it wouldn't end well.

He reached the flat rock at the bottom and turned to face his daughter. She threw herself into his arms, and for a moment, I thought maybe I'd been wrong. Maybe she really did want to be with him, to come away with him. A moment passed, and the two let go of each other. Nadia stepped back as a wicked smile crooked her lips and dread pumped into my gut like a broken water main.

And then the Master was there, standing just behind Nadia, his cloak shrouding him in dark mists.

"No!" I screamed. "Let them go!" I didn't know what was about to happen, but it would be something bad. Something terrible.

"Nadia," Demitri said. He took a step toward her, hands outstretched.

But Nadia spat in his face and turned, curling against the Master instead. It was only then that I realized I was crying and David was holding me tight to keep me from hurling myself down the cliff to help them.

"He's gonna—he's gonna—" I panted between breaths, but I couldn't seem to finish the sentence. I knew what was going to happen. Could see it. But I couldn't do anything to stop it. It was like the knowledge paralyzed me.

The Master put his hands on Nadia's arms and held her away from him. I couldn't see his face, but I watched Demitri's pale at what he must have seen written there.

"You are not worthy of my love," the Master hissed in a sound that echoed in my brain, spreading dread through every part of my being. "You only care for this…" he shook Nadia and her arms flailed, "thing." His cloak became shadow; tendrils of it diving into Nadia's eyes, nostrils and mouth until she convulsed, then went limp. Then he just…tore her apart. Just like that. He tore Demitri's daughter apart and flung her far into the sea.

My mind was screaming. Totally freaking out, but my voice was silent. All I could hear was the surge of the waves, and the rattling of Philo's breathing behind me.

Demitri stepped toward the Master, but instead of fighting him, he opened his arms, as if asking for a hug. The Master's lips twisted into something that might have been a smile as his cloak slithered around Demitri's body.

"No!" I screamed into the wind.

The Master said something to him as Demitri collapsed to the stone, boneless. Lifeless.

I must have said something. Must have drawn the Master's attention somehow, because the next thing I knew David held Philo in his arms and was urging me to run.

Behind our pounding feet, the Master roared.

Regardless of what you choose, it is of utmost importance that you continue your education. As a vampire, you could do so eternally. Just because you may no longer age, doesn't mean you're suddenly capable of thinking and acting wisely. Allow your mind to develop and grow so you can be a valuable and contributing member of vampire society for many millennia to come. *Agree with this in theory, but after MY experience I think no vamp should go back to H.S. High school's hard enough without adding VAMPIRE to the mix.*

As long as you are ingesting human blood on a regular basis, you will also be able to consume human food. If you plan to spend time amongst humans, this is desirable, as humans often gather around food. As of this writing, humans still find drinking blood, and eating jellied blood squares or blood pudding, off-putting. **Um ... Yup!**

A vampire must eat regularly. Your body relies solely on blood and without it you will become a dehydrated husk within two to three days. The process is quick, but incredibly painful as your organs

CHAPTER
NINETEEN

THE MASTER'S ROAR FOLLOWED US INTO THE NIGHT. WHILE David drove Demitri's car, I sat in the front seat, unbelted, with my knees drawn to my chest, rocking back and forth. All I could feel was the Master's rage and pain. All I could think were his thoughts.

Abruptly, the weight of it all shifted. The car swerved, nearly sending us over the side of the cliff which didn't have a guard rail in this section of the road. David corrected, but by his white-knuckled grip on the steering wheel and the grim set of his jaw, I could see something was happening. My guess was that the Master had shifted his mental attack to him.

Philo moaned from the backseat where he never should have been able to fit. It broke my heart to see him like that. The human body is so much smaller when stripped of its muscle and tissue. I moved, trying to wedge myself into the back so I could be with him, but there was no way.

Instead, I knelt facing my seat-back, and stroked the only part of Philo I could touch—his knee, I think. I crooned to him, telling him it would be okay, telling him to hang on. My voice quavered. I had no idea if anything I said was remotely true. I wanted to take him to our spot in my mind, but I was afraid. His mind had been battered and bruised before the Master began his onslaught, and from the pinched expression on Philo's face, I thought maybe he wasn't being spared.

"What are we gonna do?" I yelled at David. As soon as the words were out, I realized I hadn't needed to shout—the expensive car was pin-drop quiet; it was only in my head that the noise was deafening. David didn't answer.

We drove past a small diner in a pretty little white cottage, then David turned around so fast, I had to cling to the seat and watch helplessly as Philo slid across the backseat. David turned into the restaurant's lot and parked at the side of the building, where a couple of men stood having a smoke. They must have been cooks or staff since they both wore black aprons.

The car was still rocking from its sudden stop when David's door opened and he was stalking up to the men. I watched them straighten, wary, then their bodies sagged as if they completely relaxed. David sank his teeth into the man in the white shirt. I gripped the dashboard of Demitri's fancy car and dug my fingers into the plastic. Hunger burned within me and suddenly I felt—I *knew*—that if only I could get fresh blood, I'd be able to shut the Master out.

I opened my door and stumbled out, scraping my knee on the ground before I found my feet. I didn't ask David's permission, I just told the guy with the long beard to sit on the curb, then bent over him from behind and bit down deep into his carotid artery.

The relief was immediate as everything but the man and his thoughts filled my mind. I drank long and deep, only catching myself when I saw David return to the car.

And then I realized the relief would only be short-lived.

Though the Master no longer roared in my head, I felt the *pressure* of him there. Like he was an angry mob threatening to break down my door. I sat in the car, both my palms pressed to my forehead, and stared at the two men, who stood and sat, respectively, still completely entranced by David's thrall.

"What about Philo?" I finally managed to ask haltingly.

David finally swung his head to look at me. Though his skin glowed from his feeding, the shadows beneath his eyes were deep smudges like someone had pressed their thumbs in blue ink, then left their marks there. He was gaunt, drawn. I hadn't noticed before how terrible he looked, whether it was because of the way vampire night vision worked or because I hadn't wanted to see—hadn't allowed myself to see. I didn't know, but my heart gave a tight, hard squeeze when I looked at him.

"You're going to have to feed him." His voice was flat, nothing at all like the commanding, capable David I knew. Like the father I relied on to always know what to do. This David seemed to be holding on by a thread. Like he wanted *me* to give *him* the answers. "We'll take turns." He reversed the car and we drove away, David still demanding every bit of speed the car could give.

I stared at him for a minute, feeling as if I carried the weight of the world on my shoulders. Even though I'd just eaten and should feel strong and capable, the Master's assault hadn't stopped, and my defenses were cracking faster than I could rebuild them.

After a moment, I took a deep breath then turned in the seat again. I studied the dark, cramped area that was more like a ledge or compartment than a true backseat. Philo seemed to have shrunk into himself even more than before.

"Philo." I knew he wasn't dead, but my heart had trouble believing it. He lay sprawled, arms and legs all akimbo, one arm in an awkward position that couldn't possibly be comfortable. "Philo." He didn't respond.

"Just do it," David growled. I jumped and whipped my head toward him, but he wasn't angry with me.

I bit down deep into my wrist, deep enough the blood welled in my mouth, then wedged myself between the two front seats as best I could and shoved my wrist in front of Philo's mouth. Nothing happened while blood smeared over Philo's mouth, dripped down onto the seat, and into the carpet below.

"Philo," I begged. I tried to squeeze even more of me between the seats so I could reach him better. Somehow I managed another inch, and I pressed my bleeding wrist against his mouth. "Drink," I urged quietly as I felt his thin, dry lips part beneath my wrist. Hope flared, but a second later I realized it had only been the pressure of my wrist that had caused his mouth to open. As far as I could tell his fangs hadn't dropped and he hadn't responded at all.

I couldn't see his face, with my head pressed sideways against the seat, but fear and worry, exhaustion and hopelessness dragged me down and down and down.

"Just don't give up," David said in a tight, brittle voice.

But I was too tired to answer.

This hadn't gone at all like I'd hoped. I hadn't had a plan—if I had, none of this would have happened. None of us would have died.

I didn't know if it was my own memory, or a trick of the Master's, but the images of him tearing Nadia apart, the way Demitri broke inside at the brutal death of his daughter, the way his body had looked, limp and lifeless over the Master's knee played through my mind on repeat, all while the Master railed at me.

I was selfish. I was a liar. I knew nothing about love. Nothing about sacrifice.

And I would pay.

Over and over again as my blood dripped uselessly into Philo's mouth.

It wasn't going to work. Nothing was going to work.

For once in my life I'd been stupid, and I'd gone down in a blaze of freaking glorious stupidity.

My rescue came too late and at too great a cost—the Master's onslaught was too great for Philo to bear and David practically exuded hate toward me.

I'd ruined everything.

What had I thought I was doing, feeding the Master's paranoia like I'd done? Why hadn't I seen what it would lead to? The Master wasn't human! Of course I couldn't reason with him like a human. And then I'd made everyone run just because the Master was consumed by his own emotions. I stole his chance from him. Stole his chance to figure it out, to learn. I'd presumed too much. Thought too much of myself and my own abilities.

How could I have been so proud? So full of myself?

Now Philo would die, and David would blame me forever for bringing his Master's wrath down on us.

Whatever had been wrong before was ten thousand times worse now. No one would be safe now. No one I loved would ever be safe.

The sky grew dim as we roared through the Italian countryside, taking one-lane roads far from crowded areas.

"Can we stop?" I asked. I wasn't tired from holding out my arm—it would take a lot more effort than this to wear me down—but with every minute that passed, every mile between us and the Master, the futility of what we were doing broke my heart bit by bit. "This isn't working. We need to stop!" I didn't realize I'd started crying until I heard the sobs in my voice when I tried to speak. "David!" I shouted. "Just stop already!"

But he didn't. He wouldn't.

What is happening? I yelled into his mind. *Why aren't you answering me?*

I expected to be met with a brick wall, since he'd been so closed off and strange since before we left the cave.

Instead I recoiled at what I found there. His mind was flayed open, while some sort of...*frenzy*...filled it so completely I couldn't reach him. I couldn't see him. Couldn't recognize any of it as his. It was like his mind was Kansas and I was Dorothy screaming for Auntie Em. It seemed impossible that he was still driving, that he was functioning at all.

I had just a moment's warning, just a flash of understanding that we were far from free from the Master's clutches, before something struck the car and my whole world became chaos.

shut down one by one as they are leached of their blood content. Liver failure will come first, followed by kidneys, then brain. At least you won't be conscious as you desiccate.

I can't ... not while Philo is suffering through it.

Vampires are complicated creatures — especially old ones. You can never presume to understand them. RIGHT??

Every vampire needs a reason to live. Without it, we succumb to our base nature until we are destroyed. A purpose shapes our days, our years, our lifetimes. Find your purpose and you just might find you truly can live forever. *This is pretty much the only awesome thing about being a vamp.*

Self-awareness is an important virtue every vampire should nurture. Both old and young vampires struggle with self-awareness, but without it, inflated emotions can lead to violent and regrettable decisions. The Council has recently begun exploring the use of psychologists who specialize in vampire mental health. For more information, speak to your sire or to your local Council office.

CHAPTER TWENTY

I THINK I DIED, KIND OF. AT LEAST, WHEN I CAME TO MY senses, I had the feeling that time had passed while I'd been away—more than just asleep. *Gone*, somehow. And I hurt everywhere. The pain consumed me for a while, like I shared my body with a voracious monster and it was all I could do to keep it from devouring me whole.

My neck and collarbone were broken. All of my ribs too, so my chest cavity was filled with air and I couldn't fill my lungs. My spine was broken, all four of my limbs and my pelvis. I was forced to lie there, slipping in and out of consciousness while my body struggled to put itself together.

I have no idea how much time passed before I finally lay on my back, the night sky dotted with stars spread before me. I was alive again, it seemed.

The memory of what had happened was fuzzy. I couldn't exactly recall why I was there, or why my body was so broken. At first I thought I was home, lying in the meadow with Philo, watching the stars pass by overhead.

But these stars weren't our stars. These were…different. But I couldn't figure out why.

A sort of sibilant hissing sound came from far off, but otherwise, the night was cool and quiet.

And I slept some more.

I woke to tears clogging my throat. I coughed and choked until I got myself enough onto my side that I could let my sorrow pour into the grass beneath me. Each sob that wrenched through me sent wrenching pain through my body, each stab of pain bringing more tears to my eyes.

But it wasn't just the pain that sourced all my tears, it was the heartbreak of loss.

Gripping the grass in one fist, I poured my sorrow into the earth, but no matter how much I cried, I couldn't get the pain of what I'd done out of me.

I'd failed. I'd failed at it all. I hadn't rescued Philo and David. I'd only brought them more pain.

And I'd gotten Demitri and his daughter killed.

When I woke again, I was somewhere different, and while my body felt more or less whole, there was more pain, this time deep within my core, the center of my being.

The Master was here.

I felt his power inside my mind, so much that it bled into my body, causing my limbs to jerk and twitch, my mind to scream with pain. I grit my teeth and pushed back on his presence with all my might until I'd cleared away space enough to think. To try to make sense of it all.

What was the Master doing here? *How* was he here? Hadn't we driven far enough away that he wouldn't dare venture from his hole in the ground?

Then I remembered the accident. The way David's mind had been filled with the Master, how David had grimly driven faster and faster as if trying to escape. I hadn't understood, and a shudder of regret and shame at my stupidity raced through me.

There was no moon. The night was completely dark.

And the night was the Master's domain.

David had been trying to outrun him, to get us as far away from the lair as possible. He'd known. He'd understood that just because we escaped the cavern didn't mean we'd escaped our Maker. Now I wondered if we'd ever had a chance at all.

How stupid I'd been. How completely naïve. I should have known that David wouldn't have left me behind in Utah if there hadn't been a good reason. I should have really thought about what it meant that David and others of my family feared the Master. That if they, who were old and so much more experienced than I was, were afraid, I should have been, too.

I should have understood that David would never have let Philo linger with the Master if he hadn't had a very good reason.

But I hadn't listened to anyone. I hadn't used my brain at all.

And somehow, that was the greatest disappointment of all.

If I was so smart, so capable of this Great Future I envisioned for myself, how had I for even one second believed I stood a chance in bringing Philo home?

I'd been too proud, too full of myself. I'd let my little accomplishments of the past year convince me that I could overcome everything, when in reality, I'd done none of it alone. There'd always been someone there to help me.

When Hashiki came after me at the school dance, it had taken Philo, my family, even Thor—and then a freakin' faerie queen—to help me save the day. I couldn't have done any of it without them.

When Ying Yue followed me to Seoul, I would have been toast if it hadn't been for my family and Sang. And even they weren't enough. It had only been when Hanjo showed up in all his dragon glory that Ying Yue had finally been finished.

It hadn't even been me who stopped the stupid *kynigoi*.

I hadn't even done anything for Cheveyo, except break his heart.

And now…

I scoffed, welcoming the pain in my mind, in my body. In my heart.

Now my hubris had led to Demitri's death, to his daughter's death, and to whatever suffering the Master had in store for me and David.

At least there was some comfort in knowing Philo would be beyond it. The crash had just about broken every bone in my body; I couldn't imagine what it must have done to him. There was no way he could have survived it.

Fresh tears filled my eyes as the familiar grief washed over me.

Philo was gone. Well and truly gone.

And I…

I was just a girl in way over her head.

A foolish, stubborn girl who never seemed to know her place.

Well, I knew it now, didn't I?

Hopeless, I let my head fall to the side—and saw a body—a skeleton, really—crumpled nearby. I reached for it, and when my fingers grazed the pale, papery-thin skin still clinging to the bones, memory washed through me.

Philo kissing me in the meadow.

Philo holding my hand, hugging me close.

Philo telling me to run.

Run! Run!

His voice resonated in my head like a gong, startling me back into full awareness.

I lay next to Philo, David a couple yards away. A weighty darkness pressed down over us, blocking out the stars I'd seen earlier, blocking out my sense of anything beyond our little bubble of blackest night.

Philo opened his eyes and I gasped.

A smile drifted over his lips as our eyes met.

He was still nothing more than skin and bones, but he was alive. And I saw everything in his eyes. He was better—the bit of blood I'd been able to give him earlier had brought him back from the brink, but he needed more. So much more. But he was here with me, at least. He knew me.

And he loved me.

Oh, that love.

It lit a fire within me, making my soul burn with passion and determination.

I hadn't come all this way to give up now, had I?

Yeah, I had no right to come here without help. Or without *more* help. I should have asked my family. I could have at least tried. But I was here now, and I couldn't just give up. Not with Philo's gaze on me, not with the light pressure of his mind, so familiar, so intimate, near mine.

Even if all I could do was save him—him and David, because he'd need David to get him away and fed—then it would make all of this worth it. And maybe Demitri wouldn't hold his own death against me if I at least managed to do what I came here for.

The Master had listened to me when I'd spoken to him before. I'd felt something click between us, hadn't I? Some sort of sameness, some sort of understanding. I did. I knew I had.

Philo must have read my thoughts in my gaze because his whispered mind voice urged me to run again, to leave him and David, to save myself.

It seemed to me that I was finally thinking straight, and I wasn't about to run. I'd been so focused on myself, on all that I'd lost in becoming a vampire, of all the ways I no longer fit in as a human or a vamp, on how I would rectify all of that by proving how similar we were. It had all been about me. About how *I* felt. About where *I* belonged.

Now, as I stared into Philo's blue, blue eyes, I felt my world shift.

Life wasn't about proving how awesome I was—it was about the love that I gave and the love that was given to me. Life was about love. That's all it had ever been about.

I felt the buzz of the Master's power, felt the way he drove himself into each of us, delving into our minds, searching for something he could do to punish us for fleeing, and realized I was just like him.

I mean, not literally or anything, but he was stuck in this constant loop—a loop that had lasted for millennia. On his own world, he'd been all about his own power, his station as an heir to his world's ruling power. He believed that position guaranteed him belonging and importance. He'd viewed love as something that was owed him, and when it went to someone else, he couldn't accept it. *Wouldn't* accept it.

Hadn't I been more bothered by the threat my vampirism was to my dreams than I'd been by becoming a vampire in the first place? Hadn't I believed that I, singlehandedly, could change peoples' view of vampire-kind? Hadn't I thought that no one else but me cared enough about Philo to come for him?

And wow. That was supremely sad. For such a smart girl, I really had been clueless.

As I watched the Master, cloaked in his shadows and writhing in the dark night like a crazy person in a trance, my empathy for him grew.

"No…" Philo's voice, his whisper, was as thin and formless as the wind, but I heard it. I returned my gaze to his, and there was no pretending what was on my mind and in my heart. I'd never been a good liar, and I wasn't about to start now, so I didn't try to pretend that Philo hadn't read me perfectly.

"I have to," I whispered back. Then I rolled onto my side, cringing at the pain that still defined my body, and kissed him. His lips were dry and thin, nothing at all like their normal lush softness, but still I sighed against them.

Somehow he found the strength to lift one hand and drag his fingers through my hair before it fell useless to the ground. I cried at that particular gesture that was so familiar, so full of love.

Then with great care and determination, I pressed my feelings into his mind as gently as I could and begged him with my eyes to forgive me.

Then I rolled away from Philo, sat up, and reached a hand out to the Master.

Be sure to carry baby wipes or wet wipes with you at all times. You never know when you might need to clean up a little blood. *Redundant.*

Maybe it could go in a list of helpful items or something. though.

Do not underestimate yourself. Doing so could cost you your life. *What?*

Vampirism is truly a gift. Everything you were before is maximized as you become your best self. Not only are your physical attributes magnified, but so is your mind—and your emotions.

This whole book feels like they went around asking "Hey, I'm putting this book together—what's your best advice for noobs?" It should be a lot more professional. I'm surprised our Master let it go out like this.

THE VAMPIRE COUNCIL

CHAPTER SEVEN

The Council of Vampires has existed for millennia. With the recent changes in the world, divisions have been created to allow for improved oversight all over the world. While vampire law still rules our kind, special accommodations must now be made for human law. Where once we operated outside such mundane jurisdiction, we are currently required to

CHAPTER
TWENTY-ONE

FATHER," I CROAKED, MY THROAT STILL RAW AND SORE
from the pain, the screams, the tears.

The Master stopped, then slowly rotated before letting
the shadows around him drift to the hem of his cloak. He
floated a couple feet off the ground, his cloak pulled
tightly around him, his deep hood hiding his face. But his
blood-red eyes were clearly visible and they peered right
at me and into my soul.

What happened next went beyond my own mental
abilities to understand, as the Master invaded my being,
inhabiting every particle of my *self*. He probed, tasted,
then devoured all my thoughts, all my hopes and dreams,
my loves and losses.

I tried to share with him what I'd just realized, to help
him see as I was beginning to, that love was about so

much more than just what you *did*. It was more than who you belonged to or who belonged to you. It wasn't about *you* at all. It wasn't about *self*.

But I had no idea if I succeeded. I was completely lost within his own overwhelming presence.

With the last of my *self*, I reached out to Philo, to David—to everyone I loved and cared for. Siobhan, Fearghus, Jack, Diana and Sang. Even Tim. I sent my last thought to Master Yi, to Veyo and to Hanjo. And though I wasn't sure if they could receive it, I reached for Stacey and Junu. And I reached for my parents.

I love you, I told them.

And then all sense of self was devoured by the monster that was my Master.

사랑해
♥

We were in our den, surrounded by our children—those babes that were reMade, weak and unable to thrive on their own. We loved them, just the same. We breathed in deeply, appreciating the familiarity of blood and bodies, death and decay. These creatures were shadows of what we had once been, and we mourned the loss of all that we had once had. We had been one among many, greater than them all, but all of them so much more than the greatest of these. We wailed over the pain of it. We railed at the injustice, the indignity.

And why had our parents not come back for us? Why had we been abandoned all those years ago?

We understood the necessity of the banishment, but it had never been meant to be forever.

Had they known it would be forever?

Were our parents overthrown? Had our people turned against them?

Perhaps it had only been a moment, a moment that had already felt like forever.

Time did run differently here.

At least now we were not so alone. Not quite.

We had each other, Minnie and Master. One being. One *I*.

And until our people return for us, we have all that we need before us.

The scrape of leather against stone brought us to a sense of awareness, but we didn't move. We scented the *human* on the air, heard his heartbeat, fast with fear, as he approached. He fell to his knees at the edge of the cavern.

"I have come as-as…promised, my, um, my lord."

We drifted closer, taking measure of the human before us. He was of a young age, just old enough to take part in the ritual his people had committed him to long before his birth. He smelled familiar. His family had given themselves to us many times over the years. Then again, all of our worshipers smelled the same, having sprung from the same ones who had been first to sustain our life so long ago. We caress the young man's throat with the essence we hold manifest about us. When the young man shivers, and we taste his fear on the air, we splinter.

Just for a moment, less than a second.

In that splintering of time, we are Minnie and Master, one eschewing the fear of the man, the other reveling in it.

But then the man bends his neck, and we are of one accord once more.

We have expelled much energy this night, and we are thirsty. We are hungry.

As we drink, the man's thoughts drift past us, his dreams like tiny sparkles that make him taste sweeter on our tongue, his fears like bits of dust that satisfy the darker of our desires.

We cannot take all of him. All he has to give.

We deserve it all. We deserve everything.

We fracture once more.

As we struggle to regain our balance, our children fall upon the sacrifice. They were hungry, too.

사랑해
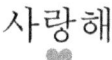

We are changing. We are changed.

As we observe our children, we feel sorrow for them. A desire for them to live for themselves and not only ourself. It isn't right for them to live like this, in this cold and damp. Besides, our bargain with the locals is that we will not kill their sacrifices, only taste, and we cannot sustain the others who linger here.

"Go," we told them one day when the winds and waves blew softly. "Return to your homes."

They looked upon us, grief and fear radiating from their eyes, etched in the frowns on their faces.

"But, we cannot go," said one man. "We belong nowhere but here."

We knew him. He had been with us a long time. A very long time. We peered at him now, our vision shifting as it sometimes did these days, to see our child, a creature of blood and bone, and a man clinging to life, his youth and beauty stripped away and replaced by tough, mottled skin, sunken eyes and greasy, listless hair.

He is human, we think.

He is ours. He should stay.

He should stay if he wishes it.

Yes, if he wishes it.

The man stayed. Others did not.

We watched them go as we struggled not to haul them back.

We are changing, we think.

We love our children, and in loving them, we should be more concerned about what is right for them, as opposed to what is right for ourself.

That is love.

That is what it means to love.

It is not about us. Not about self.

We hold…then breathe…

Then fracture once more.

사랑해

Something woke me, but I couldn't say what. I stirred, softly, carefully, within the Master's cloak until I could see outward from where we slept in the deepest corner of the den. It was morning, and I had to blink against the light, because I haven't used my eyes—my own eyes—for…I don't know.

I didn't know how long I had been one with the Master. How long it had been since saying goodbye to all that I loved. It seemed like an eternity ago. But the sea moved ceaselessly toward us, and the wind continued to blow. Our children—*his* children—still huddled together in sleep, where they would remain for the duration of the day.

At least there were fewer here, now. At least some had left the cave in search of warmth and belonging elsewhere.

I sighed and closed my eyes. I wasn't sure what I'd accomplished by going with him. I certainly never imagined I would end up like this—somehow one with the Master in all but the smallest moments, stolen from a day like this one.

Every day I tried to change his heart, to convince him that as long as he was our father, his children would always reverence him. Every day I tried to convince him that the best way to love is to give what the other person needed, as opposed to taking what you wished from them. But the truth was, I no longer knew what a day was, unaware of the passing of time. It felt like I tried to change him every day, but what was a day? And what was a changed heart when I could no longer decipher between his and my own?

I wasn't sure I even knew what I was doing it for. What my purpose had ever been.

A presence brushed across the surface of my mind, and I stiffened. It wasn't him. It was something else.

Some*one* else.

I pulled on the mental strings that would draw our cloak more completely around us until only my vision remained. I watched the entrance of the cave, the glimpse of sea I caught glimmering beneath the refracted sunlight. The Master never stirred, and he wouldn't unless I woke him. He slept more deeply now than he ever had before, knowing the daylight didn't affect me as it did him.

So I prepared myself for what might come, for the stranger who had wandered into our den.

But I wasn't at all prepared for what had come for us. Not prepared at all.

Feels kind of combative. And man. If the Council's been around for millenia, why does this book feel slapped together by a couple kids in vampire costumes?

conform. Vampire kind cannot allow the behavior of a few to endanger the survival of our race.

* No violence, of any kind, toward humans will be tolerated. Any vampire who commits such acts, including the unwilling change of a human, will be subject to the Council's judgement.

Except when they're not. My case, & Tim, is different. So I get why David wanted to keep it on the DL, but I bet this sort of thing happens a lot. :/

The Council operates in the best interest of all vampires.

Prior to the Treaty of London, the Vampire Council presided from its place of origin in Istanbul, <ins>??</ins> formerly Constantinople. In recent years an oversight committee has been created to serve North, South and Central America (the American Council). *Why'd the Master set up the Council there if he's always been in Otranto?*

A Council consists of twenty-four vampires, five of whom must be less than one hundred years old and twelve of whom must be greater than five hundred years.

CHAPTER TWENTY-TWO

A MAN APPEARED IN THE MOUTH OF THE CAVERN, BUT it was the wrong time of day for a supplicant. I tried to nudge the Master awake, but since our joining, he'd been sleeping more and more deeply during the daytime. He didn't stir, which meant I couldn't, either.

I can't explain exactly what it was I—we—had become. It was like he held me within himself, but also not. When he was awake, we were *we*, and even when he slept, I had very little awareness of my body or self. It was almost like we'd become one being with two heads, but that wasn't quite right either. Or like I saw through the Master's eyes when he slept.

Either way, despite my wakefulness, as the Master slept I was only able to watch and to think. Nothing more.

"May I enter?" The man's voice was strangely deep and resonant and somehow not human. I squinted at him, but though he had moved closer, he still appeared only as a man.

When I didn't respond, he moved closer.

There'd been a part of me that had hoped, believed, that Philo had come—but then I had to be glad that it wasn't him. I didn't want him anywhere near here. Not now, not ever. Otherwise, what would have been the point?

The point of all of this. Of what I had done.

Of what I had become.

Besides, I didn't even know if Philo had survived. Had I been here a day or a century? It was all the same to me. I chose to believe Philo had survived and gone on to find happiness. While we were bound to all of our children, there were too many strings to pull and none of them had led to Philo or any of the Aristos clan.

A secret part of me worried that the Master had them all wiped out. That somehow, in the midst of everything, he'd managed to order their deaths. Every day I expected the *kynigoi* to show up with their heads or something.

But since I'd been here, no one but our supplicants had come. No word had come to the Master of my clan— or if it had, he had managed to hide it from my view.

Now, for the first time since I'd come here, *I* was the one to know something the Master didn't, so I watched curiously as the man came further into the cavern where the light didn't reach, but my vision did.

"Hello," he said once he stood at the edge of the den. I felt a faint brush against my mind, but then it was gone. The touch had felt somehow familiar, but I didn't know the man who stood before me. If he even was a man.

He stood tall and lean, perhaps even as tall as the Master. He wore a traditional Korean *hanbok* with a *duramagi* embroidered with dragons at the hem over top. A Korean? Yet I was certain I'd never seen this man in my life. I briefly wondered if he was an ancestor come to life, but there was something vaguely inhuman in the metallic sheen of his skin, in his sharp cheekbones and eyes that reflected the light much like my own.

"Ah," he said. "I see you do not know me." He smiled then and I had no trouble seeing the glint of jagged teeth. I recoiled, mentally scrabbling for the Master—until that familiar touch once again brushed over my mind.

The being stepped forward again, then reached for the collar of his *duramagi* and pulled it down slightly to reveal the edge of a softly glowing white orb embedded in his manubrium.

My gaze jumped back up to the creature's as recognition settled over me like a comforting blanket. *Hanjo!* I wanted to scream, to shout, to fling myself into his arms, but I was trapped within the Master, unable to do any more than watch.

A slight frown tugged at Hanjo's straight, hard lips. He strolled closer, then around to one side of us. I felt the Master stir. My eyes wide with fear, I tried to warn Hanjo. *Get away! Run, now! He's waking!* But I have no idea if Hanjo heard me. If he did, he made no outward sign.

The Master's presence in my mind—my presence in his—rolled, entwining until we were once again, *one.*

"What are you doing here?" we asked in a low, sibilant tone. We stretched, wakening our muscles and sinews from our slumber, but also allowing the dragon to see our size and might. "Hanjo." His name tasted bitter on our tongue as we fought to grasp what he meant to us.

Hanjo gave a deep bow in the old, traditional way. When he stood straight once again, he said, "Forgive my intrusion, though you must have expected it."

We bowed our head in acquiescence. "We knew someone would come. Eventually. Though it will not change the outcome."

Hanjo, who had the nerve to look away from us as we spoke, had begun stepping around our children, inspecting them. He glanced up at us. "Is that so?" He made a clucking sound with his tongue and shook his head.

His wanderings took him once more to the edge of our den, causing his form to be silhouetted by the sun beyond the cave. "You really should clean up," he said with a disdainful pursing of his lips. "These conditions are deplorable." Then he turned and began the trek along the ledge that would take him outside.

We seethed as we watched him go, an uneasy sense of dread and something like confusion settling over us. At the edge of our vision, Hanjo glanced back, then he stepped into the sunlight and was gone from our view.

We sank down into our corner, but we didn't sleep. A fire raged within us, spiraling so intensely that we flexed from one, to two, and one once more.

They will try to rescue me.

You are mine! We are one!

We are one. We understand their desire to rescue Minnie because they love her, and that's what you do for someone you love.

We were never rescued. We were abandoned. Even our children do not all remain.

Many of our children are brilliant. Successful and powerful in their own right. We glory in their success and are glorified because of it.

Inside, we swelled with a feeling we struggled to name, a sensation that left us feeling both more and less powerful.

That is love, I said.

This is love, the Master agreed.

We cannot fault them for wanting to rescue Minnie, even though she requires no such rescuing.

We are one. Together.

We felt our being expand as we became aware of our children, many of them, drawing nearer. *They come! We are loved!*

We knew them, each of them, though only a few personally. David, the child who would not bow before us, whose respect had never been freely given. We understood—he should have given it!—that such a thing must be earned, and we have mistreated him and his own children in our efforts to demand it. We are proud, but a thrill ran through us as we anticipated the opportunity to earn it.

There are others of David's clan, too—Fearghus, Siobhan, Sang and Jack, Chan-ri, Samantha, Diana and Tim. Even Brandon.

Thorstein had come, along with Matteo and others from Demitri's and Thorstein's clans.

So many children! We welcome them, glad of their return.

Then other beings enter our awareness, creatures we do not know and cannot welcome. Humans. And *werewolves*.

And Hanjo. The dragon's presence sent a shiver through us that incited our rage, and we stretched and screamed, erecting a barrier around our mind, around our being.

Do not come closer, we tell the dragon. *Tell them all. Come nearer and we will destroy you.*

We listened, but no answer came. Nothing stirred beyond our cavern, and our anxiety grew.

And then...the world beyond our cavern fell away. We pushed out our senses, but there was nothing. We sensed no life, no thoughts—it was as if the entire world had disappeared. We could see it—the sun still shone beyond our cave—and we could see the ocean sloshing in through the cave mouth.

But there was no life. No world.

For a moment we splintered as I considered what Hanjo's appearance might mean and how it might be connected to the strange cessation of awareness, while the Master railed against the barrier that had closed in around us.

Two beings burst into view, seeming to appear out of nowhere, and rushed toward us, weapons raised, their mouths open wide in strident, ululating battle cries. Their presence burst upon our mind, sending us reeling back against the wall.

And they were not the last.

As our children scattered, a few to the chambers beyond where rudimentary cells held the ashes of our enemies, and a few to range themselves before us like a shield wall, the invaders poured in. They overwhelmed us with their battering, with their screams and with their demands, the cries from their minds even louder than those from their mouths.

Give her back, they demanded. *She does not belong to you.*

We blinked down at them, so puny and small compared to our greatness. They were nothing compared to us. We laughed and enjoyed the way their pale faces blanched. These mutts were so silly, so beneath us. It shamed us that they were our creations—the gift of our powers was wasted on such puny beings.

You are mistaken, a voice whispered in our mind. *I am part of you, part of us. Those humans, vampires, are brave and precious and they'll do anything for love.*

You know them? The Master snarled with distaste.

We both know them.

"Master," David's voice, strong and sure called out to us and we turned our gaze to consider him. He did not bow down before us. "We have reason to believe that Minnie Kim, my daughter, our sister and friend, lives. We have come to demand that you release her to us."

We splintered. The Master laughed.

I tried to pull away.

We laughed again.

"Who are you to demand anything of us," we said.

David faltered and searched our face, but we are one, and he cannot understand. Cannot grasp how great we have become. David set his sword on the ground and took a step closer, his hands raised and open. "Because I am your son, and she is my daughter. It is a father's responsibility to protect his children, to love them."

"Love!" We bellowed, but while the Master jeered, I pulled away.

Love, I say.

"What do you know of love?" the Master asked.

I've told you, I said. I've told you so many times. Why can't you understand?

David bows his head, and when he speaks again, it's in a low, soft tone. "I don't know everything there is to know about love. But I do know love is something that cannot be forced. Cannot be demanded. Cannot be created out of nothing."

The Master tugged on my awareness, as if to disprove David's words, but I didn't give in to him.

"I didn't love my first children—not at first. I didn't know them. I only knew that they were hurt and dying, and I felt something in them. Something that made me believe they needed what I could give them. And I wanted them because I was lonely and afraid of the long life you had given me.

"I came to love them. To admire them. To respect them for the people they were and who they were striving to be. And, in time, I believe they came to love me."

Diana stepped forward, and we noticed that Manuella had also come.

"Love is unselfish, Master," Manuella said.

"It is kind," Diana added. "And patient. None of us are perfect, but we're trying. And Minnie has reminded us of all that we'd forgotten about love. She is the best of us. The best of *vampire* and *humanity*."

We regarded Diana, an unfamiliar pain squeezing our chest. We saw Fearghus and Siobhan, those wild Celts David had picked up so long ago. And Sang and his offspring, Chan-ri. Our gaze fell on others too, and while the Master questioned who they were, I tore myself away.

"Master Yi?" I asked in my own voice. Everyone jumped, but my attention was focused on the two men who stood apart. "And Junu! What are you doing here? You shouldn't have come. It's too dangerous!"

Master Yi raised his chin a fraction and met our eyes, completely unfazed by a girl's voice from the lips of a monster. He scoffed. "Nothing is too dangerous when it comes to the people you love. Or else what is life for? What is love for but to motivate us to do and be our best? I love you. I love young Junu here." He half-turned to acknowledge Junu, whose grim expression hadn't changed. "What value would my love have, if I was not willing to sacrifice all that I had to protect it?"

I opened my mouth to respond, but the Master yanked me back so we were one once more.

We were dimly aware of the small army of vampires and humans lifting their weapons, but it was nothing next to the rage and turmoil raging within us. We were furious, incensed that anyone should dare tell us the meaning of love. That anyone should wish to divide us when we were perfected together.

We knew love. We loved each other.

No one else could understand.

Council meetings must consist of a quorum: two-thirds or greater of the current Council members. Judgements made by a quorum must be unanimous in order to stand.

All judgements made by a quorum, or the American Council, will be upheld by the General Council.

All judgements are final.

The Council of Vampires has ruled our kind for millennia. Our Grand Sire presides today just as he has since the beginning. If grievances between Council members occur, he may be called upon to exercise judgement. This must not be done for inconsequential matters. To do so would bring dire consequences.

From what Demitri has said, I can't imagine the Master doing this. Unless the "dire consequences" are just to throw people into the cave with him!

CHAPTER
Twenty-Three

WE ROSE HIGHER AND SPREAD OUR ARMS WIDE, OUR *swarga* rising with us to shroud our body. "She is not yours to love!" We—*the Master*—bellowed. I struggled to find myself, but was viciously yanked back, once again fused with the whole.

We stalked forward, allowing our *swarga* to expand until it brushed over every one of the puny, meaningless creatures. "She is mine." Our voice was the voice of thunder. Of the wild crash of the sea. Of mountains breaking asunder.

The cavern trembled, then groaned as many tiny fissures broke through and traveled across the floor, the walls, the ceiling. The invaders' faces crumpled with fear, their little bodies flinching away from the walls as they broke, from the stones, large and small, that fell.

We laughed at their fear and sent our *swarga* into the cracks to widen them, to invite the failure of this place. We could go elsewhere. Losing this horrid place would be worth seeing David and his get realize their attempt to dethrone me had not only failed, but caused the end of their meaningless little lives.

We grew, fueled by anger and rage until our head brushed the ceiling and our *swarga* reached everywhere, touched everyone.

They cried out. Begged for their lives. Begged for Minnie's life. But we laughed in their faces. We rejoiced in their suffering.

No! I screamed. *This isn't right! We don't want to hurt them!*

I fought the Master, but his presence surrounded me, encased me, and there was no escape. My thoughts were rarely my own. My—

The Master roared and swallowed me once more.

"This ends," he seethed. "This ends with the death of all of you. There is only one love. There is only one that I need. I need none of you." With a thrust of power, he sent everything—rock, people, bodies—forward, where the force hit some sort of barrier before the concussion sent the material inward.

Water rushed in through the stone at our feet and we rose above it, not limited to standing on our feet like these creatures. One of the invaders slipped, their foot catching in a crack, then fell. The sea swept away their cries before we were forced to endure them. We were not so lucky with others of them. Rocks fell, pelting these children and causing them to flee with their arms over their heads.

They tried to escape, but there would be no such release for them.

We thrust forward with our power, bidding the rocks to collapse the entrance and box them in. Our laughter rang above the crash and tumult and we reveled in the cries of our enemies.

Except...

Except.

Finding my own self this time was like fighting to the surface of the water while your ankle's tied to a cement block. During a hurricane. Or a tsunami.

The Master thrashed against me, trying to hold me down, clawing at me, choking me.

But I would not be held down.

These were my friends. My family.

Someone had slipped beneath the water—who was that? Had they survived? I looked around wildly—where were they?

Bodies lay everywhere—the walls of corpses that had built up over the years had toppled, until that was all I saw. Bodies bobbed in the water, crushed beneath rocks. So many, but were any of them alive?

You are mine! The Master roared as he fell upon my mind and tried to push me down. *You gave yourself to me in exchange for letting those others go. I gave you what you wanted and now we are one.*

We aren't one! I shouted back at him. *I came with you so I could teach you about love. So you could learn how to love your children. But you haven't even tried! You've pushed them all away!*

He laughed, tearing his claws through my spirit, tearing away my soul. *You are a child. You never had the power. I have it. I've always had it all. I am the power. You are a diversion. Nothing more.*

He crushed me, his dark presence filling me, suffocating me, tearing me apart.

I struggled, fought back…

Then…

I couldn't hold on.

The Master cackled, whispering how naïve I had been, how childish to think I could have had anything at all to teach him. He never intended to learn from me, he'd only wanted what he could take from me. My companionship, my gifts, my love.

But his understanding of love was so twisted and wrong. I thought I'd been making a difference, but now…How could I have been so wrong?

I knew my love for Philo was real. I knew he loved me.

And David had called me his daughter. He'd come for me—they'd all come for me.

Because they loved me.

And now they were dying.

For me.

And…

And I couldn't let them.

But what could I do? The Master's mental powers were so beyond my own, and even if I did have a chance, it was too late now. Far too late.

Wasn't it?

From the shadows, a figure stumbled forward. Even though he was covered in dust, there was no mistaking Fearghus's hulking form and long red beard. "Now see here, ya right ba—" A tendril of the Master's *swarga* whipped out and yanked on Fearghus's ankle, sending the big man hard onto his back. I winced, imagining how that must've hurt with all the rock and debris on the ground. The Master laughed and bile rose in my throat.

But Fearghus struggled back to his feet and faced us again. "Ya cannae keep her, Lord. She's just a wee girl. She needs her family."

The Master leaned down and down, until his face—our face—was nearly nose-to-nose with Fearghus. "Are we not all family?" he asked in a sibilant, too-sweet voice. I felt his intentions rise within him, and horror made me momentarily numb.

"Aye, Master. But she's just a wee girl—"

Fury built within him, washing over me like a vile wave, drowning me in his putrid emotions. His twisted, nonsensical rationales.

Fearghus! I tried, but the Master refused to let me speak. But for just a moment, I think Fearghus saw me in the Master's eyes because his mouth dropped open in horror, and his eyes grew wide.

"Min—"

The *swarga* engulfed my friend, my brother, drawing him close within our embrace, then we *drew* the life out of him.

My heart, my mind, imploded with fury and pain.

With all the will I could muster, I pushed aside my pain. I needed to think more clearly. To be rational and sane. To be the opposite of the Master.

I didn't know how it had been done, but he'd somehow *absorbed* me, body, mind and spirit—but I was still here. For this moment in time at least, I was still here.

I knew there was no rescuing me, and I couldn't risk my family any longer. This had to stop.

I might not be as strong as him. I might not have a clue what I was doing. I might not stand a chance.

But I had to try.

The Master wasn't capable of love as we humans loved, but I was. I let that love fuel me now, let it build me up, let it strengthen and inspire me.

I would not stand by as the Master destroyed everyone I loved.

And even if I couldn't stop him from spending another eternity destroying love and life on Earth, I would at least go out having proved myself faithful to those who deserved it.

Once I had drawn all that I could into the center of my mind—every touch, every kiss from Philo, every smile and laugh from Junu, every hug and smile from Stacey, all of it and more—I thrust it outward in every direction. I shoved it with all my force of will, determined to tear down the wall that protected the Master's mind.

At first, I thought it hadn't worked. The Master didn't even react. He dropped Fearghus's broken body at his feet as David approached. I wanted to warn him away, but I couldn't divide my attention. Not now.

Instead, I caught the rebounding wave of my power and shoved again against the Master's barriers.

They cracked beneath my onslaught.

I needed to get inside. I needed to end his rule of tyranny and terror.

I pushed and pushed again.

And then I felt another presence, just before I was about to give in and give up.

I am here, Hanjo said, and I could have sworn I saw him standing by my side, both hands pressed against the enormous barrier that was the Master's essence.

Renewed by my friend's presence, I pushed harder.

The wall began to collapse, but it wasn't enough. Not nearly enough.

And then someone else joined us—David. And then Thor and Master Yi.

Love added to our combined power and intention as we beat against the Master's mind.

Together, we brought his walls down.

And our own battle began.

We scattered, throwing ourselves against the Master's will in whatever way came natural to us, in whatever way we could. I heard him roar in frustration or pain, and felt his body list to one side.

You cannot defeat me, he roared inside his mind. The pressure of it, the power, drove me to my knees, yet still I pressed on. *I am far too powerful for you, for any of you!*

But together we are more, I hissed before a blast blew outward from the core of his mind, driving me back and back, and I felt Master Yi's and then David's presence wink out.

They aren't dead, I told myself. *They can't be dead. They've only been shoved out of his mind.*

Hanjo, Thor and I redoubled our efforts.

The Master fell to his knees.

The battle went on and on and on until I had no sense of anyone else with me. Until every ounce of my energy had been spilled on the battleground of my mind.

I found myself standing in a vast cavern, cold seeping into me through my bare feet, through my body, and through my very soul until my internal landscape was utterly frozen and barren. I stood in that unknown, yet somehow familiar environment for a long, long while.

Eventually, a being appeared from the shadows and walked toward me.

Fear rushed through me, but I resisted the urge to recoil. The Master stood before me, and I refused to cower.

He was just as tall here as in reality, but he wore no *swarga*, drew no shadows about him. His skin was gray and pebbled, stretched tight over a skeletal frame that seemed too large. His joints were exaggerated, making him appear a little like a gangly teenager. Those over-large joints allowed his limbs to move in almost every direction.

His hands, too, were overlarge, as were his feet, and from his shoulder joints and hip joints other appendages hung. He had no visible sex, and his legs, while long, were not quite as long as his torso. My gaze swung upward to his blood-red eyes that saw so much more in the darkness than I could, even with his blood running through my veins. He had no lips, but I thought he smiled at me with those long thin teeth.

He lifted his hands in an elegant, smooth gesture. "And so it is just you and I."

He was right, I realized. Thor and Hanjo were gone. I wondered what he had done to expel them, since surely Hanjo was a match for him, but I didn't let my curiosity or fear show on my face. I was just so tired.

"Despite all your talk of love and family, you have turned against me. As fickle and counterfeit as any human I have ever known."

He flicked his wrist as if to dismiss me before turning away.

I lunged forward and grabbed his wrist. "Wait." He turned to face me again, his brow crinkled in the way I associated with the raising of one eyebrow, though he had none. "I didn't lie," I told him. "Everything I said was true.

"I was faithful, while you—" I dropped his wrist in disgust, "you are not capable of love. You don't receive it and you cannot give it. You call it love, what you felt for your family, for the partners you were to bond with— but it's not. It wasn't. It was ownership. Command over another being." I shrugged. "That's not love.

"Anyone can own a thing. Anyone can command a thing. Like a dog. Or a cat. Or a snake." I watched with satisfaction as he curled his lip. "Anyone can command a lesser being. But to gain the respect, admiration and love of an equal? That takes something you just don't have.

"That takes courage and faith." I crossed my arms over my chest and sneered at him. "You don't have either of those things. And you never will. You never can. Because you are not my equal."

He was before me in an instant, so close our bodies touched. He gripped my face in his hands, so large they practically wrapped around my whole skull. Tilting my head at an uncomfortable angle he peered down at me and into my soul. "You are *nothing* to me. You are the dirt beneath my feet. I will devour you until there is nothing of you left. Nothing left at all."

I shut my eyes as he bent his head toward me. I didn't need to watch his jaw dislocating and his mouth opening impossibly wide to know what he planned to do. He was going to devour me—just like he said.

But I had no intentions of going down without taking him with me.

OTHER SUPERNATURAL CREATURES

At the time of this printing, the Council does not feel it is appropriate to publish information about other magical creatures as they have not yet been revealed to humans. However, we feel it is important for you, the young vampire, to know that as a supernatural being, you are not alone in this world. As more information is released on this

I don't think this info should even be in this book. Even saying what they did it puts other SUPs in a bad situation. IDK. So much will depend on this "unmasking" that's going on. But I think if a species wants to stay hidden — they should be able to.

topic, we will update this edition.

Please also check out our eBook,

which will receive updates more

often.

Obviously, the world isn't quite ready to know.

Generally, different magical species
do not get along well together.
Should you meet one, despite how
charming they may initially seem, it
is best to keep your distance.
Vampires are not the only predators
in this world.

How do you know when you've met another magical? How do you know when to keep your distance?? Sheesh.

Should you chance to meet another
magical creature, be wary. You

CHAPTER
TWENTY-FOUR

THIS TIME, INSTEAD OF PUSHING AGAINST HIM, I FILLED my heart and mind with the ones I loved. As I called the memories to me, they became real and alive, and I welcomed them, filling each memory with life and light and love. My mind held them all, however small and trivial.

I stand on the top of the colorful play structure, my hands on my hips in my Wonder Woman pose. With a raised fist I pump the air and proclaim, "I'm the queen of all the land!"

"Hey! You can't be queen. I am!" Stacey, the girl from across the street climbs out of the tube that's supposed to be a slide. She puts her fists on her hips just like me and shouts, much louder than I did, "I'm the

queen of the castle and all the land, as far as my eye can see!" She's wearing a bright yellow cape over her white T-shirt and it flows dramatically out behind her. I fervently wish I had a cape like that.

I frown at her.

She smiles at me.

"Okay," she says, putting her arm around my waist. Then she lifts her other arm and faces outward. "We are the queens of the castle and all the land!"

I grin, amazed at her kindness, at her brilliance and awesomeness. Then I pump my own fist, and shout, "We are both the queens of the castle!"

"Well done, Minnie!" Mr. Pike says. He even stands and claps. "Well done, indeed." He turns and faces the other kids at drama camp and announces, "We have found our Lucy!" I grin so wide, so proud, even as Stacey folds her arms and pouts. I know she'll get over it because she loves me, and in that moment I feel so full of love for myself that I jump up and down and all around, squealing with delight. It isn't even a full minute before Stacey is rushing toward me and throwing her arms around me, shouting for joy right along with me.

"Hey," a guy says as I shut my locker door and find him leaning against the one next to mine. I nearly jump out of my skin because I'd been so lost in thoughts about *my upcoming math test. Besides, every nerdy girl knows the football quarterback does not notice her—especially not with a few of his buddies lingering nearby.*

I stammer out a hello, sure that something terrible is about to happen. But he sticks out his hand and says, "I'm Daniel. You're Minnie, right? Minnie Kim?"

My gaze flickers toward the two other boys who are quietly snickering behind Daniel's back. Daniel glances at them. "Hey, I'll meet you guys in the locker room, 'k?" They glance between him and me and I can see they have no more idea why he wants to talk to me than I do. Daniel's a junior, I think, and I'm just a freshman.

"Never mind them," he says with a smile that warms me through and through. "Mr. Arthur said you might be able to help me with math."

I nearly roll my eyes. I'm busy. Beyond busy. The last thing I need is to tutor some jock who's not even gonna try to do a good job. And I sure as heck wasn't gonna do his homework for him.

He must see my reaction on my face, though I'm sure I haven't given anything away—I am a pretty darn good actress, after all—because he leans forward a little and puts his hand on my shoulder. "I swear I'll do the work. I want to learn it—and not just so I can play on the team."

I fold my arms and look up at him, considering. "Seriously?"

"Seriously," he says. "Dead serious. I want to get better at math. I want to be good at math. And Mr. Arthur says you're the best."

I quirk a smile. I am the best, but it would probably be too snooty of me to agree.

My heart filled as I remembered my love for my friends and their love for me. I remembered my parents, and the times my dad went running with me in the morning to help my brain be alert and ready to learn. I remembered Junu, Hanjo and my friendship with Master Yi. I never expected to find either one of them on my trip to Seoul and now I couldn't imagine my life without them.

I remember Philo, putting on the latest BTS album, which is filled entirely with love songs. He turns off the light before he joins me on his soft love seat, the room lighting up with the soft, warm glow of candlelight. As he pulls me into his embrace, my head pressed against his wide, solid chest, I think how he makes me feel like the room—warm, and glowing. This is what love feels like, I think, just before Philo tells me he loves me.

And I glowed then, so full of all the love I'd been given. I was still so young, yet I was positive I had more love in my life than most people felt in a lifetime. It's so real, so profound and huge, that I couldn't contain it, couldn't hold it in a moment longer, even if I tried.

But I didn't want to try. Whatever happened next, I knew it had to be done with all this love shining forth from my heart.

And so I let myself shine. Let the love flow in and out, over and through—not only myself, but the Master as well.

I no longer had any sense of him, or myself, as physical beings. I only knew that his darkness surrounded me. I suspected he really had devoured me, and that there was nothing of my *self* left at all, but I could be okay with that, so long as I could stop him from doing the same to my loved ones.

I heard him growl—a low rumbling sound that built and built until it was a keening cry that made my cells quake and my grasp on my own emotions splinter. And so, I let go.

I felt myself scatter, the *me* of me fly into a thousand pieces in the vast darkness of the Master's mind. It reminded me of what Master Yi had taught me about the universe and my role in it. I felt as if I were the stars and the Master the blackest night. I thought of my ancestors, the other lights in the sky, and called upon them to help me.

I knew that—freely given and received—love was the manna that could heal a person, a family, a generation forever and ever.

I let go of my resentment of my parents for not accepting me as I am, and instead focused on the love they'd had for me when they counted me as their daughter.

I let go of my resentment of Tim and Brandon for my reMaking. I no longer felt as if something had been taken, because the reality was that I had been given the greatest gift. Being a vampire did not mean I needed to remove myself from my humanity—being a vampire meant I needed my humanity now more than ever.

The Master had no such grounding. His world, his *self*, required sacrifice and humility in order to build themselves up beyond their peers. There were no friends, no loves, nothing of true value because of their constant struggle to be better than the other.

At the end, just as I felt the last of my awareness fading, I imagined the familiar warmth of Philo's hand in mine. *I'm here,* he seemed to say. Overwhelmed by joy and gratitude that I should have this sweet thought for my last, I gave myself all away.

should never make assumptions based on myth or speculation. Instead, invite them to join you in conversation as a way to get to know them and to avoid alienating them due to misinformation. You are now one of the elites and we are glad to have you with us

Well this pretty much goes for everyone! Straight / Gay, Black / White. Everyone's always jumping to conclusions or listening to others' opinions instead of making their own.

Vampires are not the only magical creatures on Earth, but we are the only ones who have revealed ourselves to the humans. For this reason, we felt it unwise to do more than mention them in this

49

volume. If you have questions, you know what to do. Ask your sire!

Check, check & check!

CHAPTER
TWENTY-FIVE

A SEA-SCENTED BREEZE BLEW OVER MY SKIN, BRINGING with it the fresh, sharp scent of burning wood and sap. The fire bathed my side with warmth, while my other side was warmed by a body curled against me. My brow furrowed as I opened my eyes. The vast night sky above me, with its brilliant display of stars didn't surprise me, but everything else did.

People sat nearby, gathered around a moderate fire burning in the center of the tableau. Master Yi and Junu, David, and others of my family—I thought I even glimpsed Matteo's bright hair which made me think the dark figure tucked to his side was Bianca. So many people I cared about, that the ones missing stood out in stark relief. Fearghus. *Philo*. If this was my next life, it was awfully strange. I had always believed I'd be reborn as a baby—or some other creature if I had not earned life as a human. Maybe none of that was possible when you died a vampire. Hadn't thought of that, before. I should have asked Master Yi while I still had the chance.

Still, if this was the afterlife the universe had gifted me, then I wasn't going to complain, not when just about everyone I loved was represented here. Master Yi had told me that while the universe demanded much of us, it was not unkind, not without its mercies. I hadn't exactly understood what he meant by that but now, as I sighed and let myself relax into this beautiful surreal moment, I thought I did. I just hoped I'd earned it by doing some good with the last moments of my life.

I knew I'd have to come to terms with it all at some point. Even if I was gifted this little moment in the middle of nowhere, a small spot created by the gods or some other great being who took mercy upon my soul, it made sense that I'd have to face what I had lost—*who* I had lost. I squeezed my eyes shut, hoping to stay in the peace of the moment a while longer.

The person behind me stirred. I'd forgotten they were there, but as soon as I felt his fingers combing through my hair, I knew. "Minnie Kim." Philo's voice near my ear made me shiver. "I know you're awake."

"Mmm." I rolled toward him and snuggled closer. My relief and gratitude that he was here, that I'd have a chance to say goodbye to him, was so great that my chest constricted, and I had to fight the flow of tears. Maybe I could make the moment last if I just didn't open my eyes.

His chuckle hummed through his body and into mine and I realized that even though I'd never believed in heaven the way Christians did, I believed in it now. *This.* This was *my* heaven.

The tips of his fingers grazed my neck as he drew my hair away, like he always did. He kissed my neck and longing, so profound and deep, rushed through me.

Reluctantly, I opened my eyes and said, "Philo, I—" But my words died in my mouth. The night was dark and the shadows cast by the firelight were deep, but I could still see.

He watched me, his fingertips lightly resting on my cheek, his bright blue eyes as familiar to me as my own—but his short hair was gray, and his skin clung tightly to every bone in his face. His lips, more plump than they had a right to be in that thin, drawn face, quirked up on one side in my favorite smile.

Shouldn't he look well and whole, then?

"I know I still do not look quite like myself." Sudden doubt and shame shadowed his eyes. "I-I hope you can bear with me as I heal. I have improved a great deal over the past two months, but I still have a long way to go." He leaned in and kissed my nose. He smelled like himself and I drank him in. "Especially with you by my side."

"But…" I searched his eyes, then rolled onto my back and looked up at the sky, then turned my head to the people who sat around the fire, and beyond them to the vast expanse I knew was the Mediterranean Sea. Dread dropped into my stomach like oily stones and I suddenly rolled over and was sick into the dirt beside me.

Philo rubbed circles on my back, while the others stood and one figure came near. He crouched down in front of me and I knew who it was just from his shoes—even though the fine Italian leather was scuffed and muddy.

"Minnie," David said in a tone so gentle the tears I'd been holding back sprang to my eyes. He stroked my cheek and smiled, his eyes wide with…what? I thought wonder, but why would he look at me like that? "I'm so glad you are all right, my child. You *are* all right, aren't you?"

Slowly, I nodded. I felt fine, but…

I struggled to sit up and both David and Philo helped me. I looked around the fire, at all the faces staring back at me, as the pieces fell into place. "This isn't heaven, then?"

Chuckles sounded out from the darkness and even David smiled into my eyes. "You did it, my dear one." He shook his head and this time I knew the gleam in his eyes was wonder. "You saved yourself, and all of us." He gestured toward the now-silent group.

Philo tightened his arms around me and I leaned against him. He might still be thin, but he still felt like my Philo.

"The Master?" My voice came out scratchy and hoarse, as if I'd been screaming, screaming, screaming—which, I supposed, I had.

David glanced over his shoulder to the others, who had pressed nearer. I couldn't bear to meet their gazes. I'd failed them. Let them all down. And now the Master would have even more reason to punish them, if only to bring me pain.

David shrugged his shoulders slightly. "He's gone."

I frowned. That didn't seem quite right. The Master wasn't gone. I could still feel him . . .

Philo's arms tightened around me. "You are here. I can feel your confusion, but whatever you did to destroy him, he is gone and you remain. I'm sure of it," he whispered, his warm breath tickling my ear.

David gripped my hand. "He's right, Minnie. I don't know how you did it, but you defeated him. The Master is gone."

The words washed over and through me, while the truth whispered from somewhere inside me. I needed time to think. To discover for myself why I felt so different inside.

Siobhan dropped to her knees next to David and grinned at me, but it didn't quite reach her eyes. "Hey,

Squirt," she said. "Nice of you ta join us." Her eyes sparked then with genuine love, before winking out again. Then I remembered. *Fearghus*.

I lunged forward, throwing my arms around her neck. "I'm so sorry," I cried against her neck. "I'm so, so sorry."

She squeezed me tight and held me a long time. "It was a good death," she finally said, her voice breaking with her own tears. "He made himself—and me—proud. Now he'll be with his Mary and wee bairn. He'll be glad for it, I'm sure." She patted my back in that sort of awkward, *I'm ready for you to let go now* way I was all-too familiar with since it was usually my move.

I withdrew from Siobhan and somehow, Philo knew that his arms were the only ones I could stand to be in for an extended period of time and right then I needed his embrace more than ever. He was right there to wrap his arm around me and draw me to his side. I pressed my ear to the soft sweater he wore, and his arms wrapped around me in a way that was so familiar and so completely his.

For a long time, I sat there, half on my knees, half lying in Philo's arms. The rest of my loved ones had gathered near—including Diana, who'd survived her fall into the ocean. They all encircled us now, instead of the fire. I couldn't feel its warmth anymore, but I felt theirs and it was more than enough.

Finally, I thought I ought to face the music, so I took a deep breath and straightened, leaving the warmth of

Philo's embrace. Sitting cross-legged on the soft sleeping bag I'd been lying on, I called upon all the courage I could muster, and lifted my eyes. I forced myself to meet each gaze, and to give and accept their smiles. Then I faced David. "Tell me what happened."

And he did.

APPENDIX A
IMPORTANT TERMS

Blood Lust: The overwhelming need for human blood directly from the source. Particularly common among young vampires. *Another reason not to go back to school. There should be a specific waiting period.*

Blood Hunger: A vampire's state of frenzied anger and rage.

Blood Rage: A vampire's overwhelming need to feed from a human.

Maker: The vampire who makes another vampire.

reMaking | reMade: The act of making a vampire.

Then again, I know I would have hated it & would have pushed back. It might feel like a parental thing where you just CAN'T take their advice, ya know?

APPENDIX B
VAMPIRE GIFTS

Vita Ambulare (mind-walker)
Frequency — rare
The mind-walker is capable of transporting his presence and mentally, sometimes even physically, influencing another person's mind.

This feels so childish — even to me!

Memoriae Ambulare (memory-walker)
Frequency — moderate
A vampire who can view another being's memories for their point of view.

CHAPTER
TWENTY-SIX

HANJO KEPT THE FIRE BURNING BRIGHT THROUGH THE night, even though there was little wood to be had. It still boggled my mind to see him in this human-like form. Every now and then I'd catch his luminescent purple gaze from across the fire and he'd grin at me— his teeth too white, his grin too wide to be strictly human. I still wasn't sure whether to be awed or frightened. Turned out I was far too tired to be frightened.

Though David told the story, others chimed in from time to time to explain their part, or correct David's retelling—though that was really just Hanjo.

It seemed that Hanjo hadn't left me when I entered the cave that very first time, even though I couldn't remember him being with me. Apparently, he'd bonded with me in some sort of way—he started to explain it, but the story went on and on and David ended up redirecting him, and I couldn't remember any of what he'd said—and when I approached the Master's lair, he'd sensed a presence almost as powerful as his own. That's when he contacted me. I remembered that part.

But when the Master chased David, Philo and I down and caused the accident, and I…That part was blurry for me, and from the way Philo's arms trembled as they tightened around me, I figured it was just as well I couldn't really remember. But that was the moment Hanjo's connection with me was severed. As he explained it, he knew I was still alive somehow, but it was as if my mind had been shut off. He actually flew to Italy, finding shelter in one of the other sea caves that dotted the coast, expecting me to return to his awareness, but when I still hadn't many days later—he couldn't be sure how long since dragons don't really keep track of human time—he flew home and got in touch with Master Yi.

Meanwhile, David got Philo home and began plans for rescuing me. It took longer than expected because Philo wanted to be there, but he needed to heal at least to a point where his survival was assured. And when Siobhan told Veyo what had happened, he and Jonah wanted to be included as well. Apparently Stacey even got wind of it—Veyo didn't fess up, but he was a terrible liar and really, who else could it have been?—and was only restrained from joining in with the rescue party after getting a talking-to from her mom. I was on strict orders to call her as soon as we were done talking, no matter the time. Veyo had already texted her to let her know they had me, but she'd kill me for sure if I didn't call her soon.

And that wasn't all. When a month or so had passed, Bianca contacted Matteo—after I left, they broke up because he didn't want to risk her safety and she didn't want to be a vampire. She wondered if he knew anything about what had happened to me. Though I hadn't promised I would see her again, she'd been hurt that I never returned her call and texts. Matteo hadn't been worried—until he felt his connection to Demitri sever. He'd hoped that I was okay, but he hadn't wanted to say anything to Bianca. When she reached out to him, though, he found David's number and called him.

Hanjo, Master Yi, and of course Junu—because Master Yi felt he had a right to know what was going on—also contacted David. And so the rescue efforts began.

As I listened to the story, I'm sure I had my mouth hanging open the whole time. I know I shook my head in disbelief and amazement practically constantly. The story, their heroics—it was almost too much to bear.

Almost, but not quite.

I was overwhelmed by their love for me. That so many would love me enough to sacrifice their lives for me. It would take me many lifetimes to adequately thank them all.

We had a long moment of silence to mark Fearghus's passing, but the pain was still too fresh for us to speak of him just then. And with their story done, everyone wanted to hear mine.

I'd known it would come. Knew I owed them some sort of explanation of what had happened. From their perspective, they thought the Master had me locked up somewhere. Or that he used a kind of magic that let him manifest me, then hide me away. They were confused and wanted answers.

But I needed time to think. Time to process and take measure of just what to say to them. I made the excuse of wanting to call Stacey before more time passed, and walked away from the group. I meandered along the ragged plateau, taking care not to get too close to the edge, for at least ten minutes, before I stopped and stared out at the sea, which was a dark mass of undulating waves illuminated only by the flicker of stars and the wedge of a waning moon.

They wanted to know what had happened to me, but I still wasn't entirely sure even I knew.

I know I gave myself to the Master, thinking that we had a moment there that we'd connected, that we'd understood one another. I thought maybe he would take me to his den, and maybe, after a little while, he'd come to understand humans better and want to care for his children better.

Instead…

My mind kind of fritzed when I tried to think of it. Because I *couldn't* think about it. The memory was there, but it was fuzzy and slippery. All I knew was that the Master had wrapped his weird cloak around me and held me tight. And then…

I frowned into the darkness. It just didn't make sense. All my memories from that point weren't just my own, they were the Master's, too. And what should have been his private thoughts and feelings, I remembered now as mine.

I took in a long, slow breath, held it for ten seconds, then expelled it in a noisy *whoosh. Just do it, Minnie. Just say it*. With my arms wrapped tightly around my middle, I closed my eyes and fought down the bile that churned restlessly in my gut.

He'd taken me into himself.

Literally.

"That's how he did it," I told the quiet night, the constant push and pull of the tide. "That's how his species marry. How they breed. They literally become one being until they're ready to become parents. When they're ready, they create a third being within their oneness, and then they separate to become three." My whole body shivered violently. Had the Master thought I was his mate?

Had he thought we would create a new life together?

"Gah," I groaned. *Gross*.

At least I knew we hadn't created a new life. *Thank goodness*.

What I was less sure of, though, was myself.

I mean, I was still me. Totally.

But I was also something else. And I wasn't the only one who knew it, either. David and Thor looked at me strangely, and I was more acutely aware of them and Philo than I'd ever been before. I knew that all I had to do was turn my attention to them, and I'd know their minds without ever having to mind walk. I'd know them in a different way than I ever could before.

And it wasn't just that, either. I felt…larger. Felt my reach extend far beyond my little family. Somehow, I was aware of dozens of other vampires. Hundreds, even.

And while I didn't feel them in the same way I felt David, Thor, and Philo, even my own family had been casting questioning gazes at me tonight that went beyond just an unknowing of what had happened to me. It was like they no longer knew *me*. Or were afraid they no longer knew me.

And I thought I knew why.

As I gazed sightlessly out toward the ocean, I peered into myself. The Master and I had been one for a long time. Two months, I guess, according to my rescuers. There were moments I remembered that were mine alone and not at all the Master's, but mostly every thought, every action had belonged to *us*. And the connection hadn't only been mental.

When he'd absorbed me into his self, he had taken on the responsibility of my life, nourishing me with his own body. His own blood.

And when I'd stepped into his mind in an effort to destroy him, I'd only partially succeeded.

The Master as we knew him was gone. He'd never return. I felt sure of that. In the way that was only possible with his species, I had literally absorbed his body into my own.

But I hadn't known anything of his kind and how they worked. If I had, maybe I would have or could have done things differently. But I hadn't known.

Maybe if I'd taken the time to know him better, if I'd tried to understand his people's way better…

Well. I supposed I knew now.

As easy as thought, I let the *swarga* unfurl from my body, letting it stretch and expand, a thing almost alive. A thing that had been his, that was now entirely my own.

As were his gifts, his power, and much of his knowledge.

Just as his children were now my own.

Because in his culture, should a couple fail to bond, one will absorb the other in order to break the connection. After that, they're free to seek another partner, but they will forever be changed by the assimilation of their former bond-mate.

With a gentle, experimental tug, I tested the many connections tethered to my core, and felt their responses. Because *I* was their master now.

Mens Moderator (mind-controller)

Frequency: rare

A vampire who can control another being through their mind.

Imperium Protestate (ruler of another)

Frequency: extremely rare

A vampire who can control not only your mind, but your body as well. Extremely rare.

Note: Be careful of mind-work. You may inadvertently create a bond that is very difficult to break.

Well this is scary. ":"
How do you practice without creating that bond?
I worried about it all the time with Thor.
* It would be awesome if there was a school for vamps where you could have multiple teachers so you wouldn't get too close to anyone. Hogwarts FTW..

CHAPTER
TWENTY-SEVEN

About an hour later, I walked into our little camp. The sun was just rising, casting the cliffs and sea into shades of pale pinks and gentle purples. Everyone but Hanjo had been sleeping, but as soon as I rejoined them, the vampires woke.

They jumped to their feet, even Philo—though Manuella had to support him when he wobbled. They stared at me with wide, wary eyes.

"What?" I asked, glancing down at myself. I was gross and dirty, but I still had clothes on. I shuddered to think how long I'd been wearing these same clothes. *Ew.*

I looked back up, smiling, but the smile fell away at the expressions on their faces. I sighed. "None of you seemed to notice before."

And then my jaw began to tremble and my eyes welled with tears. David was there in an instant and I fell into his arms. "Shh," he murmured while I cried. "Shh."

"I don't want it. I don't want to be like him."

"I know," he said. "And you won't be. It'll be all right. You'll see."

As I cried, and David held me, I felt Philo slip his thin arms around us both. Then Siobhan was there, crying even harder than me. Jack's strong arms were next, and I realized I hadn't even known he was there. But as each new person joined in this weird hug with me at the middle, I marked them. I knew them. And in my heart, I thanked them.

"Well," drawled Thor from somewhere in the pile, "at least I won't dread a summons from the Master as much as I used to. It used to make me piss my pants."

We chuckled, our compressed bodies shaking together.

"When I was very young, he summoned me," Philo said. "I was so determined not to heed the call, that I got on a ship and sailed away. By the time I reached the New World, I was so sick I could not stand, and I had to get right onto a return vessel as soon as I disembarked. I felt better after three or four days, but I'd certainly learned my lesson. I never ignored a summons after that. But I agree with you, Thor." Several people chuckled because Thor and Philo never agreed on anything. "I imagine a summons from our new Master will not be nearly so painful." He kissed my cheek and whispered against my ear, "In fact, if she will allow it, I will never leave her side."

I closed my eyes and let my forehead fall against David's chest. A moment later, the hug began to melt away as people stepped back. I still stood in the center of them, and they still looked at me with unfamiliar expressions, but I no longer felt alienated like I had before. I snorted a laugh. *Alienated*.

"So," I said in my usual lame manner. "I guess you guys all know, now? I mean, I wasn't even positive myself until I went away for that little bit. And I really want to reassure you guys that while I have, um, absorbed him, for lack of a better word, he really is gone. I have his powers, his blood and the connections that go along with that, but I'm still me." I tried to make eye contact with each of them as I gestured my way through my little speech. I needed them to know that I was still me. "I'm just…Minnie 3.0, I guess."

Someone barked out a laugh and though I couldn't see him beyond the people standing around me, I recognized Veyo's voice, his laugh. It made me grin.

"And you do have that—" Philo said softly, gesturing to my body.

I looked down and at first didn't notice what he was referring to. And then I understood.

"Oh." I drew in the *swarga* until it sank beneath my skin. "Guess I'll have to work on controlling that."

"Wait," Thor said. "I always thought that was the Master's cloak. You weren't wearing it before, then you were, and now you're not. I don't understand."

I released the *swarga* and commanded it to take the form of a long evening gown. I held the skirt out with one arm. "It's a shield of sorts. Almost like clothing. But it's a part of the Master's species' mental capacity. It's called a *swarga*. It can operate independently too, if I allow it, but it will always seek to do my will. It's mine now. Totally mine. It came from the Master, like a gift, and now it's mine. It doesn't belong to him in any way, so you don't need to fear it."

I watched them and felt for their reactions, and while they were cautious, they seemed to accept what I said to be true and none of them feared *me*.

Thor stepped forward and took my hand, holding it as if he would kiss it. I stared into his pale gray eyes as he returned the gaze. I knew him now. Knew all his hopes, his wishes and dreams. "I knew I should have worked harder to make you love me. Now I'd be—" he cast a wary glance at Philo who scowled at him. His frown looked extra dark on his lean, drawn face. "Well, we'd have been quite the power couple."

I grinned up at him, feeling relaxed in his presence for the first time since I'd met him. His attention to me had always kind of creeped me out, even when I thought I liked him. Even though Philo was way older than Thor, and I felt totally okay being his girlfriend, Thor had always seemed more…dangerous or something. I mentally rolled my eyes. I could never let Philo know I thought that. Or Thor, for that matter. He'd view it as some kind of compliment.

Now I saw that he'd been honest with me all along. He had been a bit enamored with my innocence, but mostly he felt like he wasn't being utilized in the Council as he should, that he wasn't being recognized for his power and strength. He really had thought that if he paired up with me, my strength combined with his would be just the leg up he needed to do the things he wanted to do. Which weren't dark and nefarious but legitimate ways that vampires could co-exist in the human, post-Treaty world. I made a mental note to make time to speak with him soon.

While in Italy, I hadn't seen any sign of the supernatural unrest that had dominated my newsfeed at home, but I knew it hadn't gone away. The Master should have stepped up right away and set about creating order from the chaos the video of Veyo and I had caused. But of course, he'd never been that kind of leader.

I wondered if Thor or David, or anyone else for that matter, knew who had established the Councils. Or who had been responsible for the Treaty, or that stupid *Ultimate Guide*. My guess was they'd be shocked when they found out it certainly hadn't been the Master's doing. None of it had.

Thor kissed the back of my hand, lingering just a hair too long until I had to yank my hand away.

"Ew," I complained. But Thor grinned as he stepped back and winked. I could only shake my head at him.

Philo wrapped his arms around me possessively. It was just a show of manliness for Thor's sake, but I didn't care. His arms might not be as big and strong as they once were, but none of us had come out of this experience unscathed or unchanged. I was just so grateful he was here with me at all, and I never wanted to be without him again.

Plus, I had a lot to think about, like tracking down the real "head" of the Councils, and getting the *Guide* replaced as soon as possible. Who knew what other snakes I'd uncover once I set about putting the Master's house to rights.

My house now, I guess.

And it sure as heck wasn't gonna be in some ancient sea cave.

APPENDIX C
FAMOUS VAMPIRES

Note: Vampires currently living do not appear on this list, nor do those whose families' have refused to publicize their progenitor's status.

Alexander the Great
Boudicca
Charlemagne
Eleanor of Aquitane
Elizabeth the 1st
Elvis Presley
Emily Dickinson
Ernest Shackleton
Francis Drake
Plato
Ulysses S. Grant
Vlad III
William Shakespeare

CHAPTER
TWENTY-EIGHT

ON THE TARMAC OF A PRIVATE AIRSTRIP NOT FAR FROM Otranto, Master Yi hugged me tight in his arms and held me for a long, long moment. "I have faith in you, *naui jag-eun kkoch*. But do not forget you still need your *seogsa*."

I laughed, the sound muffled against his robe. "I won't." It was all I could do not to cry—at least his robe was black, so if I did happen to get some tears on it, they wouldn't be totally noticeable.

And then Junu had me in his arms, spinning me around before setting me on my feet and holding me at arm's length so he could peer down into my eyes. I hadn't had nearly enough time with him, and I didn't want to let him go.

Emotions swam in his eyes, and though he smiled, it was too broad, too tight to be wholly honest. But I smiled back at him, because I knew that's what he needed. He needed me to be strong for him, and that, at least, was something I could do.

"It's okay, *oppa*. I promise to do my best to stay the same."

He scoffed then pulled me into an almost too-tight hug. "Well, you were super annoying and bossy, so if you change a little, that'd be okay."

"Hey!" I shoved away and slugged his arm, because that's what he needed.

Passing by, Thor muttered, "Don't be too sure. Now that she's the new Master, she'll probably be even more bossy."

I glared at Thor's back before smiling at Junu and giving him another quick hug. As he walked away, I said, "I'll miss you, dummy."

He threw me a grin over his shoulder and waved, then let Master Yi put his arm around him and draw him toward the small plane David had ordered for them. They'd fly from here to Russia, where they'd board a commercial flight to take them the rest of the way home. Hanjo had offered to take them home himself, but neither of them were keen to take him up on it. I think Hanjo was secretly relieved, too.

Philo slipped his hand into mine and together we watched them board the plane, me waving wildly all the time, even though they only looked back at me once at the top of the stairs. Philo squeezed my hand. "We'll go see them. Often."

His use of "we" was like Cupid's arrow straight to my heart and I turned and threw my arms around him. He stumbled back and I immediately loosened my grip—he was still far too weak to support my weight.

"Sorry," I said sheepishly as I let go. I grinned up at him. "But you said, *we*."

His answering smile was radiant, warming me in all the cold and lonely places and I hugged him again—gentler and longer this time.

The rest of our entourage were already on board the larger private plane that bore the Aristos Industries logo on the side. Earlier, Matteo and Bianca had left on their long drive back home. I hadn't had a chance to ask about Freddy, but I figured it was probably better that way.

Philo and I walked toward the plane slowly, hand in hand, and each step brought me closer and closer to a sense of peace.

"Thank you," Philo said with a little tug on my hand.

"For what?" I looked up at him, smiling as I did. I was just so happy to be with him again. Even his gaunt appearance was dear to me. He just looked like Philo. It was still him I saw shining in his eyes.

He stopped, so I did too, each of us turning to face the other. "For coming to get me."

I snorted and rolled my eyes. Hey, I might have absorbed the essence of an ancient alien creature, but I was still me. Mostly. "As if I wouldn't." I pulled up short when I saw the dark expression on his face and the pain and regret that shone in his eyes.

"You shouldn't have done it." He shook his head as if he was still battling with the reality of it all. "It was so dangerous. Too dangerous. You could have died—you…you should have died."

I stepped closer to him, taking his other hand and giving them both a gentle squeeze. "I didn't, though. I'm right here. We made it."

He dropped my hands and cupped my face, moving so quickly I gasped a little when his warm palms enveloped me. His gaze on mine was so intense it stole my breath. "It was so dangerous, and I never wanted you to get hurt. I felt you coming, felt you near—those couple times I managed to reach out to you before I grew too weak, I never meant for you to come after me. I only wanted to say goodbye. To feel you with me one last time."

He bent his forehead to mine, and I closed my eyes. So much lay between us, but it didn't divide us, it strengthened us. But we were just human enough that the fear of how close we came to losing it all—to losing each other—still resonated painfully within us. I felt a tear, his tear, fall on my cheek.

"I know." My voice was low, choked by my own tears. "I love you." It was all I could manage to say, but my feelings were so much more than that. They filled me and overflowed from me and I grasped the front of his sweater and held it in my fists, needing to hold on, to hold on and on and never let go.

Philo pulled me to him in a crushing embrace and in his arms, with his beating heart beneath my cheek, I knew everything I felt, all that love, was felt by him, too.

"Oh, my Minnie Kim. I love you so."

I was dimly aware of the other plane taxiing down the runway away from us, but I didn't look up. It was only when Siobhan shouted at us from the door of our plane that we finally pulled apart. Philo's gaze, softer now, dove into my eyes as he ran the back of his knuckles along my jaw, while Siobhan swore at us in Gaelic.

In mute defiance of her pushiness, Philo leaned down to kiss me, and I leaned up to kiss him.

I know we'd kissed before that moment, but just then, that was the kiss I wanted to remember. That kiss wasn't just born of desperation, or a strange sort of elation. That kiss promised forever.

On board the plane, I found everyone waiting, steam billowing out from numerous mugs on the tables and the biggest bloody steaks I'd ever seen in front of the two werewolves. All conversation stopped when I joined them and I felt the tension, the worry, the anxiety, hanging in the air, mingling with the steam. Most of them were more than a little nervous about how their lives would change now that I was their Master.

"Wow," I said brightly. I needed them to know that despite the giant elephant in the room, I was still me. You know, in all the ways that matter most, anyway. "You really know how to travel in style."

David gave a deep bow, with a flourish and everything, that made me laugh. The others laughed too, and soon mugs were in hands and the tension fell away like a heavy coat on a hot summer's day.

"To Master Minnie, the greatest littlest master the world has ever known!" Veyo called, and we all laughed and clinked our mugs while Jack and a few others said, "Hear, hear."

"To Philo, the longest lasting!" Jack said that one, but it was mostly met with groans. I didn't get why it was groan-worthy, but I happily clinked my mug, anyway. Philo blushed, which was super cute and made me kiss him—to a new chorus of cheers and mug-clinking.

"To Minnie," David said, once the noise had died down. "The most remarkable young woman, who became the world's most remarkable vampire. We owe you our lives, and freely give our love and servitude." Then he bowed again, but it felt different this time.

The cabin fell silent as each of them, even the werewolves, bowed or lowered their heads toward me. I didn't know what to say, or what to do. I looked to Philo, who hadn't bowed, and found him watching me, a soft smile on his mouth and his eyes glittering. He gave me a short nod that seemed to say, *It's okay. You've got this. You've earned this.*

When David rose, the others followed. "To Minnie," he said again and lifted his mug into the air.

"To Minnie," the others said. Then we clinked our mugs and drank.

Shortly after, Philo led me toward the back of the plane and into a room that was small but comfy, including a double bed and a compact shower and washroom. There was a stack of clothes on the bed, folded neatly so the *drama llama* on the front of the shirt showed. I glanced down at myself and realized that the drama llama shirt I currently wore was beyond ruined.

"Why don't you get a shower," Philo said. "Then…sleep."

I stared at the bed, then at him.

"Is it all right if I sleep with you? I need to rest and, well…" He gestured to an IV pole standing next to the far side of the bed that I hadn't noticed until then.

"Oh!" My body practically jumped into motion, grabbing up my clothes and pressing them to my chest. "Of course! Totally okay!"

Shut up, Minnie!

Philo just grinned at me as I backed into the bathroom.

I shut the door and turned—and came face to face with the first reflection I'd seen of myself since…well, I honestly couldn't remember. Since before I went down to meet with the Master in his cave, at least.

I groaned. "Why didn't anyone tell me?" I called out to Philo.

His voice was faint, but I still heard his chuckle.

I was…a wreck. There just wasn't another word for it.

My hair lay heavy and listless around my face, highlighting my sunken cheeks and faded skin. I'd fed, sort of, while bonded with the Master, but obviously not enough, since my arms looked like sticks and my leggings hung like limp skin around my legs.

I turned on the shower, suddenly wanting to remove anything Master-ish that might still cling to me. I might have to live with the remnants of his spirit or whatever inside me, but I didn't ever want to smell that smell again. How had anyone managed to be close to me at all?

How in the world had Philo been able to snuggle me—to kiss me!—when I looked and smelled like this?

I stripped off my clothes as fast as I could, wishing I had a way to burn them right then and there, and stepped into the shower.

I scrubbed and soaped and soaped and scrubbed until I was certain I no longer smelled like that den of death I'd been trapped in and the creature whose home it had been. Then I stood under the stinging hot water and let it wash away the past months as best a shower could.

All that sorrow and self-pity while I refused to mourn Philo's death.

All that time learning and honing my skills that in the end, hadn't really mattered at all. Well, except for Thor's training. If it hadn't been for him and Master Yi and all the mind work they had me do, I probably wouldn't have been able to get so close to the Master, and I'm sure I wouldn't have been able to outwit him in the end.

But there was no way I'd ever tell Thor that.

The water grew cold and I figured that even David's luxury airplane couldn't do everything, so I sighed and turned it off.

I dressed in my T-shirt from a couple camp seasons ago and the pair of comfy leggings that had been brought for me, then contemplated my hair. I was suddenly just too tired to try drying it, so I put it up into a bun on the top of my head. I figured if Philo could love me stinking of death and looking like something from *The Walking Dead*, then he could handle me like this.

In the room, Philo lay under the sheets, propped up on some pillows with a blood bag flowing into his arm. Our eyes met, and in that moment, I knew I was exactly where I was supposed to be, with the person I was always meant to be with.

As I slipped under the sheets and snuggled against him, and his arm wrapped snuggly around me, holding me close, I realized something else.

I was the person I was meant to be.

Vampire or human, it didn't matter. Not as long as I stayed true to myself and to the ones I loved.

Epilogue

STACEY, MAC, AND EVEN DANIEL WERE WAITING AT THE airport for us. Mac and Daniel held a hand-painted sign that read *Welcome Home Minnie & Fam!* with lots of girly embellishments *à la* Stacey. I felt kinda bad for Mac and Daniel—they didn't look too comfortable holding a sign with ribbons and glitter on it.

As soon as she was able, Stacey threw herself at me so hard the impact would've knocked me to the ground if I'd been human. As it was, I still had to take a step back to regain my balance. Stacey curled around me and pressed her face into the crook of my neck. No easy feat considering she was a head taller than me.

At first our hug was excited and fun, but soon we just held onto each other, sharing our gratitude for life, for being together again.

"I was so scared," she whispered. "I thought I'd lost you and I never got to say goodbye." She pushed back and glared at me. "What were you thinking running off like that with nothing but a stupid text? And then you just go and disappear for two frickin' months? I'd kill you myself if I wasn't so relieved you're alive."

I opened my mouth to respond with all the apologies I could muster but she crushed me to her again. "I'm sorry, Stace," I said into her armpit instead. "It really was the stupidest thing I've ever done, and I promise—I'll never do anything like that again." I meant every word and I pressed my sincerity into my words and hoped she felt them.

Running away like I had, thinking I could take on the Master like I had—it was a miracle I was still alive. Like, really. The odds had been stacked against me from the beginning and it was just a stroke of good luck, or fate, that changed those odds. I didn't understand it, but I wasn't going to question it.

When Stacey pulled back again, she eyed me a little warily. "So…are you…" She trailed off and she blushed. I felt her worry tinged with sadness, like a tangible thing between us. A gift from the Master, I guess. After waking up from the best sleep I think I'd ever had, I'd been sensing a lot more about the people around me. It had been good so far, but I knew it was just another thing I would have to spend some time working on and learning how to control.

I took one of Stacey's hands in both of mine and peered into her eyes. "I'm still me," I told her and she immediately relaxed. "And you're still my best friend. That's never gonna change."

She smiled and squeezed my hands back, but she still seemed unsure. "But you're…you're the Master now, right?"

We'd only joked about it before—at least, I thought we were joking—but since I woke up a couple hours ago, I'd done little else but think about it. One thing I knew for sure was that I did not want to be known as the Master, or even the Mistress. *Yuck*. Not only did it make me think of him, but it made me feel dark and vampy—and not the good kind of vampy, either.

But there was no doubting I was changed—even then I felt the threads that connected me to every single vampire alive. I was definitely going to need to come to terms with my new role and the responsibility that now lay in my hands.

I'd been silent too long, I could tell, and concern had reappeared on Stacey's face. Plus the family had all passed me, and Mac and Daniel were kind of awkwardly trying to fold up the sign, but obviously weren't quite sure what to do with it.

"She'll be all right," Philo said, coming to stand beside us. He took my hand and gave it a gentle squeeze. "I'll be with her every step of the way."

Stacey glanced between us, her eyes brightening again. "I'm so glad you're back," she told Philo as she leaned forward and gave him a gentle squeeze. He gave her a one-armed hug because he didn't let go of my hand. "She was impossible to deal with when we thought you were gone."

They both looked at me then, Stacey with a mock serious expression, and Philo with a tenderness that made me want to melt into his arms.

"I'm glad I'm back, too. I'm glad we're both back." He tugged on my hand, propelling me into his arms. "Despite appearances, I've never felt more alive, and it's all because of my Minnie Kim."

I gazed stupidly up into his azure eyes and sighed. Hey, I was still a sixteen—wait, I forgot I had a birthday—*seventeen*-year-old girl and Philo was still my first boyfriend. My first and only boyfriend, ever. I knew I'd never need or want anyone but him.

Stacey clapped her hands together and bounced on her toes. "Aww!"

"Stace!" Mac called, and Stacey bounded out of my peripheral view. I didn't look away from Philo.

He smiled a slow, delicious smile, then kissed the tip of my nose. "They've all left us, you know."

"They have?"

"Mmhmm. And people are starting to stare."

"They are?"

"Yes."

I sighed. "Does that mean it's time to go?"

He chuckled and tightened his arms around me. "Let's go home. That way we won't have an audience." His grin tilted up on one side in that special smile that was just for me.

"For what?" My heart thumped heavily in my chest as my excitement grew.

"Well, for all the kisses I plan to give you."

"Oh." My cheeks burned, but I didn't care. His blue eyes sparkled mischievously, and I wished we were already away and alone. "I plan to give you kisses, too. Is it weird that we got each other the same gift?" I grinned, loving the way his smile grew in response to mine.

"Not strange at all." Philo slowly pulled away and we walked side-by-side, hand-in-hand. "I have to warn you though, I'm a little out of practice."

I laughed and squeezed his hand, joy and hope buoying my steps. "That's okay. I have a most excellent memory, and I happen to have had the best teacher ever. I'll help you remember."

We stepped out of the airport and into the sunshine where my family and friends waited for us. I turned my face into the light and felt the familiar, intoxicating prickle of delicious heat and light. Vampires had lived in the dark since before time began, but not anymore. We deserved to live, to have the same opportunities as any other person out there, and now I was in the very unique and very awesome position of being the person who could make that happen.

And I would.

ALSO BY
ALI ARCHER

DESOLATION
Sacrifice (prequel)
Become (book 1)
Desolate (book 2)
Destined (book 3)
Desolation Diaries (v. 1-3)

MINNIE KIM: VAMPIRE GIRL
First Kisses Suck (book 1)
Deadly Sweethearts (book 2)
Seoul Demon (book 3)
Blood Moon (book 4)
Den of Death (book 5)

THE EDEN PROJECT
Dragon Protocol

Dear Reader,

When I first set out to write Minnie's story, I imagined a series that would dgo on and on, for as long as there were bad guys to fight and supernatural creatures to meet. so it came as a surprise to discover late last year that there would probably only be seven books. And then even more of a surprise when I finished writing this book and realized...the story was over. At least, it's the end of the story as it is now.

There WILL be a "continuation" of sorts of Minnie and Philo's story, it just won't be Minnie Kim Vampire Girl anymore. If you're reading this after completing Den of Death, you'll know why. so the context will change, but Minnie's story will continue. I haven't finalized the details yet, so unfortunately, I can't announce it just yet, but please join me in one (or all!) of the following places where you'll be sure to be among the first to learn of the new series.

Facebook Group
(always the first to know)
facebook.com/groups/alicats

Newsletter
(second to know)
https://alicross.kit.com/thiscreativelife

Website
(typically the last to be updated!)
aliarcher.com

Many thanks for reading Minnie and staying with her story! I appreciate each and every one of you.

Love,
    Ali

ABOUT THE AUTHOR

Ali Archer is the USA Today bestselling author of young adult fantasy and science fiction, including the Desolation series and the Minnie Kim: Vampire Girl series.

Ali's always loved science fiction and fantasy, as the first books she read were by such greats as Isaac Asimov, Ray Bradbury, and Lloyd Alexander. But when she discovered *Dragonriders of Pern* by Anne McCaffrey—a perfect blend of fantasy and science fiction—her own imagination was set aflame.

At eleven, Ali met Ms. McCaffrey in one of the single most illuminating moments of her life. When she told the eminent writer she wanted to be an author when she grew up, Ms. McCaffrey said, "Never let anything stand in the way of your dreams." Ali's been following that advice ever since.

LET'S CONNECT!

www.aliarcher.com
www.Facebook.com/aliarcherbooks
www.Facebook.com/groups/AliCats
www.Instagram.com/aliarcherbooks